Sharon Marie Provost

I0658706

DARK ARTS

Sharon Marie Provost

No part of this book may be reproduced, or stored in a retrieval system, or transmitted in any form or by any means, electronic, mechanical, photocopying, recording, or otherwise, without the express written permission of the publisher.

Front cover art by Luke Spooner / Carrion House
Interior images from Pixabay, public domain
Cover and interior design: Stephen H. Provost, Sharon Marie Provost

The contents of this volume and all other works by Stephen H. Provost and Sharon Marie Provost are entirely the work of the authors, with the exception of direct quotations, attributed material used with permission, and items in the public domain. No artificial intelligence ("AI") programs were used to generate content in the creation of this work. No portion of this book, or any of the author's works, may be used to train or provide content for artificial intelligence (AI) programs.

©2024 Sharon Marie Provost
Dragon Crown Books 2024
All rights reserved.

ISBN: 978-1-949971-55-2

Dedication

This book is dedicated to all those wannabe horror writers who live in the darkness with their terrifying stories but are too afraid to give writing a try. Bring your creatures into the light—we want to see them.

"Hell is empty and all the devils are here."
— William Shakespeare
"The Tempest"

"I delight in what I fear."
— Shirley Jackson

Contents

Dark Arts

Foreword

𝔍've been impressed by many people over the years, but by none more than Sharon Marie Provost, who makes her debut as a novelist with this present work, *Dark Arts*.

It's the latest stop in an incredible journey for Sharon, who produced her first short story, "Shining Night," just a year ago. Since then, she has published one collection of short stories (*Shadow's Gate*) and collaborated with me on two others in the *Nightmare's Eve* series. She has done all this while undergoing biweekly chemotherapy treatments, helping me with my own research, and running the business side of Dragon Crown Books.

Shadow's Gate? *Nightmare's Eve*? If you're sensing a pattern in the titles she's produced, you're not imagining it: Sharon writes horror. Exclusively. And it's a genre to which she brings a broad and unique perspective.

She's been a fan of scary movies and disturbing tales since childhood, many of which have informed her writing. Already, in her short-story collections, she has led her readers on adventures across a broad spectrum of horror, from classical to myth-based; from paranormal thrillers to graphic gore.

Sharon has the chops to tackle it all. Over a period of several years, she embarked on a number of paranormal investigations braving such haunts as Nevada's Gold Hill Hotel, Goldfield High School, and Washoe Club. Then there were overnight stays in Iowa's Villisca Axe Murder House and Edinburgh Manor asylum: solo investigations that would have scared the goosebumps off of the hardiest souls. I've stayed with her at several haunted hotels myself, but sadly, as a skeptic (though not a denier), I seem to scare the spirits away.

Sharon, on the other hand, has experienced the supernatural firsthand on many occasions. She is, however—by her own admission—more intrigued by the kind of horror inflicted by demons who wear human skin... the villain in this present story being a shining example.

Sharon's background studying human horror is just as impressive as her experience with the paranormal—if not more so—and goes far beyond her love of true crime TV and *Dexter*. She earned an associate's degree in Criminal Justice from Western Nevada College, giving her insights into forensics and police procedures that play a key role in a number of her stories— including *Dark Arts*.

Sharon's training and experience make her uniquely qualified to tell stories such as this. And she imbues each of them with a passion for all things terrifying and macabre in a way few others can. I invite you to join her on this journey through a true night gallery of deviant art, an exhibition so grotesque and terrifying that you dare not look away.

Log on to—and become entangled in—Sharon's twisted and dark web of horrors. This is your ticket to the *Dark Arts*. It's showtime!

Stephen H. Provost
October 15, 2024

One

A Chance Encounter

April 2021

Stellan couldn't take his eyes off her. He had been walking through the Los Angeles Farmers Market, buying the finest ingredients for his seafood feast, when he first spotted her. Then he nearly ran her down later when he turned his cart away from the fingerling potatoes and fresh corn on the cob he had been selecting at the Farm Boy Produce stall. The flaxen-haired beauty had the most enchanting emerald-green eyes he had ever seen.

"Begging your pardon, Miss."

"No worries. This place is a madhouse on Saturdays."

With that, she turned her cart and headed over to the check stand. Stellan had a lot on his mind as he contemplated his next big project, but he found himself staring at her again. With regret, he returned to the task at hand and selected a large Vidalia onion, a bulb of garlic, and some lemons before proceeding to the checkout counter.

He swung the bag of groceries in his hand as he whistled "Green-Eyed Lady" while walking across the market to Monsieur Marcel's Seafood stall. He was at the counter, selecting large Alaskan king crab legs, shrimp and clams when he felt a tap on his shoulder.

"I could swear you were following me," said a sultry voice from behind him.

He turned to see *her* standing there smiling at him.

"Well, not exactly following you, but this is certainly a

3

happy accident. I must admit I am glad to run into you again."

"I saw you looking at me earlier when you were buying spices, and then you ran into me at the produce stand. When I saw you walk in here a few minutes ago, I just knew I couldn't let this opportunity pass."

"I'm glad you didn't."

"If I am not being too presumptuous, it appears you are making a seafood boil. Am I correct?"

"Why yes, you are. Good eye."

"It appears there is enough for two?" she asked as she held up a brown butcher paper-wrapped package labeled "kielbasa." "I always did like a little sausage, too."

Stellan's smile widened as he shook his head in the affirmative.

Her eyes sparkled in the sunlight as they walked to the parking lot after checking out. He followed her to her Tango Red Audi R8 with the top down and loaded the groceries into the backseat.

"I suppose I should introduce myself. I am Stellan Erikkson. It is very nice to meet you."

"Meredith... Meredith Price."

"I could swear I have heard that name before."

"Hmmm... maybe. I have a lovely little place right on the beach. How does 6 sound? We can watch the sunset while we enjoy some wine. Then make dinner and eat it out on the deck."

"That sounds perfect."

Meredith reached into her purse, extracting a business card and a pen. She scrawled her address onto the back of the card and tucked it into the breast pocket of his button-down Oxford shirt. "See you later, sexy," she whispered with a wink before climbing into her car and zipping out of the spot.

Dark Arts

Stellan stood there and watched her drive away before turning over the card. He quickly realized why he recognized her name. Meredith Price was one of the most sought-after art agents in the country... in the world actually. She worked with the biggest galleries in Los Angeles, New York, Paris, Vienna, London, Venice, and Florence.

What luck! I meet my own Venus de Milo, and she could be the key to my success... all in one day.

Stellan had a spring in his step as he walked to his Carpathian Grey Jaguar F-type and popped the trunk to load the groceries. As he rounded the back of the car, he noticed a flower stall at the edge of the market. He ran over and bought a large, colorful bouquet with three white rosebuds. He felt confident that it would be a good day.

Stellan returned home and unloaded the groceries into the refrigerator before walking downstairs to the basement storage area to find his Yeti cooler for the 45-minute drive to the coast later. When he returned upstairs, he strolled through his art installations, taking pictures from the most flattering angles. It couldn't hurt to have some photos available for Meredith to peruse should the subject come up. He had just finished a three-part Gothic series with Lovecraftian creatures rising from the tumultuous sea.

He spent the rest of the afternoon preparing canvases for his next series. It would be a reimagining of the Victorian-era Penny Dreadfuls, with stark black-and-white serialized images sensationalizing the exploits of Sweeney Todd, Jack the Ripper, Frankenstein, and Dracula. The only touch of color would be the crimson of blood from the vicious murder scenes depicted.

At 4 p.m., he began the process of cleaning the studio before heading upstairs to his loft to take a shower. He dressed in a khaki cotton chino suit with a pale blue button-down shirt and loafers. He carefully packed the seafood on ice and arranged the flowers in a vase he had picked up some time ago from Pottery Barn.

The drive along the coast was fraught with traffic as he had predicted, but he had left the loft early enough to make it on time. Meredith had a lovely beach bungalow in Malibu with a blue-and-white mosaic tile fountain in front, surrounded by hibiscus, hydrangeas, and bougainvillea bushes. As he drove up, he saw her sitting on a lounger on the white deck out back.

He grabbed the cooler from the trunk and the vase of flowers before heading to the deck to greet her. She rose from the chaise lounge, drink in hand, beaming as she wrapped one arm around him in a half-hug before kissing him on the cheek. She then led him into the kitchen to place the seafood in the refrigerator while she poured him a glass of Chardonnay. They returned to the deck and seated themselves on the canopied double chaise lounge to watch the brilliant reds, oranges and pinks of the sun setting on the horizon.

"So, what do you think?" Meredith asked with a smile.

"Your place is lovely. I can't think of a better way to spend this evening."

"I agree. So, tell me about yourself. What do you do for a living?"

"Funny enough, I realized how I recognized your name when you gave me your card earlier. I am an artist. I specialize in large immersive installations that need a dedicated site. Most of my collection is broken up into different series that need to be experienced as a whole to guide you along the psychological journey."

"That sounds utterly fascinating! Would I have seen your work anywhere?"

"Regretfully, no. I don't mean to sound pompous, but I think I am just too advanced... too far beyond the L.A. art scene." Stellan was surprised by the throaty laugh that erupted from Meredith.

"Why don't you let me be the judge of that? Do you have any photos of your work with you?"

"Oh no! I don't want you to think I was trying to get you to look at my work."

"You have me fascinated with your descriptions. And to be honest, I know exactly what you mean about the L.A. art scene. I'm surprised you've stayed in the area rather than moving on to New York or onto the world stage where avant-garde works of art are more readily appreciated. If Los Angeles wasn't my childhood home, I'd have left here completely long ago... So, do you?"

Stellan reached into his jacket pocket, extracting his cell phone with a sheepish smile. "I do have a few photos of my latest Gothic series, plus some of my earlier collections."

Meredith took the phone and began scrolling through the gallery; her brow furrowed as she zoomed in and out, focusing on all the little details on each canvas. She released a loud sigh as she handed him back the phone. "These are absolutely groundbreaking, fantastic works of art. I'd say that I'm heartbroken that you weren't discovered earlier. Except I'm not... you're my greatest discovery of the past decade. We're going to turn the art world on its head."

"Are you serious?"

"Serious as a heart attack, as they say. I simply must see your *entire* collection in person as soon as possible. Then, I will need to schedule a professional art photographer and videographer to come in and document your installations so I can show them off to all the biggest art galleries in New York. I am going on a business trip there next week for a month to represent some of my other clients. If we weren't about to make dinner, I would suggest that we draw up a formal representation contract and sign it tonight."

"This is amazing! I never expected this to happen. I was just excited to have dinner with such a beautiful, intelligent, alluring woman."

"One thing though, and this is non-negotiable. I never mix business and pleasure. I admit I am very attracted to you, but to be brutally honest, I am even more drawn to your art. What can I say? Art is my life. Art is my passion. Clearly, it is the same for you. We will have dinner tonight, but strictly to celebrate our new collaboration. It is all business from here on out. *Capiche*?"

"I agree!" Stellan gushed as he reached out to shake her hand.

Meredith met him the next morning at his loft downtown, and he escorted her through the intricate displays that took up most of the first floor. She was astounded that he hadn't been picked up by any of the local galleries, even if it wasn't their usual fare. After the tour through the installations, Meredith was even more certain she could get him in for a big debut show in one of the premier galleries in New York City.

The next day, she scheduled a videographer to meet them at his loft to create a virtual showing of his installation that she could share with galleries on her trip to New York.

Dark Arts

A month later, Stellan received an exciting call from Meredith. She had a private debut showing scheduled for him at the Nouveau Galley in the West Village in six months, which would give him time to prepare additional pieces. Initially set for a one-month run, the showing could be extended depending on how it was received. Meredith had planned a huge opening-night gala with all the biggest name art critics in attendance, along with several local artists of note and celebrity collectors.

She had already arranged for a shipping company that was familiar with moving delicate pieces of art to pack up the installation at his loft 2½ weeks before the show. Stellan was expected to arrive two weeks prior to opening night to oversee the set-up of his art and start schmoozing with the curator and other movers and shakers in the New York art world.

Stellan already envisioned creating four additional works for the show.

The next six months would be a busy time.

Sharon Marie Provost

Two

Special Delivery

October 2021
Six months later

Phwap! He pulled off the gloves with a loud snap after dropping the last envelope into the bag. The letter-sized manila envelope stood out amongst the others. The bag was filled with fancy gold foil envelopes containing invitations to his first major solo art show, *Stellan Erikkson—When the Lights Go Out*. He had been on the art scene, ignored by everyone, for the past 15 years. But all of that changed when he hired Meredith as his agent. She had the connections and the balls-to-the-wall enthusiasm that made people—the right people—pay attention.

Stellan was looking forward to his show next month. But he was tired of waiting. He was tired of being ignored. His art had deserved recognition all along. As confident as he was in its merit, he was tired of holding back from his true passion... the real art he was meant to create.

That one envelope would make them pay attention now and recognize the genius of *Le Créateur*.

What it contained was special... an introduction to his new art installations. Installations designed to be an immersive experience into surrealistic nightmares—dreamscape sculptures of fantastical creatures—born of beauty and horror. These creations could never be displayed for the world at large to see. However, there was an audience, a group of discriminating people, that paid handsomely to see them.

Stellan knew this one invitation—a special delivery of sorts—could not be linked to this area. He would drop the others off at his local post office, but this one would go across country with him on his drive to New York, where he would be spending the next two weeks setting up his lights installation. He would drop it off at some random post office box where he would not be observed, or recorded on security cameras.

Stellan had been careful not to leave fingerprints or any other trace evidence for the police to find. All they would receive was the photo of his first creation, titled "*La Sirène,*" from his *Dark Arts* collection along with a short note.

You can call off your search. You shall never find her. She has taken a place of honor in my collection as La Sirène.

Yours Truly, Le Créateur

There was no need to identify her—after all, her picture had graced most newscasts for three weeks solid after she'd disappeared without a trace. His creations were already bringing him the fame and fortune he desired... now to live in infamy.

Three

Annalise

June 2022

nnalise drummed her fingers on the desktop as she stared at her phone, waiting for the little blue download wheel to stop spinning. *How did I ever let Mendy talk me into trying this in the first place? I know the local dive bar dating pool has been a little shallow lately—that, along with my penchant for being picky, has led to very few dates. But life has been busy over the past six months anyhow, ever since my promotion. Who has had time for dating?*

Finally, the download completed, and the installation began. Annalise's anxiety ramped up as she saw the percentage climb next to the app's predictable icon: a white flame on a red background. A match on Tinder leads to a flaming love... or more likely, a hookup. *Hurk... Huuurkkkk... makes me gag!* Annalise always hated it when things were too cutesy.

Annalise remembered her conversation with Mendy starting out so innocent. Mendy was hosting her usual Fourth of July bash, and she asked if Annalise would be bringing a date. Before she knew it, she was getting the hard sell about how she should try Tinder. Mendy had tried a range of arguments: assuring her that the party was going to be all couples, then following that with the "you're not getting any younger" cliché, and the time-honored classic, her biological clock.

Annalise finally caved just to shut Mendy up. The two of them planned to meet for lunch on the patio at Garibaldi's, the new restaurant in town, on Saturday at noon. She had agreed to let Mendy help her create her profile. She had done a little research into Tinder during lunch on Thursday. The profile setup was surprisingly detailed, including photos, bio, lifestyle and interests, relationship goals, languages, job, school, and living situation. This lunch date would definitely have to include margaritas at this rate.

Annalise had set aside Friday night to download the app, create her log-in and sign up for Tinder Gold for one month. For less than twenty bucks, Tinder Gold would notify her of anyone who had swiped right (signifying they liked her), which would allow her to focus on the profiles of those who were already interested in her. Most importantly, she wouldn't have to waste her precious time watching ads. Her anxiety lessened when the initial setup turned out to be quick and easy. She went to bed early, pushing her worries out of her mind. Those would be back soon enough when the next day dawned.

Memories of bad blind dates plagued Annalise's sleep that night. At 3 a.m., she got up to make some warm milk while she attempted to Facetime with her sister Belinda in Sydney, Australia. Her young niece and nephew should have been put to bed an hour ago, allowing her time to have a private chat with her sister.

Belinda answered the video call and set the phone up on the windowsill as she washed the dinner dishes. "Hey there. Long time no talk, sis," Belinda chided as Annalise's face appeared on the screen.

"I know, I know. I'm sorry. Work has just been so crazy lately... and with the new responsibilities that came with my promotion. Never mind... no excuses. I have missed you, though, I swear."

Belinda laughed and blew her a kiss. "I understand. To be honest, the lapse isn't just your fault. The kids have been busy with school, sports, and other activities. I wouldn't mind trading you for a busy work schedule."

"Why couldn't we be twins? Trade jobs for a few weeks, and no one would know the difference. It would be spectacular!"

"Talk to me, sis. It is the middle of the night there. What are you doing up calling me? You only call your big sis at this hour when something is on your mind. Spill it."

"You know me, I have never been big on the dating scene. To tell the truth, I can't say when I last went on a date, but it was months before my promotion."

"So, a year..."

"Not a year exactly."

"Close enough. Get real, Annie. This is me you're talking to."

"Okay, basically a year. Anyhow, my co-worker talked me into trying Tinder to get back on the dating scene. I'm just not sure if I'm ready for that."

"*You* will never be ready for that. That is precisely the point. She's right to encourage you to get back out there—although I am not sure if I'm a fan of Tinder, per se. But... thinking about it... it might be just right for you. You are much too shy in person. Look up 'wallflower' in the dictionary, and there is a picture of you. Maybe the actual distance will be enough to give you a little boost of confidence. Plus, you can be swiping left and right during lunch or while you are watching TV at night—you can multitask to your heart's content—I know how busy you are."

"That is a valid point. I knew you could make me feel better."

"As independent and introverted as you are, I know you *do* want a family someday. I know you are lonely at times and wish you had a partner. Everyone in this life needs someone to come home to at night. You deserve that, too."

"Thanks, big sis. You are right, as usual. I love you so much. Give the rugrats a kiss and hug for me. Maybe one day soon, I will come out to visit—maybe I will even have someone to accompany me. I am overdue for a vacation."

"I love you, too. Now go get some rest. I will talk to you again soon, right?"

"Yes, I promise. Night."

Annalise rose early as the sun's first rays began to shine through her window. She went for a jog on the seaside trail only a quarter-mile from her home. She had always found exercise, especially jogging, helped clear her mind. The talk with her sister the previous night had been enlightening. Belinda was right—annoyingly she was always right—now she just needed to calm her nerves.

If an introvert must date, then Tinder, in a way, could be an introvert's dream solution. People did not know if you had chosen to swipe left and discard them. Unless they subscribed to one of the higher tiers, they didn't even know if you had chosen to swipe right to like them, unless they liked you, too. No embarrassing disclosure of a crush, only to be laughed at, like she experienced in high school. That same measure would let her save time looking through profiles because she could choose to only look through those that had already swiped right on her.

Annalise returned home feeling much better. She made herself an egg white omelet and drank her coffee in the breakfast nook as she scrolled through her photos. She made a folder in her photos app on the phone to set aside her most flattering selfies. Mendy probably wouldn't agree, but these would be her choices, just the same.

Annalise arrived for lunch fifteen minutes early and found an eager Mendy waiting for her. Mendy insisted on looking through her pictures as they waited for the server to come take their order. To Annalise's surprise, Mendy quickly chose the picture of her at the Great Barrier Reef when she'd visited Belinda a year and a half ago. Annalise had to admit her body did look good in the bikini her sister had bought for her. More importantly, she looked happy and relaxed—rare for her these days.

They ordered lunch and began to discuss what Annalise's bio should say while they waited for it to arrive. Annalise was pleased to find that Mendy didn't expect her to post false information; she just wanted to jazz it up a bit. After lunch, they ordered margaritas and began to create her profile. She had to admit that Mendy did have a certain flourish to her writing, so she was quite pleased with the results when they finished an hour later.

Mendy looked over at her with a big smile. "You ready to go live?"

"Yes... no... I guess so," Annalise stammered.

Mendy stabbed the enter key with one of her long fingernails. "And we're off. I can't wait to see how this goes. You have to keep me updated. Better yet, let me help you decide who to date. We can swipe like mad at lunch."

"Whoa! Cool your jets, Iceman! We don't know that anybody is even going to be interested. One step at a time here. You got me to sign up."

"I bet you'll have a list of men waiting to date you by the time the day is through. You are a catch, Annalise Sophia Fischer. I

17

mean it!"

Annalise's eyes filled with tears. She turned away, blinking rapidly to clear them, then turned back with a smile. "Thank you, Mendy. You're like a sister to me... a pushy, annoying, bossy big sister that I wouldn't give up for all the world. Your care and concern mean so much to me, especially with my sister living so far away."

"You stop that shit right now, sister. If you make me cry, so help me..." Mendy threatened with a wink.

Annalise snatched up the check as the server dropped it off. "My treat! It's the least I can do for all your help."

"You got that right. We both know you need all the help you can get." Mendy cackled as she reached over to hug Annalise.

"Well, I need to be getting home now. Morris is waiting for me."

"Morris—your cat—is waiting for you. Why aren't we signing you up for Tinder as well?"

"You know me, Annalise. I'm never without a man for long. I will have 'Mr. Right Now' by the time my party arrives. I'm not one to be tied down. I turned off my biological clock... kids are not my jam. Now *that* is my jam." Mendy pointed toward the speaker behind her, as the infectious beat of "Feel Good Inc." by the Gorillaz began to play. Mendy stood up and began to dance, drawing the attention of all the men on the patio.

"I take it back. I can see you don't need any help," Annalise giggled as she stood up. She took Mendy's hand, leading her dancing friend off the patio before one of the wives with daggers in their eyes—sitting alongside those entranced men—pulled one for real. As they reached Mendy's car, Annalise drew her into a bear hug. "I will see you on Monday, you troublemaker!"

"I can't help it if they can't hold their men's attention," she said, batting her eyelashes innocently, before climbing in her electric blue convertible. She lifted her arm, waving as she backed out and took off with a brief screech of the tires.

How did I ever become friends with that wild thing? Annalise returned to her car smiling and shaking her head. She spent the rest of the afternoon working on her distance education classes for work. She was, admittedly, a workaholic, but she truly enjoyed her career. Besides, it was the best way to distract her from overwhelming thoughts about what might be happening on Tinder.

Monday rolled around, and she still hadn't had any response to her Tinder profile. When Mendy came bounding up to her, bubbling with excitement, she smiled and pretended she didn't care.

"It was the first hot weekend and the official start of summer. Everybody was probably at the beach or on vacation. I wouldn't take it to heart. I'm sure you will get lots of matches this week. Besides, we're going to look through the available men at lunch and start swiping right."

"Pfft... I totally don't care," Annalise said with a wave of her hand.

A few hours later, Mendy arrived at her desk with lunch in hand for both of them. "Scoot over." She pulled a chair over from an unoccupied cubicle across the way. As bold and brassy as she might be, she understood Annalise's private nature and desire to keep this part of her life from their co-workers. They spent the next hour devouring the delicious ramen and spring rolls she had delivered from Ijji Noodle House, as they scrolled an endless stream of available men.

Most were a quick swipe to the left. It was clear from their pictures or a quick peek through their profile that they were either arrogant alpha males or the sporty, outdoorsy type... neither of which matched Annalise's personality. Camping trips just weren't her thing. By the end of lunch, they had swiped right on a handful of men who seemed more like the intellectual, introspective type that interested Annalise.

"I told you we'd find somebody to pique your curiosity. Now, it's just a waiting game to see if you found a match. Anna, stop looking so serious. This is a good thing... I promise."

Annalise smiled and nodded. "Well, nose back to the grindstone. Thanks, Mendy."

Annalise made a point of not looking at her phone until after dinner that night. When she sat down to watch her guilty pleasures, *Catfish* and *Help! I'm in a Secret Relationship!*, she finally pulled out her phone to check Tinder. She was surprised to find a list of 12 men that had swiped right on her. She had promised Mendy that she would wait to go through those with her, but she did sneak a quick peek at their pictures. And to her delight, although she would never admit it, she had matched with two of the men they had liked earlier in the day.

Annalise could picture Mendy's gloating face already. She decided she might as well get it over with, so she texted Mendy with the news. She received a flurry of different happy face emojis and then an eggplant. *Leave it to Mendy to get crude.* Annalise rolled her eyes and texted back "LOL."

"I told you we would find you a husband... or at least get you laid," Mendy texted back.

"Let's start small. Okay? How about we find me a date for your party and go from there?"

"Whatever you say... for now. I can't wait to see those other guys tomorrow. Anybody look interesting?"

"Well, I didn't look at their profiles, and I only just briefly looked at their pictures. But... Anthony Carreras was attractive."

Annalise waited for a response and jumped when her phone rang instead. She was greeted with Mendy's excited screech. "Ooohhh... tell me more, tell me more..." Mendy sang to the beat of "Summer Nights."

"Oh my God, you and your obsession with *Grease*! Anyhow... he had wavy dark brown hair; icy blue eyes; a strong, chiseled jawline, and he was clean shaven. He looked so mature and intelligent in that blazer with the blue plaid button-up shirt that accentuated his eyes."

"For a brief look, you sure have a lot of specifics," Mendy said suggestively.

"Mendy, what I am going to do with you?"

"Tell me all the juicy details. Let me live vicariously through your torrid love affair!"

"Mennnnndy!"

"Okay, okay. Well, how about a compromise? Meet me for breakfast tomorrow at Annette's Cafe across from work at 7 a.m. That'll give us an hour to go through the list. And of course, send a message to lover boy Anthony... see if we can make a little magic happen by lunchtime."

"Fine. I'll see you then. Night, Mendy."

"Goodnight. Sweet dreams," Mendy replied through giggles, hanging up before she could respond.

Annalise rose at 5 a.m. and jogged over to work. She used the showers in the office gym and then walked across the street, arriving for breakfast 15 minutes early. Mendy, never one to be a morning person, had beaten her there. *Did she even sleep for Pete's sake? You would swear she was the one about to go on a date.*

Mendy jumped up and ran over, dragging Annalise to the table. "I ordered the usual breakfast burrito with bacon and a blended mocha with caramel for you. Let me see," she begged, as she reached for Annalise's phone. Annalise barely had time to swipe her fingerprint before the phone was gone.

As they ate, the two women pored over the list of men who had liked Annalise's profile, in fact, two more had appeared overnight. Mendy was disgruntled when she found that she agreed with Annalise's assessment... most of them were not right for her. Annalise swiped right on another man, named Clarence, although neither woman felt confident in that choice.

For the two matches that had reciprocated her like from yesterday, they came up with an introductory message to send to them. It was short and sweet. "Hi. I hope you are doing well. I would love to chat some when you have time. Tell me more about yourself."

Annalise could see that Mendy was somewhat disappointed, but they agreed to meet for lunch again, at Mendy's desk this time. The smile returned to Mendy's face when she remembered that they might find a response from Anthony, and she practically skipped to her desk as Annalise boarded the elevator to the second floor. *She is more invested in my love life than I am!*

The phones were busier than usual, so the morning passed quickly for Annalise. When lunch arrived, she took the elevator down to the first floor and found a smiling Mendy. They walked down the hall to an empty interview room to eat their lunch.

Mendy grabbed Annalise's phone when she set it down to pass out their food.

"Hey, I haven't even looked yet!" Annalise implored.

"I knew it. I will look for you while you deal with our lunch. Let's see..."

"Don't you dare send a message to anyone. Look with your eyes only."

"Well, Clarence is a dud, just like we thought. Listen to this... 'Hello, Annalise.' He sounds like freaking Hannibal Lecter."

"Be nice, Mendy. Maybe he didn't realize how it sounds."

"I shall continue... 'I am so happy to meet you. I told my mom that I had met a pretty girl online. Maybe you can come over for dinner next week. You wanted to know more about me, but I don't really know what to say. I like to read technical manuals and watch *Masterpiece Theater*. I have three cats. My favorite dinner is grilled cheese sandwiches with tomato soup. How about we chat online later tonight?' Oh yes, I can definitely see how very wrong I was, Annalise. He is a regular Don Juan. Shall I set up a date for you?"

Try as she might, Annalise couldn't keep a smile and then a giggle from escaping. "Fine. Fine. I get it. Did anybody else respond?" Annalise asked with a nervous tremor in her voice.

"Hmmm... anybody in particular? Maybe Anthony, perhaps?"

"Yesssss!"

"Well, those other two guys that you matched with... nothing from them, yet. Nothing new either."

"Dammit! Just get to it already, Mendy."

Mendy giggled before turning the phone toward Annalise. "It seems a Mr. Anthony Carreras is quite pleased that you matched with him. He would like to chat online with you tonight. Apparently, he is a senior associate at a marketing firm here in town. He enjoys jogging, candlelit dinners, reality television, and traveling. He sounds perfect for you. We have to write him back."

"Okay, chill out. Let me text him."

"What are you going to say?"

Annalise bent over her phone, as her fingers quickly tapped out a message. She turned the phone toward Mendy for her approval.

"Perfect! Short and sweet works. Seven o'clock is past the dinner hour but not too late. I am proud of you. I will stay up late tonight. I don't care what time you get done texting him... you call me. I am dying to know how it goes."

"How did I know you were going to say that?"

"Because you know I am a nosy bitch? Because I told you I was going to live vicariously through you?"

"All of the above. Anyhow, I need to get back up to my desk. Work is calling to me. I will talk to you later tonight. Thanks, Mendy."

As Annalise turned to leave, Mendy slapped her on the ass. "Don't forget, you are one hot babe. Put on a sexy top and some makeup... just in case your texting turns into a video chat."

Annalise shook her head and walked away. "We'll see. I'm not sure I am ready to jump right into a video chat." She waved goodbye as she stepped onto the elevator.

Annalise's caseload kept her busy throughout the afternoon, so she didn't have time to be anxious about her upcoming chat.

Annalise rushed in the door at 6 p.m., dropping off her knapsack and purse on the table, as she headed to her room to change. Mendy's suggestion to look presentable in case they video chatted had been running through her head all day. She had finally decided on changing into a pink silk camisole and tan cargo shorts, with her hair up in a ponytail. Her light daytime makeup still seemed appropriate, so she headed out to the table to scarf down some leftover salad.

As she rinsed her plate, she heard a faint message chime. She dried her hands before picking up her phone and saw a chat bubble on her screen. She took a deep breath and then clicked on it.

"Hi, Annalise. Is this still a good time to talk?"

"Hey, Anthony. Yes, I am free. Is it convenient for you?"

"It is perfect. I just sat down to relax after a long day at work. How better to spend my time than chatting with an intelligent, beautiful woman?"

"Ahh, thank you. That is very sweet of you. I don't know about the beautiful part though."

"I do. Or wait? Am I talking to an impostor? Are you catfishing me? Are you really an ogre?"

"Funny man! Here... I will send you my picture with the clock behind me. You can see it really is me in living color."

Annalise smiled nervously and tilted her head slightly, accentuating her best side. She snapped the selfie and sent it before she had too much time to think about it. She watched the little circle spin as the percentage climbed... 100%... the moment of truth. She chewed her fingernails as she watched the flashing ellipsis in the thought bubble appear.

"Wow! You look just as beautiful as you did in that picture at the, uh, Great Barrier Reef? Am I right?"

"You nailed it. Well, thank you very much. Your turn now. Gotta make sure you aren't some killer clown or Ted Bundy."

"Just a second. I do mean it though. You really are my type... attractive, witty and an intellectual."

A few seconds later, a file appeared on the screen, and Annalise pressed the download button. Before long, a picture appeared. Anthony was seated on a couch, holding that day's newspaper, looking just as handsome as he did in his profile picture. *Why is this hot guy interested in me?*

"So now that we have that out of the way, tell me more about yourself, Anthony."

"Well, like I said in my message, I am a senior associate at a marketing firm. I work long hours most days, so my guilty pleasure is unwinding while I watch those reality TV dating shows. I usually start my day with a jog to the office. My favorite pastime is traveling, and I am fortunate that I do get six weeks off a year at my office."

"I guess it is my turn then. I am a data processor and call center operator at my office. I'm taking online classes to finish my degree for a promotion at work. I am a bit of a workaholic myself, so I also work long hours. I'm normally a bit of an introvert, so I frequently go to new places to jog or hike by myself. That trip to the ocean was an anomaly... visiting family. I have to admit that I do like to relax at night by watching some awful reality TV show or true crime documentaries."

"So, do you socialize with friends or family much? Date very often?"

"This is embarrassing, but I haven't been on a date in, like, a year. The only family I have is my sister, brother-in law, and a niece and nephew who live in Australia. I have one close friend I work with, but we mostly socialize at work, except for her periodic parties. To be honest, that is why I am on here now. She insisted that I must bring a date to her annual Fourth of July extravaganza. I think she just wants me to get married."

Annalise looked horrified as she saw what she had just

typed.

"God! Did I just say that? I didn't mean anything by it."

"No. No. Don't worry. I find your candor quite refreshing. I can tell you are not out on the prowl for a husband. You seem very much like me. You would like to get married... someday... but right now, your career is your priority. But that doesn't mean that either one of us should be holed up inside all the time alone. Dating can be fun, at least that's what they say."

Annalise sighed in relief when she read his response. "Thank you for understanding. You're really quite easy to talk to. I must admit I'm having fun."

"So, Annalise, what do you think about going out on a very casual, no expectations, date?"

"What were you thinking?"

"Well, we both like to jog, right? I think I remember seeing that in your profile."

"Yes, I do."

"I was thinking on Saturday we could go up to Sanford Meadows State Park. With all the trees and the higher elevation, it should be the perfect temperature for a casual jog. Then we can have a picnic lunch out on the meadow and just get to know each other a little better in a quiet, non-stressful environment. How does that sound?"

"That sounds delightful. I haven't been out there in years. What should I bring?"

"Yourself. Did I mention I love to cook? I will bring the picnic and some wine with me and pick you up about 10 a.m.?"

"Yes. I will be ready. Do you like dessert?"

"What normal human doesn't?"

"Great. I know just what to bring."

Over the next couple of hours, the two of them exchanged pleasantries, told childhood stories and expressed excitement over their upcoming date. Their conversation had proceeded so naturally that neither one realized she hadn't given him her address. They bid each other goodnight, and Annalise began to make a list for the store.

She jumped when her phone rang and looked at the clock, surprised to see it was already 9:30 p.m. *Damn! It must be Mendy. I promised to call her when I was done.* As she was about to answer the call, the chat bubble popped up again. She clicked on it and giggled when she saw the message.

"Now, I am an intelligent, intuitive man and all, but I must confess I'm not psychic."

"Neither am I."

"So... where shall I pick you up on Saturday?"

"I promise I am not a blond. Well, I am... but not a bimbo. Never mind! I am all flustered now."

"Hey, I didn't think of it either. I was so entranced talking with you that I didn't think to ask."

"You live in the city, right?"

"Yes. Don't you?"

"No, I actually live in the rural area out on Route 60. Do you want me to meet you at the park or somewhere in the city?"

"No, that is perfect. I could use the drive to calm my nerves before we meet."

"LOL. And here, I thought it was just me feeling anxious."

"Nope. Now, I ruined my smooth guy image. You sure you still want to go out with me? LMAO."

"Even more so. 1525 Elmwood Drive. I will see you on Saturday, Anthony. Goodnight."

Annalise dialed Mendy, her mind and body swirling with electricity.

"I thought you were never going to call. I was about to head over there and kick your ass."

"We just finished chatting."

"Really? Two and a half hours? I'm impressed, my dear! So...?"

"He is amazing. He was so easy to talk to... very kind and considerate. He didn't laugh at any of the silly things I said... or at least he didn't tell me he did. He is not at all like the typical men I have dated. It seems like we have a lot in common. In fact, he is picking me up Saturday morning to go out on a very low-key jogging and picnic date!"

"Only you would go out for a picnic in the daytime for a first date."

"It was his idea. I told you... he is different."

"So, what are you going to wear?"

"I was thinking my pink Nike jogging shorts and cropped tank top since we are going jogging."

"Makes sense and sounds cute... and shows a little skin. I approve. Anyhow, I won't be in the office tomorrow. If you want to discuss anything before your date, call me in the evening, and we will talk. But you have to call me Saturday as soon as you get home and tell me *everything!*"

"I promise. Night, Mendy!"

Sharon Marie Provost

Four

Anthony

June 2022

A nthony clapped his hands in delight after he finished typing "Goodnight" to Annalise. He couldn't believe his luck. She was just his type, beautiful and intelligent, with a sweet personality.

A jog and a picnic—the perfect first date for them—now he just needed to prepare for it. He realized he had been so busy at work and with his side job that he hadn't been out on a date in four months. It had been much too long since he'd had some real true fun.

Anthony opened the hall closet and dug around until he found the picnic basket. He set it aside on the dining room table as he grabbed a tablet to make a grocery list. He had promised her a good meal, so he had better live up to that.

Why did I have to mention that I am a good cook? It's not like I can make any food out there.

Anthony shook his head as he mentally berated himself for his lapse in judgment. Clearly, he was out of practice.

He decided to prepare a basket full of tapas—a sampling of delicious *hors d'oeuvres:* delectable little bites of different delicacies with something sure to please any palate. His shopping list included a bottle of Pinot Grigio, various cheeses, prosciutto, grapes, crostini, caviar, *crudités, naan,* pickled mushrooms; and the ingredients to make *foie gras,* stuffed olives, and meatballs.

Pleased with his selections, he set the list aside, next to his wallet and keys.

He then moved around the kitchen, gathering silverware, serving spoons, saucers, napkins, wine glasses, a bottle opener, and his set of divided charcuterie "snackle" boxes, and he placed them in the picnic basket. He knew she wouldn't be expecting such a lavish first date, but he was hoping Annalise would enjoy it as much as he knew he would. Luckily, he didn't have work tomorrow, so he had time to complete all these preparations for Saturday.

Anthony's dates over the past year hadn't gone quite as planned. He had met most of the women on Tinder, like he had with Annalise. He always seemed to find girls who were more interested in outside activities than pursuing a serious relationship, or women with radical political views. He was willing to give this dating app one more try because he hoped this date would go better than his past several attempts.

Anthony was confident that Annalise would show her true colors one way or the other, hopefully sooner rather than later. He wanted to find a partner in life who might share his passions, but being a busy man, his schedule just didn't leave him time to waste on fruitless endeavors. He wanted to pursue his dreams with reckless abandon, yet still make enough money to enjoy life and travel.

Anthony felt sure he wasn't being too picky or discriminating in his tastes. He'd been raised by a liberal hand that left him open-minded. Anthony knew what he wanted in life and that he deserved more than settling for second best. His mother had taught him that.

Anthony's mother had been a beacon of love and light

throughout his life. She had expanded his horizons from an early age, exposing him to literature, fine music, art, philosophy, world travel, and culinary exploration. She had acquainted him with members of society the world over, and introduced him to everything from the dregs of humankind to the political, financial, and societal pillars of communities. He had seen all manners of religious practices, from dark and blended monotheistic Voodoo rites to "enlightened" Christianity and all manner of beliefs in between.

During their world travels, they had lived in the lap of luxury at times, while other times had been spent in primitive native encampments. He'd learned not to judge a person based on their religious or political beliefs, wealth or lack thereof, or cultural norms that differed from those he had accepted from society in the highly developed United States. He took all these lessons with him into every interaction with family members, co-workers, potential life partners, and the public in general.

But sometimes late at night, Anthony worried that his drive to succeed, his overarching ambition, made him less patient and willing to tolerate the kind of differences he had been raised to accept. The past few years, his fiercely independent nature and nose-to-the-grindstone work ethic might have made him a bit more narcissistic and self-indulgent than his mother would have preferred. At times, he felt like he was sacrificing everything his mother's upbringing had sought to instill in him. Her passing two years ago had been immensely hard on Anthony. He no longer had that sounding board... the mirror to reflect his inadequacies.

Anthony decided to go to bed in hopes of getting a good night's rest. Exhaustion would do nothing to improve his personality and behavior. Besides, he had a full day of cooking and preparations ahead of him before the big day on Saturday.

Anthony rose fifteen minutes before his alarm at 7 a.m., as usual. He spent an hour tidying up the house, just in case he and Annalise should decide to come back after the picnic. Afterward, he grabbed his car keys and grocery list and headed out to the store. He drove downtown to Charbonnau's Delicatessen, the local gourmet food shop, to pick up most of the items he needed for the menu. Then, it was just a quick stop at Whole Foods to gather the grapes and some of the vegetables.

Anthony spent the rest of the afternoon cooking the food to perfection before carefully placing them in the "snackle" boxes. One box contained all the items that needed to be kept cool, and it fit in a special bag that held ice packs just for that purpose. The other one contained grapes, *crudités*, and vegetable *hors d'oeuvres*, with room to add the crostini and *naan* in the morning. He placed them both in the fridge overnight.

That evening, as he watched his favorite reality TV shows, Anthony texted Annalise one more time. "We still on for tomorrow?"

"Yes! I have to say I'm excited for our date. Thanks for choosing such a low-pressure date. You sure you don't want me to meet you at the park? I hate to make you drive out of the way just to pick me up."

"I am happy to do it. To be honest, I love driving out of the city... getting away from all the people and traffic. Besides, it gives us more time to talk. But if you're uncomfortable with not having a, shall we say, escape hatch, I totally understand."

"No, I appreciate the gallant gesture, kind sir. I will see you at 10 then."

"On the dot."

"Oh! I hope you like double chocolate chunk brownies?"

"Oh yes, my dear. Chocolate isn't just the way to a woman's *heart*. I can't wait to try them. See you tomorrow."

Anthony set his phone on the coffee table with a smile on his face. Sleep would come easily tonight. He had a wonderful day ahead of him tomorrow with a beautiful woman running at his side.

Sharon Marie Provost

Five

Free as a Bird

June 2022

nnalise rose with the sun on Saturday morning. She hadn't slept much the night before because she was a bit anxious about her upcoming date. Anthony seemed like the perfect man for her—kind and considerate, handsome, intelligent, and a hard worker. Her only concern... what made him interested in her.

Annalise was a humble person, but she knew that she was attractive, physically at least. It just seemed that once she started talking to a guy, no one ever seemed interested enough to ask her out. Even if they did, she didn't hear back for a second date. But Anthony was different: He truly seemed interested in her, even after texting for hours.

Annalise felt like a teenager again as she spent the next hour rummaging through her closet, looking for the perfect outfit to bring in case their date extended past the jogging and picnic. She couldn't very well be seen around town in a crop top and jogging shorts. She finally settled on a bright yellow off-the-shoulder top with flared sleeves, distressed skinny jeans and pair of white Keds. She placed the outfit in a bright Great Barrier Reef print tote, along with a small compact, makeup case and a comb.

She set the bag on the round table by the front door after tucking in her small wristlet purse and keys, then she walked to the kitchen to grab the canister of brownies and placed them next to the bag. As she passed the living room, searching for her baseball cap, she heard her phone begin to ring up in her bedroom, where she'd left it.

Annalise bounced up the stairs. She was not surprised to see Mendy's name on the caller ID.

"Hey, Men! Who else should be on my phone at this hour on a Saturday morning but you?"

"Don't 'hey' me all cool, calm and collected there, missy. I know you're bound to be a mass of nervous energy."

"I'm actually doing pretty good right now. I'll confess I was up most of the night worrying, but I settled down as I picked out an outfit for later."

"Later, huh? I thought this was just a picnic. What haven't you told me?"

"Nothing. I swear! I just thought maybe if it went well, we might decide to do something afterward. I thought it was a good idea to pick out something casual to wear... you know, just in case."

Mendy couldn't stop herself from giggling. "Oooohhhh! Annalise has a crush on Anthony."

"So help me, you better stop it before I cancel this date."

"You wouldn't dare... you like him. But in all seriousness, I'm proud of you, Annalise. That's a really big step for you. It's about time you find yourself a man."

"Thanks for the push, Mendy. I will deny it if you ever tell someone, but maybe, for once, you were right. I'll call you later when I get home and spill the tea."

"I'll be waiting here by the phone."

Annalise burst out laughing. "Somehow, I knew you would say that. I'm picturing a gargoyle perched over the phone, staring at it intensely, just waiting to dive down on the innocent, unsuspecting device."

Annalise had spent the next two hours engrossed in her distance education classes when she was startled by the friendly rat-tat-tat at her door. She looked down at her watch, surprised to find that it was 9:59 a.m. She called out, "Just a moment," as she jumped up, before tightening her ponytail as she glanced at her reflection on the microwave door.

Annalise opened the door with a smile to find Anthony looking hot in a tight pair of black jogging shorts and a tank top. She was surprised when he leaned forward and enveloped her in a loose hug with his right arm wrapped around her shoulders.

"Hi there, gorgeous... I mean Annalise. I hope I'm not being too forward, but your beauty had me at a loss for words."

Annalise's cheeks blushed a crimson red, as she smiled and looked down at her shoes. "No, that is... uh... fine. You just surprised me. You aren't looking too bad there yourself."

"Well, now that the awkward hellos are out of the way, these are for you." Anthony pulled his left hand out from behind his back and presented her with a bouquet of six large fiery orange roses.

"Those are absolutely stunning! You really didn't have to do that, Anthony. Thank you so much," Annalise said, breathless as she turned to walk into the kitchen. "Please have a seat at the table while I find a vase."

Annalise breathed in deeply over the flowers as she stretched on tiptoe to retrieve the vase from the top shelf of the cabinet by the sink.

"Please, let me," Anthony said as he grabbed the vase, his side pressed comfortably against hers.

Annalise's eyes met his and held them for a few seconds,

neither of them breathing as she took the vase from his hand. "Thank you," she whispered, before looking down at her trembling hands. He held his position there another few seconds before turning and taking a seat at the table. She turned on the tap and set the vase in the sink to fill as she pulled out a drawer and grabbed a pair of scissors to trim the stems.

Annalise poured the packet of flower food into the vase and turned off the faucet, then began to remove the plastic overwrap. "I've never seen roses in such a vibrant shade of orange before," she said.

"Neither had I. I must confess... But I have a connection: My friend owns My Secret Garden, the best flower shop in a 500-mile radius. Apparently, these are called Heart's Desire. I met her at the office... she supplies flowers for all my needs."

"So, I guess you buy all the girls flowers? Uhh... excuse me. That was rude to ask."

"No pardons needed. That was an entirely reasonable assumption, especially after my own comment. Open mouth, insert entire leg, Anthony! Although, I didn't mean it that way. You are the only woman I have bought a bouquet of roses for on the first date. You are special. You deserve them."

Annalise smiled at him as she finished arranging the flowers in the vase, then placed them in the center of the table. "I really do appreciate them. Thanks again. Shall we go?"

Anthony's wide smile returned, his eyes sparkling to match. He held out his hand when he rose and took hers, leading her to the door. She turned to grab her tote bag and the canister of brownies before proceeding out the door. "May I set these in the trunk, out of the sun?"

"Let me take care of that for you." Anthony led her to the passenger seat and opened the door. Annalise sat down and placed the items in his proffered hand. He closed the door gently after making sure she was out of the way, then walked back to the trunk, placing the items inside and clicking it shut.

Anthony climbed into the driver's seat, his brow furrowed. "What's in the tote bag anyway?"

"Oh, I just brought a change of clothes for after the run... in case I wanted it."

"A woman after my own heart. I have my own duffel bag back there with some essentials as well. Off we go!" he exclaimed as his Jaguar backed out of the driveway in one smooth motion.

Annalise's joyous laugh swept through the car often as the two of them chatted about the ridiculous couples on this season's episodes of *Help! I'm in a Secret Relationship!* The 20-minute drive back into town, followed by the hourlong drive up the mountain, to Sanford Meadows State Park passed in a blur of easy conversation.

Anthony chose a parking space in the shade, then came around to open the door for Annalise. His fingers interlocked with hers as he grabbed her hand to lead her over to the jogging path. They stopped, and both began to stretch, almost as if on cue. Annalise couldn't believe how seamless their interactions had been so far.

"So, how difficult of a jog were you interested in? We can do the five-mile Hillary Trail with the 1,000-foot change in elevation or the two-mile Messner Trail that is mostly flat. By the way, I hope you have an appetite. I have prepared quite the feast for us today."

"Well, let's build up that appetite. Are you coming?" Annalise called out with a wink, her feet already pounding up the steep path of the Hillary Trail.

Anthony shook his head and charged up the path to catch

up. It rapidly became clear that they were both in shape, their powerful legs carrying them up the path without pause, with neither straining to catch their breath. Annalise stopped at the summit, and Anthony took a picture of the smiling, triumphant woman with the valley below her. Annalise considered asking him for a selfie of the two of them, but she didn't want to appear too presumptuous.

Halfway down the descent, Anthony took off with a wink and an impromptu race for lunch began. After a couple of moments, he looked back because he could no longer hear her footfalls behind him. He quickened his pace as he rounded the last bend. It was natural that he should have begun to worry about her. Where had she gone?

Then he looked up to see Annalise casually leaning against his Jag. "Guess you don't know about that alternate shortcut down the hill?" she giggled. "Oh, it is a bit steeper."

"You're a competitive one, aren't you? And quite independent, too. It's as if you stretched your wings and soared down that last stretch." He shook his head, and Annalise saw a flare in his eye. But she shrugged it off, deciding he was merely returning her playful banter. He opened the trunk and removed the picnic basket and a blanket, then turned to her with the canister in hand. "Brownies... I presume?"

"Yes. Thank you."

The two of them walked down the path in the other direction toward the meadow. Anthony chose a spot in the center of a large fairy ring embedded in the grass and laid out the blanket. Long, wispy strands of moss hung just above their heads from the giant pine trees near the forest's edge. The sunlight filtered through the branches, casting ever-moving beams of light upon their faces as the branches swayed in the breeze.

"This spot is really quite magical. Thank you for bringing me out here."

"You are welcome. I am glad you're enjoying yourself. I hope you are enjoying the company as well. You were in your own world up there on that hill. I almost thought you forgot you weren't out here alone at one point."

"I'm sorry. I didn't mean to seem like that. I'm quite independent by nature... always have been. I feel as free as a bird, soaring across the sky, held aloft by the thermals. Jogging has become my escape. It is when I am most at peace with myself. I guess you could say it is my Zen."

"I guess I can understand that."

"I thought you were focused on running as well and intended for us to interact at lunch."

"Maybe I am just being too sensitive. One of my last attempts at dating... well, she cared more about surfing and spending time at the ocean, *her* Zen place, than spending time with me."

"I truly apologize. I didn't realize I'd been that preoccupied. I do want to spend time with you. I've been looking forward to it for the last day and a half. Can we start fresh?"

"Of course... of course. Here, let me get the food out for you. We can talk as we eat our lunch."

Anthony spent the next five minutes removing the containers and detailing every tasty morsel he had prepared. Then he passed out the plates and napkins. "Please, dig in while I open the wine. I hope you like Pinot Grigio?"

"Fabulous!" Annalise reached over to open the tin of brownies. The delightful aroma of warm chocolate washed over them.

"Are you trying to corrupt me? My mother taught me that I must eat my meal before dessert, but I'm not sure that I can resist."

"I won't tell if you don't."

Anthony snatched up a large brownie full of chocolate chunks and took a big bite. Annalise giggled as she filled her plate with crostini pieces, some covered in *foie gras* and others with caviar, and then rolled up pieces of prosciutto with the different cheeses inside. Anthony enjoyed watching her face as she explored some culinary delights for the first time, her mouth rolling the flavors across her tongue.

Before they knew it, two hours had passed while they chatted about their childhoods, experiences in college and their current career paths. The sun had passed over them, leaving shadows at their backs.

Anthony was impressed with Annalise's beauty, intelligence and spirit, but it began to dawn on him that they didn't seem to be a match.

While Annalise did want a husband and family, it didn't seem to be a pressing issue for her anytime soon. She seemed focused almost exclusively on moving forward in her career. She had received a promotion six months ago; to help her prepare for further advancement, her employer was paying for her to take extensive distance learning classes. She would be finishing those in the coming months, at which point she would receive another promotion to a hands-on position.

With everything that was happening at work, Annalise didn't seem available to pursue any kind of relationship. She worked long hours, had schoolwork in the evenings, and would soon be on call with the next promotion. It was clear that she was looking for a man to fill her "dance card" in those rare moments when she took a break, such as that friend's upcoming party she had mentioned the other night. A space filler... not an actual priority in her life.

While Annalise might not become his partner, though, that didn't mean she couldn't still be part of his life.

Anthony had become quieter as the afternoon progressed, so Annalise began to clear up their dishes and stow the food back in the picnic basket for him.

"Thanks for helping clean up."

"It was the least I could do after the trouble you went to preparing all those gourmet foods."

"Thank you for the brownies. They were delicious."

"I put the tin in the basket as well. Please enjoy the rest of them."

"You are spoiling me."

Annalise smiled and climbed to her feet.

"Hey, would you like to stop by my workshop on the way back to your house?" he asked. "I want to show you a project I've been working on."

"Sure. I would love that." Annalise sighed in relief.

When they reached the car, Anthony escorted Annalise to her seat before returning the picnic basket and blanket to the trunk. He met her eyes in the rearview mirror, waving just before he closed it.

Anthony sat down and turned to Annalise.

"My workshop is on the edge of town. It is pretty much on the way to your house. We should be there in about an hour."

"Sounds good."

Their easy conversation resumed as they turned to another mutual favorite, *Catfish*. Neither one of them could understand how people could be so gullible... so accepting of obvious huge red flags. Anthony turned off the highway and onto a road headed toward an industrial center. The area was full of what appeared to be long-abandoned old warehouses.

A mile farther down the road, he stopped in front of a large, dark grey metal warehouse with a sturdy padlock chaining the door closed. "It's larger than I need, but it is cheap. I have a surprise for you. Let me grab it out of the back before we head inside."

Annalise smiled and nodded her head. Anthony jumped out of the car and returned to the trunk. Annalise watched him in the visor mirror shuffle through a duffel bag in the back, as she smoothed her hair. Before long, he approached her door with an object wrapped in cloth.

He opened her door with a smile on his face. As she turned to swing her legs out of the car, she saw the cloth in his hand near her cheek. She was overwhelmed by the sweet-smelling ether-like odor as the cloth was pressed against her mouth. Within seconds, her eyes began to blink and burn.

Then everything faded to black.

Six

Awakenings

June 2022

Annalise's head was spinning and throbbing from the worst headache of her life. Her eyelids felt so heavy, the exhaustion dragging her back down to tranquil sleep, but her mind a chaotic swirl of fear and confusion. Every time she tried to move her head, a wave of dizziness overcame her. If only she could open her eyes to see where she was or identify the noises she heard surrounding her... but she felt hopeless.

"I see you are awake again. Welcome back, sleepyhead."

The voice echoed in the room around her, making it impossible to pinpoint its location. Annalise could hear the clattering of metal objects and footsteps moving back and forth. A shiver ran through her body, whether from the unnaturally cool temperature in the room or out of sheer terror, she didn't know. Although she still couldn't open her eyes, she could sense bright lights surrounding her.

She fought a wave of nausea and dizziness as she tried to shift her body and assess her ability to escape. Fear washed over as she realized that she was reclining in a seat that felt eerily similar to a dentist's chair, but her arms and legs were bound tightly. There was even a strap across her chest that prevented her from trying to rise. All she could do was lift her head.

After a few minutes, she was able to squint her eyelids open a little. She could see that she was deep in a large, empty warehouse. The windows had all been blacked out with paint and metal panels riveted to the wall. She could see the door that must have been the entrance, but it was securely locked with chains and padlocks, as well as a deadbolt that locked with a key. There were even large metal drawbars at the top and bottom to prevent it from being opened from the outside. The warehouse appeared inescapable... or impenetrable... or maybe it was meant to be both.

Above her she could see large high bay light fixtures, with metal cages covering the 100-watt bulbs installed every six feet between industrial strip lights. As she looked around the room, she saw ring and other video filming lights on tripods situated on both sides of her and in front. The reason became apparent as she noticed a large, professional-looking video camera mounted on a heavy rolling tripod about ten feet in front of her. Against the wall to the far left, she noticed a sophisticated computer system set up with a bank of monitors.

Annalise had heard footsteps only moments ago, but whoever was making them was out of sight behind her at the moment. Her eyes widened as she saw the cause of all the metal clattering sounds she had heard. Off to her right, some kind of large hoist system was suspended from the ceiling; seven thin metal cables hung down from it, each with a sharp, terrifying hook at the end. Between her and the hoist, she saw a large rolling tray of medical instruments and power tools alongside what appeared to be a surgical table.

"Anthony? Where are you? Is this some kind of sick game? Your idea of a joke? You succeeded... I am afraid. You win! Now let me go."

"Who said it was a game?"

Anthony—or someone who sounded like him—appeared from behind her and came around to stand next to her. The man was wearing a black cotton jumpsuit and a shiny, black polyester hoodie. A fine black mesh had been sewn into the hood, covering his face. It was the kind of mesh used on fly masks for horses that allowed him to see out, but kept others from seeing his features.

"Why are you dressed like that?"

"Well, I can't have people seeing who I am. Plus, I can't very well walk around covered in your blood."

"What the fuck, Anthony? Why would you be covered in my blood? This is really not funny. This is a truly sick, demented game, and I don't appreciate it."

"When did I or anyone else say this was a game? Does it feel like a game? You look terrified to me... as you should be. And for fuck's sake, quit calling me Anthony!"

"What's your name then?"

"That doesn't concern you."

"What're you going to do to me?"

"That's not your concern either. You won't be around much longer to care."

"Anthony... uhh... whoever you are, I will do anything. I will pay you whatever you want. Just please let me go. I haven't done anything to deserve this."

"Your money doesn't concern me. Besides, you don't have enough to turn my head. But you are worth... or should I say... what I do with your body will compensate me fairly for what my work is worth."

"And what work is that?

"You will find out soon enough. I should really be getting the show started. We are running late as it is."

"Show? You sick fuck, what show are you talking about? That's why you have all the lights and cameras? You're going to broadcast from your little torture chamber?"

"That's correct. You are the next contestant on.... the *Dark*

Arts. Yay! Woohoooo! Are you excited?" Anthony yelled as he ran around her excitedly.

"You're going to pay for this. They'll find you and lock you up until they strap you down in the electric chair!"

"And who might they be?"

"The police... my other family."

"What are you talking about?"

"I never told you, did I? I just mentioned I did data entry and worked in the phone center... the phone center being 911 dispatch and the police tipline. The data entry? That's me entering information from the tipline into the case log. I am finishing up classes for my promotion to become an entry-level forensic technician.

"They will notice that I am missing. They will come looking for me. They won't stop until they solve the crime. That is what I mean by my other family.

"Oh, Anthony, my best friend—who, by the way knows that I went out with you—is a detective. She will make it her personal mission to find me and make you pay. I wouldn't want to be you. This is your last chance."

"I told you my name isn't Anthony. You don't know shit about me, and neither does she. I have covered my tracks well. Nobody will ever find me, least of all, your friend. You will vanish off the face of the Earth, never to be seen again. For all intents and purposes, I don't exist. They can't catch someone who doesn't exist. I am done talking."

"I'm not done with you."

"Oh yes, you are, my dear. I'm quite done with you talking," Anthony growled as he tore a large piece of duct tape from the roll, slapping it across her mouth.

Anthony walked behind the camera and looked through the

50

viewfinder. He made some final adjustments to make sure Annalise, the surgical table and the hoist apparatus were all in view. Then he walked over to the computer station and grabbed a mic off the desk, clipping it to his hoodie at the top of the zipper and testing to make sure he could be heard clearly.

"I just need to connect to the VPN and then route it through proxy servers around the world to make my IP untraceable. Now, to log in to Dark Arts on Tor. Done and done. Are you ready, Annalise? We are going live in just about seven minutes."

On one of the monitors across the room, Annalise could see a dark blood-red background with the words "Dark Arts" in a crimson-colored gothic font across the screen. A countdown on the screen stood at 6 minutes, 43 seconds.

Anthony removed a syringe filled with milky white liquid from the pocket of his hoodie. "I need to move you over to the table now, and I don't trust you not to misbehave. I am going to give you this propofol, and you will be back with me—or should I say us—in about 3-5 minutes." Anthony injected the liquid into her cephalic vein in her right arm. Annalise's head dropped almost instantly. One last thought passed through her mind before unconsciousness set in. *He is a monster.*

Anthony removed the ligatures from Annalise's arms and legs and released the strap across her chest. He scooped up her limp form and carried her over to the table, placing her on her stomach. He slid out the arm rests that were connected to the underside of the table and set her arms on them. Multiple ligatures were placed on each arm at the wrist and elbow, and a long strap was connected across her shoulders.

He then slid each leg over to the sides of the table. A rail on each side of the table ran along the length of it, allowing Anthony to bind her legs securely at the ankle and knee. Finally, he secured a long strap around the table and her body, holding her down at the hips. The result: her body could wiggle no more than a quarter of an inch—and only with great effort. The final step involved tilting her head up and resting her chin on the table so she faced the camera directly... every grimace of pain and every tear would be on full display.

As Annalise began to stir, Anthony looked over at the monitor and was pleased to see the countdown had reached 1 minute, 15 seconds. He walked around to Annalise's side and stood next to her, his hand resting on her shoulder.

He smiled down at and bellowed, "It's showtime!"

Seven

The Eagle Soars

June 2022

Anthony reached into his pocket and pressed the small button on the remote to activate the camera's recording function. He stroked Annalise's hair as he stared into the camera.

"Welcome, loyal followers, to the third episode of *Dark Arts* hosted by me, *Le Créateur*. As always, I want to thank you for your patronage. I have a special installment for you tonight. We are returning to the theme of transformation, as we did in Episode 1 '*La Sirène.*'

"Tonight, we have something sure to please everyone. For all my gore lovers out there, this episode promises plenty of blood and graphic body horror. For those who love history, we will be exploring my artistic interpretation of the Viking torture ritual, the blood eagle. If you are not familiar with this practice, you are in for a treat.

"As I am sure you can see, our subject tonight is very much alive and conscious. I know a lot of you out there enjoy the spectacle—the ruthless subjugation, terror, and pain experienced by my subjects. This episode will make all your nerves tingle, send your pulse racing, and satisfy even your basest, most deviant need for gratification. You see, since the blood eagle was a form of Viking punishment, it was performed on a live person, as we will be doing tonight.

"I will be activating the aerial camera as well, so you will have a split-screen view of the process. If everyone is ready, let's make some art!"

Le Créateur walked offscreen over to the computer bank. With a few swift keystrokes, he activated the camera mounted over the table, made a few quick adjustments to center the picture over Annalise's back, and then created a split-screen view showing both camera angles. He returned to the screen and drew the instrument tray closer to the surgical table.

He leaned over so his face was only an inch from Annalise's tear-streaked, terrified face. "This is going to hurt a bit. Well, quite a lot more than just a bit. Are you ready?"

Annalise's muffled scream and whimpers could be heard through the tape across her mouth. Her body wiggled ever so slightly as she fought to free herself from her bonds... to no avail.

Dear God, what is he going to do to me? This can't be happening. It must be some terrible nightmare. Wake up, goddammit!

Annalise blinked her eyes repeatedly and then opened them wide, willing herself to wake up and find herself safe and sound in bed. She screamed again in frustration, but Anthony just laughed at her —which only fueled her resolve to free herself and make him pay for what he was doing. She twisted her wrists but could not slip them from the restraints, only managing to make them hurt worse.

"Shush, my dear," she heard him say. "You will be as free as a bird, ready to take flight and soar from this cage soon enough."

Le Créateur returned to the side of the table and retrieved a very sharp scalpel from the tray. He pressed the blade into the skin of her lower back at the tailbone and watched in awe as the blood blossomed around the blade. She couldn't see his expression, but she could imagine it. She couldn't see the blood either, but she could feel it oozing out of her as her flesh was sliced apart.

Annalise yelped and the skin of her back twitched as the pain took over. "Bastard!" she screamed into the tape, but producing only an unintelligible mumble. He pressed the scalpel deep into her skin and began the long trek up the center of her back until he reached the top of her ribcage. Blood flowed from the long incision and pooled in that most seductive divot on a woman's lower back as rivulets traced their way down her abdomen and breasts, and began to collect on the table.

Annalise fought to get away from the sharp blade, even if only a fraction of an inch. Her tiny movements were barely noticeable and certainly didn't impede *Le Créateur*'s work. Her faint cries went unheeded as her respirations increased and the flesh on her back twitched in pain. She fought against the restraints again, making herself bleed where they cut deeply into her skin. She manipulated her head until she slid her chin into her body, so her head could rest at a normal angle facedown, attempting to hide from the prying eyes of the audience.

I won't let these sick, morbid assholes see my pain.

Le Créateur put the scalpel down and returned her head to the previous position, placing a restraint over the top of it and through an eyebolt on the table to hold it in place. Annalise screamed in frustration. *How could he not even allow me a little dignity?*

At the top and bottom of that long incision, *Le Créateur* began to carve perpendicular cuts deep into her flesh, creating a large "I" across her back. He grabbed one corner of the left flap he had just created and began to flay back the skin and muscles.

Fuck! He is fucking skinning me. I'm not an animal. What is he going to do to me next? Her head felt fuzzy. The room was beginning to spin.

Don't pass o...

Then he proceeded to do the same on the right side.

After he had cut through the trapezius and levator scapulae muscles in the shoulder area and the latissimus dorsi muscle in the lower back, he was able to clearly see her ribcage.

Blood was pouring out of her ruined flesh. The shallow reservoir of the table had filled with blood, and it had begun to cascade in a crimson waterfall over the edges down onto the floor, where a downward slope guided any fluids to the drain directly under the center of the table.

The holes of the drain were beginning to clog with large clots of blood.

Halfway through the flaying process, Annalise had passed out from the pain. Her already light complexion began to grow paler as she began to exsanguinate, and her breathing had become shallower.

Le Créateur reached back over to the instrument table and set down the scalpel before grabbing a large pair of pruning shears. He began, systematically, to cut each rib from the spinal column on both sides. After the first bone-crunching crack, Annalise awoke with a scream. The tape ripped away the skin around her lips from the violent motion of her mouth opening to shriek. With the second crack, her body went limp, and she grew still as unconsciousness overwhelmed her.

After he cut through the last rib, *Le Créateur* severed the last of the muscles attaching the ribs to the lower back. Starting at the top, he grabbed each rib and brutally wrenched it to the side of the body with a resounding crack as each rib broke within the body cavity. This opened up the ribcage, so Annalise's ribs looked like outstretched fingers projecting from her body. As he progressed, Annalise's breathing became much slower and more irregular before finally stopping just as he fully exposed the lungs. The camera revealed one brief flutter of the lungs, like a bird's wings, before they collapsed and ceased to move forever.

"Well, faithful audience, you just saw the last breath of our subject there. I will remove the restraints now, so I can complete the rest of the transformation more easily."

Le Créateur removed the restraints and dropped them into a bucket off to the side. Then he reached down into the chest cavity and used the scalpel to cut the pulmonary veins and arteries and the primary bronchi to allow the lungs to be removed. He placed them on the tops of the ribs to look like wings.

"I have one final step to complete the transformation."

Le Créateur adjusted the overhead camera manually, directing the lens toward Annalise's feet. He grabbed the scalpel and began to cut open the pad of the foot just above the arch so he could reach the cuneiform and cuboid bones. He cut away any muscles and tissue that prevented him from seeing the bones. Then, exchanging the scalpel for the drill on the tray, he proceeded to drill into each of the three cuneiform bones and bore two holes in the larger cuboid bone.

He threaded thick, unyielding galvanized wire through the holes and secured it by wrapping it around the bone. Then he pushed the wire through the tissues of the foot and phalanges until it was about three-eighths of an inch from exiting each toe. He used fine suture to close the incisions in both feet. Once that was complete, he was able to bend the wire to curl the toes, forming the curved, taloned feet of the eagle.

"The transformation is complete... now to put on her display."

Le Créateur unlocked the wheels of the surgical table and rolled it under the hoist system to the right. He used the hydraulic lift under the table to raise Annalise's body to the proper height so that he could begin securing the hooks into her body. The first two hooks were on the longest cables in the back and were embedded deep in the flesh of her heels.

He then placed some supports under her upper body to raise it to the proper height. The hook on the shortest cable in the very front was pushed through the back of her neck and turned to hook under the occipital bone on the skull to keep her head upright. The arms were suspended, stretched out fully at her sides to extend her wingspan. Hooks were passed through each wrist to hold them in place, and the rails on the hoist were spread out horizontally until the proper wingspan was obtained. The last two hooks were embedded in her back and turned to hook around her spine; one was placed in the shoulder area and the other in the lower back to support the weight of her body.

Le Créateur stepped back to admire his work. The effect was stunning. Annalise had been transformed into a majestic soaring eagle—her head held high in the air as she searched the ground below. Her wings spread wide, held aloft by the thermals passing under them. Her feet were outstretched below her: the curved talons prepared to snatch up some prey below.

"Well, ladies and gentleman, I present to you *The Eagle Soars.* I will be putting up five limited edition prints for auction later this evening at 8 p.m. PDT at the main Dark Arts site on the dark web at the address displayed on your screen. Remember, when placing your bids, that our website ends in '.onion,' not '.com.' As per usual, only cryptocurrency will be accepted, and secure anonymous delivery will be arranged. This video will be up for streaming on the Dark Arts gallery for the next 24 hours. After that, a heavily encrypted digital download can be purchased for $2,000 USD. I hope you enjoyed tonight's presentation. Goodnight and sweet screams to you all!"

Le Créateur pressed the button on the remote in his pocket to end the streaming session. Then he walked over to the computer bank and shut down the overhead camera. There was much work left to do before the evening was through, but it was time to take a break.

Stellan Erikkson unzipped the hoodie and slipped it over his head. The mask was functional and required when he performed as *Le Créateur*, but he couldn't wait to get it off at the end of each session and return to himself. He stripped out of the bloodied coveralls and walked to the back of the warehouse.

It was time to wash his hands and prepare a little dinner. All traces of Anthony needed to disappear from Annalise's life, but he had hours, if not days, before she would be missed. That all could wait an hour until he made some Truffle Tagliatelle in cream sauce. He'd earned it.

Sharon Marie Provost

Eight
Love Me Tinder

June 2022

Much of what Stellan had told Annalise about himself was true. He was an excellent cook: His Truffle Tagliatelle could have been served in the finest Italian restaurant. It was one of many skills he had picked up along the line—this one from a chef that his mother and he had lived with for a year during their travels.

He had also worked in marketing, albeit nearly five years ago now. For the past five years, he had lived the life of the struggling artist. Although, thanks to his mother's way with finances, money had never been part of that struggle. The hard part of being an artist—getting noticed and appreciated—had proved to be more difficult than he'd expected.

Stellan's art installations with lights and dark imagery were meant to put the viewer on edge—feel unsure if they were safe. The goal was to evoke emotion and spur discussion. Some paintings depicted bleak environments such as deep fog obscuring someone, or something, just beginning to appear. In others, the sun was a terrifying fiery ball about to incinerate all life. Or all light from the sun was blocked, and life was slowly being extinguished, as creatures of the dark rose to power. Staircases to nowhere, piers that ended in the ocean's fury with Cthulhu-like creatures rising from the depths, roads that fell off to nothingness, and scary inhabitants that were not quite human reigned supreme.

The light installations that accompanied the art were designed to further the viewer's unease. Blinding lights raised the tension in some pieces, while dim lighting created shadows that instilled fear in others. Red lights were included to inspire strong emotions, potentially signaling danger and creating a sensation of heat.

Stellan's artistic works were true installations that needed an entire gallery to immerse the viewer in his world. One had to experience the entirety of his vision to truly understand his genius. There were plenty of galleries on the West Coast, but he had come to realize his style of art was not meant for the audience he found there.

His art was more tailored to the fine, sophisticated tastes of New York or the great cities of the world: Paris, London, Salzburg, Geneva, Rome, or Venice. Unfortunately, he had lacked the connections to land an exhibit at any of the influential New York galleries, yet alone on the world stage.

All that had changed, though, over a year ago when Meredith had come into his life after their chance encounter at the grocery store.

In February of 2021, he had come up with the idea for his *Dark Arts* collection. They, too, conveyed his immersive vision of a phantasmagoric nightmare, using human sculptures of fantastical creatures... at once beautiful and grotesque.

He could never display his *Dark Arts* collection for the general public. However, it was ideal for the discriminating tastes found on the dark web... an audience happy to pay—handsomely at that—for the opportunity to view his work. Or, even better, to own one of his pieces.

Dark Arts

That was another skill he had garnered during his adventures with his mother. Not all those they met and associated with were fine, upstanding citizens. Many were on the fringes of society, whether it be socioeconomically, in their religious beliefs, or being on the wrong side of the law. He had always been tech savvy, so he learned quickly from those mentors, gaining both superior hacking skills and the means necessary to traverse and transact on the dark web.

He had created his Dark Arts site and put the word out on the dark web, advertising on sites that catered to murder, snuff films, the S&M underground, taboo art, and other socially unacceptable practices. He offered a discount for those who subscribed before he unveiled his first creation. He advertised to collectors of taboo art that prints or, sometimes, even the art piece itself would be available for purchase. More importantly, he announced that downloads of the video could be purchased 24 hours after it aired.

Stellan hadn't initially known how he was going to recruit his subjects, but then the perfect opportunity presented itself. He had created an alternate identity profile on Tinder. He'd felt that he was ready to settle down and start a family while he continued to pursue his art career. If it worked out with one of his matches, he thought, he would explain the fake name by telling her he hadn't wanted someone to fall for him because of his money.

He'd met a beautiful, blond, green-eyed California beach babe, ironically named Arizona. She loved the ocean and, more specifically, surfing—that is when she wasn't busy working to create the latest technologically innovative app for iPhones. It had all seemed perfect at first, but then she was always busy. She called off multiple dates after he'd put a lot of planning and hard work into them. When he found out a month later that her priority had been a "day of killer waves," he could no longer tolerate her excuses, so he planned to break it off.

Then it came to him... she would be the perfect subject for the first *Dark Arts* piece he had been contemplating, *La Sirène*. She would make an absolutely stunning mermaid. Even though she was a beautiful, gregarious girl, she had formed no real, meaningful attachments. Her parents had died a few years ago in a car accident. She had no girlfriends and dated infrequently (and, as he had learned the hard way, not seriously). She performed her tech job developing apps from home. The only people she ever really interacted with—and only on a superficial level—were the surfer dudes who frequented the same beach. She would not be missed soon and had very likely told no one about him... not that it mattered, since he was using a false identity.

He lured her out with him by promising her a big surprise. He explained that he needed to stop at his workshop to pick something up and then drugged her with chloroform when he came around to open her door. She had been his first piece of art, so he had not developed his showmanship at that point. He injected her with an overdose of potassium to stop her heart rather than putting her through a more gruesome end—the kind that viewers came to demand.

Stellan had sewn her legs together to form the body of the tail fluke. To form the classic fin shape, he had used a sledgehammer to break her ankles so they would twist to the side and then smashed the bones of the feet to flatten them. He had then meticulously carved patterns of semi-circles into the flesh of her torso and down her legs, creating the impression of scales.

Even though he loved her blond hair, he dyed it a beautiful shade of teal and placed small orange morning glories in her hair to cement her look as a temptress of the deep. Then, after he had washed the blood off her skin and dried her, he had applied several coats of a light aquamarine paint with a faint metallic cast. Then he added accents of electric blue and fuchsia to her tail. To complete the look, he had glued clam shells to her breasts.

The last step had been to position her body for the prints. He had created a beach scene in one of the rooms of the warehouse, complete with sand, seashells and a surrealistic ocean mural with a spectacular sunset at the horizon. He had affixed two large metal rings with detachable meat hooks onto the wall. He slid the first hook deep into the middle of her back and hooked it around her thoracic spine. The second hook he speared through her neck at the level of the C1 vertebrae through the atlanto-occipital joint and turned it to catch under the lip of the skull's occipital bone.

Once the hooks were placed, he attached them to the rings. Then he positioned her body so that her tail fluke was off to the side and bent slightly at the knee joints to create an alluring pose for his bewitching sea-maiden.

His first episode had been a hit. He'd made more on that one video than he had in his entire ten years in marketing. The prints sold out five minutes after being posted. Word of mouth spread on the dark web, and he was flooded with new subscribers. Five hundred people purchased the digital download, just in the first 48 hours. Fans filled his comments page with ideas for future pieces, requests for more prints and, of course, requests for more blood and torture of the subject.

His hacker skills came in handy when he began the process of wiping all digital traces of his existence from Arizona's life. Fortunately, he had never been to her place, met any of her surfer buddies or bought her anything, so he did not have to worry about any physical or eyewitness evidence. Disposing of the body was not difficult because the warehouse he had bought had been involved in the destruction of medical waste, so it was outfitted with a rotary kiln that burned hot enough to destroy a human body.

While he planned out his next work of art, he once again attempted to find a life partner... or, potentially, his next *Dark Arts* subject. He protected his identity further by changing his Tinder profile to incognito mode. This allowed his profile to only be seen by those he had swiped right on, so no one could find him unless he wanted them to.

As excited as he was for his debut exhibition in New York, Stellan missed the art that had become a part of his very being... his true passion. So back in July of 2021, while he was finishing the new pieces, he began to look for a date (or a new subject for *Dark Arts*, since Tinder had worked out so well the first time.)

This time, he found a girl who was outside his normal tastes—she had dyed her hair brunette, although she was a natural blonde—but her intelligence and sweet personality seemed perfect. She was a bit of a loner, which was perfect for his purposes if it didn't work out between them. She was not an outdoorsy gal, so he set up a dinner date at a small out-of-the-way place that did a bustling business just outside of town, where they were unlikely to be noticed or remembered.

The dinner went well at first... until the subject of politics came up. She was a passionate Trump supporter and went on a tirade that drew unwanted attention from those seated around them. He could still hear her shrill voice ringing through his ears, "Trump is a hero. He's a great businessman who saved the economy. He's a strong leader who finally drained the swamp. He fights to protect us from all the illegal immigrants streaming over the border."

In her eyes, Trump and the MAGA movement could do no wrong. She began to spew hateful statements toward those who did not agree with her in the restaurant, calling them all losers and vermin—and then toward Anthony himself when he didn't defend her.

It was like she had removed the mask of intelligence, reasonable thought, and common sense she'd been wearing, and her true face had emerged. She became dark and scary as she railed about the merits of Trump and his promise to "make America great again." Anthony had remained quiet and non-confrontational during her tirade. He was not one to discuss politics in general, but her single-minded, utter reverence for one person made her soliloquy even more disconcerting.

Her two-faced dark side gave him the perfect inspiration for his next work of art.

He needed to gather some items in preparation, so he invited her to see his workshop on the weekend. Millie still seemed angry at him, plus she already had plans for later in the day, so she refused to let him pick her up. Instead, she insisted on taking the bus and then walking over to her friend's house when she was done. Rather than giving her the exact address that would lead back to him if she was found to be missing, he had her meet him at the bus stop by the industrial district so he could walk her over from there.

On Saturday, he arrived at the bus stop to find Millie standing there with a friend. Apparently, they decided to get lunch before going to a MAGA rally later in the afternoon, so they had traveled together. Stellan had not planned for this development, but as he thought about it, he realized that it might just enhance his piece and please the audience even more when he offered them a surprise.

They walked back to the warehouse, and he asked the girls to wait a moment outside as he prepared the surprise unveiling for them. He ran inside and grabbed another rag and soaked it, along with the one he was already carrying, in chloroform before stuffing them both in his pockets. He went outside and asked the girls if he could cover their eyes and lead them inside. They agreed readily, so he walked around behind them, reaching into his pockets with both hands surreptitiously to palm the rags. He quickly wrapped one arm around each girl's neck and placed the rags over their noses and mouths. Within seconds, they dropped into his arms, and he guided them carefully to the ground.

He grabbed an arm of each girl and began to drag them into the warehouse before anyone could witness the scene. He placed each of them in a chair and bound their arms and legs and gagged them.

Then he started his show.

He began with a speech about how often people hide their true character until, one day, it rears its ugly head. He explained that this piece would be an amalgamation of the two girls.

He then further incapacitated each girl by placing tight straps around their foreheads and necks, so they couldn't move. His artistic process started with the friend, whose face he began crudely hacking away, following the edges of her scalp, along her ears and then removing the skin under her chin. After he was finished, he slit her throat so he didn't have to listen to her screams and the gurgling of swallowed blood in her throat.

Millie couldn't see what was happening to her friend, but she could certainly hear her screams and cries for help. When he approached Millie with a razor-sharp scalpel in his hand, her eyes grew wide, and she began to babble incoherently. The removal of her face had to be much more precise, so he injected her with pancuronium. This drug left her conscious and able to feel pain, but unable to cry out or move.

He began by making a vertical incision down the center of her face from the forehead at the hairline down the underside of her chin until it reached the neckline. He then made a careful incision around the sides of the nose to remove it from the tissue he wanted to collect. Returning to where his previous incision had ended, he cut the skin all the way around her throat. At that point, he began to exhaustively peel back and dissect her face and scalp from her skull and connective tissue.

Once he had obtained the flesh covering her skull, he placed it on the instrument table so he could clean off the blood and then dry the tissue. When that was complete, he carried it over to a sewing machine, where he attached a zipper down the vertical cut on her face so it could be zipped shut as a mask. He carried that mask over to the body of her friend and placed it over her mangled features and zipped the new "mask" closed, down to the start of the nose. He named this particular piece *Two-faced.*

The second episode was a huge success. Given the special nature of this particular piece, he placed ten prints up for auction, and there was still a bidding war. His subscriptions increased dramatically as word of mouth once again spread. The site actually crashed briefly when the digital downloads went up for sale 24 hours after the show aired. Over 2,000 download purchases were processed that first day alone.

Stellan hated to neglect *Dark Arts* over the next four months, but he still had two pieces to finish for his public showing in New York. As his gallery debut approached, he began to contemplate a very special debut of his *Dark Arts* collection to the police investigating Arizona's disappearance. Her story had been broadcast all over the news for weeks after her disappearance, but he hadn't heard anything about her in months.

Then, one month before his show, he decided to mail a print of *La Sirène* to the police. What better way to celebrate his genius work than becoming famous in the New York art scene and infamous to the police?

His showing at the gallery was a critical hit in New York. After a month on display, the items had been put up for sale, and they sold out over the next two months. He spent three months in New York meeting with collectors seeking custom works and curators from other galleries hoping to lure him away for his next big show. His agent Meredith represented him in all those discussions and promised to speak to all of them before his next show.

Stellan returned home a much richer man who had developed a name and reputation for himself. To his dismay, he found that had not been the case for *Le Créateur*. Arizona's disappearance was being mentioned periodically on the news again, but the police were not telling the public that she had been murdered, yet alone mentioning that they had been contacted by the perpetrator.

He watched the news over the next seven months as summer returned, and he feverishly worked on pieces for a future exhibition, but nothing changed. *Le Créateur* could not accept the total news blackout about his existence. It was time to create a new work of art. And it was certainly high time that he send the police the photo of *Two-faced*. As he searched for his next subject, he worked on crafting a letter sure to provoke their ire. He mailed it while on a road trip to New Mexico to pick up some supplies for his latest light installation.

The note read:

Dark Arts

You ignored my first communication with you. You are hiding the murder of Arizona Hutchins from the public. If you continue to hide the truth, I will contact the press. In the meantime, I give to you my next grand work of art, Two-faced.

Ever Yours, Le Créateur

Stellan returned from his trip the day before his date with Annalise, just in time for the preparations needed in case a relationship was possible this time. Alas, time with her had proven that not to be the case. The police would receive their second special delivery soon, and he had work to do to clean up after his date with Annalise.

After he finished his pasta, Stellan returned to the filming area to take pictures for the five prints he would be offering online at the auction later that night. He impressed himself with how well his latest work of art had turned out. After that was done, he began the laborious process of cleaning up. He put on a clean pair of coveralls to protect his clothes while disposing of the body.

He had bought this particular warehouse for a variety of reasons, including its isolated location, size, and most importantly the rotary kiln. He removed her body from the hoist and laid it in a wheelbarrow before wheeling her over to the kiln and depositing her inside.

He had installed a heavy rubber curtain that could be drawn around the artistic space to protect all the expensive equipment from water. He drew it closed and then uncoiled the hose from the hanger in the back corner and began to carefully spray down the floor, surgical table, instrument tray, wheelbarrow and hoist cables.

Now that the cleanup was finished, it was time to edit the video and upload it to the gallery for the next 24 hours and on the downloads page on the main site to be released for sale after the gallery streaming had ended. After that was complete, he looked through the pictures and chose the one for the prints, uploading that image into the auction page and setting it to start at 8 p.m.

The most intense and critical phase of the cleanup was next. He hacked into the Tinder server to remove all traces of any communication between Annalise and Anthony. His Anthony profile was already incognito to the public at large, but more precautions were needed this time since Annalise had said the police would be looking for her. He inserted code into the server that made his profile disappear completely as far as anyone could see on the Tinder administrative and technical side. However, he could still search through profiles and contact users as usual while being a ghost in the system. He couldn't fathom why he hadn't thought of that before.

Stellan's last task required him to hack into T-Mobile's server to remove all the text messages that had passed between the two of them. Stellan stretched and rubbed the knots out of his neck. He was exhausted, and it was time to go home and get some much-needed sleep.

Tomorrow would be another busy day. He would need to arrange discreet, anonymous delivery of the prints because the auctions would close at noon. The ashes from Annalise's cremation would need to be dumped in the river, where they would never be discovered.

Most importantly, he needed to get to work and finish the last two and most complex pieces for his next show. Meredith was pushing him to be done in the next month, so that she could hopefully set up an exhibition over the Christmas season at the prestigious Weimar Gallery on the Upper East Side. There would be a lot of preparations to come over the next six months for that showing, so if he wanted time to complete any more works for his *Dark Arts* collection during that time, he had no time to waste.

Stellan gathered his belongings and headed home for the night, excited to see the response to *Two-faced* over the next few days. But he found himself even more exhilarated contemplating the reaction when another blond, green-eyed beauty was found to be missing.

Nine

Mendy

June 2022

Mendy tried to keep herself busy planning the menu for her Fourth of July party, but she was eager to hear how Annalise's date had gone. She knew they had planned to meet at 10 a.m. to run and then have lunch, but she couldn't fathom how long the date might last. She was tempted to call Annalise, but Annalise had promised to call her as soon as she got home.

Just as Mendy finally focused on picking out recipes for the hors d'oeuvres, she was called in to work because there had been a break in one of her cases.

A detective in the Missing Persons Unit, Mendy had recently applied for a promotion to Homicide, but she hadn't heard back yet. Apparently, some evidence had been found that had prompted a change in the status of Millie Simpson from missing to a homicide, and the detective assigned to investigate wanted her to come in and go over all her findings.

This was the second missing person's case this year to be upgraded to a homicide, and Mendy wondered if they could be related. But she dismissed the idea from her head. There was no way for her to know: The Arizona Hutchins case had been assigned to another detective, so she wasn't privy to any details about her disappearance and murder.

When Mendy arrived at the station, she found Detective Mills standing at a corkboard in the corner of the squad room. She was shocked to see a gruesome picture of her missing person,

Millie, hanging on the top right corner of the board. The murderer had sewn a zipper on her face and then zipped it halfway down over the flayed face of another victim.

"My God! Now I see why you called me right down here. That's horrific."

"Uhh, yes. Hello, um... uhh.."

"Detective Hoffman, but you can call me Mendy."

"Excuse my distraction, Detective. I have been up all night with my daughter... she has croup. It was supposed to be my day off, but this changed everything. The package arrived first thing this morning addressed to the 'Inept Homicide Squad,' so I was called in immediately once we opened it and found this picture."

"I can certainly see why. She went missing nearly a year ago, and he is just now sending us a picture. What gives?"

"He seems to be angry that we haven't reported on the murder of Arizona Hutchins."

"So, the two cases *are* related?"

"Apparently, yes."

"My colleague told me that she had been murdered, and I did wonder why I hadn't heard it reported on the news."

"Because of this...," Detective Mills said as he pointed to another alarming picture in the top left corner, stepping aside so she could see it. Mendy gasped as she recognized Arizona and saw she'd been mutilated to look like a mermaid.

"What kind of sick monster is this bastard?"

"He calls himself *Le Créateur.* This is what he considers 'art.' He uses women as his artistic medium. He's looking for attention—notoriety—and we damn sure weren't going to give it to him. He sent us this picture eight months after she disappeared, once the media coverage had died down. We've been investigating artists in the area ever since, but haven't found any leads.

"It has been eight months since we have heard from him, so to be honest, we were hoping something had happened to him. Now, he's back and threatening to go to the press if we don't report the murder of Arizona... and presumably Millie as well."

"And do we know who the other victim is... underneath the mask? Why does he wait so long to send us pictures of his 'work'? Millie went missing 11 months ago, and I am assuming she has been dead just as long. Why now?"

"We haven't figured that out yet. He waited eight months to send us the picture of Arizona, then we didn't hear from him for eight more months after that. We thought maybe he had been incarcerated for some other crime, but we haven't hit on any leads from that angle—at least, not yet. We'll keep investigating to see if any perp has been locked up during both of those time spans. Maybe he is a real mainstream artist and was out of town for an art show? Maybe he is married with a family that keeps him busy? I wish I fucking knew!" Detective Mills slammed his fist on the desk next to him.

"As for your other question... that's part of the reason I asked you down here. I saw that you questioned her family and friends. The report mentioned that a roommate of Millie's best friend said the two women were going out to a MAGA rally the afternoon of the disappearance after meeting up with someone Millie was dating. However, I didn't see any information about you interviewing the man Millie was dating or her best friend."

"Well, we never found any evidence that Millie had been dating anyone or who he might be. We checked her computer and cell phone, but we didn't find any text messages or social media activity. She had Tinder on her phone, but the last activity showing was a year ago. We questioned family, work associates and acquaintances, but no one had heard anything about a new

77

man in her life.

"We wanted to question the best friend, but we haven't been able to find her."

"Are you saying she is missing as well?"

"Maybe... we just don't know. We talked to the friend's roommate, and she told us the friend is very spontaneous. She often disappears for weeks or months at a time, joining up with some new group of friends on an adventure to... well, just about anywhere. Her parents are rich, so they pay her rent and utilities. She has the money to go anywhere she wants, anytime she wants. She isn't one to keep in touch with anyone on a regular basis, so at this point, no one has become concerned enough to report her missing. Do you think that the second victim could be her friend?"

"I'm starting to think so. The questions now are... did they go to meet up with a man dating Millie? If so, is he the perpetrator, or did they go missing at some point before or after meeting up with him?"

"Fuck! I hate this. I want to catch this bastard so bad I can taste it. But it is no longer my case. Why can't that fucking promotion go through?"

"You applied for Homicide?"

"Yes, about three weeks ago. I haven't heard anything yet."

"I know they're starting to look over the candidates in depth. I will put in a good word for you. I don't know why, but I like you, and I don't like anyone. You have a good head on your shoulders. You ask the right questions, and that's what we need around here. Besides, I have heard good things about you over in Missing Persons."

Over the next several hours, Mendy and Detective Mills went over the evidence and interviews in the case file until he was well-versed in the details. Mendy's mind raced with all the questions she had about this murderer—either from all the jet-fuel coffee she'd drunk or the sheer mind-boggling details of the case. When they were finished, she rose from the table and shook hands with Mills.

"Thanks for putting in a good word for me, Detective Mills. Please, let me know if you have any more questions. I'd be happy to come back by anytime."

Mendy returned home and jumped onto her treadmill in her home gym. She needed to burn off all her pent-up frustration. She finally stopped five miles later when her empty stomach growled angrily. She realized she hadn't eaten all day when she looked at her watch, surprised to see it was after 5 p.m.

Fuck! Dinnertime already? Where the hell is Annalise? Could they really still be on their date? I don't want to interrupt, but it's just not like her. Although... she does seem to be crushing on him hard. Stop it, Mendy Sue Hoffman! Butt out. She is an adult, so act like it and be patient.

Mendy walked into the living room and turned on the evening news before going to the kitchen to make dinner, taking her time cutting up the vegetables and tomatoes to make spaghetti sauce from scratch. As it simmered on the stove, she folded the laundry she'd put in the dryer just before leaving the house earlier.

As she walked back through the living room toward the kitchen after putting away the clothes, she stopped mid-stride when she heard Millie's name on TV. She recognized Detective Mills' voice as he spoke at a press conference regarding the disappearances of Arizona and Millie: The families had been notified of the two women's deaths, he said. He didn't give many details other than to say that the police had received evidence that both women had been murdered.

The detective's voice was drowned out by a cacophony of voices from reporters as they began to yell a litany of questions.

Had the bodies had been found?

What were the causes of death?

Were the cases related?

Was there a serial killer in the area?

Who sent the evidence?

Mills held up his hand, asking for quiet.

"We don't have any more details to report at this time. We're still in the early stages of our investigation. We haven't recovered the bodies, so I can't comment about the causes of death right now. We're asking the public to please call the Police Department if they have tips regarding these cases. All tips are kept confidential, so please don't hesitate to give us any information you may have.

"We are also seeking the whereabouts of Alexandria Watts, a friend of Millie Simpson's, who was reported to be the last person with her before her disappearance. We are hoping she may have some information that might prove helpful. If you can help us locate her, please give us a call or ask her to call us. Thank you for your time."

Mendy returned to the kitchen and began cooking the pasta as she prepared a salad. She looked down at her watch, once again surprised to see the passage of time. It was a quarter to seven, and Annalise still hadn't checked in. She decided, intrusive or not, she would give Annalise a call if she hadn't heard from her by the time she cleaned up after dinner.

Her watch read 8 p.m. as she washed the last dish and placed it in the dish drainer to dry. She dried her hands on the towel and walked over to her cell phone on the table. She picked it up and verified that she hadn't missed a message, before quickly dialing Annalise's number. The line rang six times before she heard Annalise's sing-song voice as her voicemail answered.

"Hey, Anna! Call me paranoid. No, never mind that! Let's be real here. This is not like you. I find it hard to believe you are still out on your date. I'm worried about you. If it didn't go well, and you're embarrassed... just please send me a text message letting me know you're okay. Please? I love you."

Mendy hung up the phone and fought the temptation to drive over to Annalise's house then and there. She went over to the couch and began channel-surfing, trying to find a show to take her mind off her worries. As 9 p.m. approached with no word, she could no longer resist the urge to check on Annalise in person. She grabbed her keys, strapped on her service pistol and headed out the door.

Mendy pulled up to Annalise's house fifteen minutes later to find it dark and empty-looking. Annalise always turned the porch light on at twilight, but it was dark outside as well. She approached the house, looking for any signs of distress or any potential evidence on the ground. Everything appeared undisturbed, and the house was deathly quiet as she stepped onto the porch.

Mendy rapped her knuckles hard on the door as she pressed the doorbell, then waited at the door for several minutes.

There was no answer.

Mendy pulled out her phone and texted Annalise once more: "I am right outside. Please come talk to me. If you don't answer, I am using the key." She pressed "send" and waited for a response; anxiety written on her face. Again, there was no answer. Mendy pulled out her keys and found the bright yellow happy face key with the words Don't Worry, Be Happy printed on it.

Only Annalise would choose such an annoyingly chipper key to give to her best friend.

She placed the key in the lock and turned it, trying not to make any noise as she did. She pulled out her service pistol before twisting the knob and pushing the door open. Then, as she entered, she swiveled from side to side, looking for an intruder or any signs of a struggle.

Even in the dark, she could tell that the house looked untouched. She searched through the entire house without finding Annalise, nor any signs of trouble, but that failed to calm the sick feeling in her stomach.

Annalise *didn't* go out on a first date for this long, not even with a hot guy she had a crush on. Even if she had, for some reason, changed her behavior, she would *never* go this long without contacting her. She would *know* that Mendy would be worried.

Mendy turned on the kitchen light and powered on Annalise's laptop, which she found sitting on the kitchen table. The password was so easy that it was sickening. What else but her beloved cat's name... Freya? She brought up the Tinder website, desperate to find contact information for this Anthony Carreras guy. However, when she brought up her messages, there were none from Anthony.

That's strange. Why would she delete his messages? Did something go wrong on the date? Did she delete his messages and go back out somewhere?

She brought up her profile to find her matches, but he was missing there as well. In fact, she could find no sign that Annalise had ever matched or otherwise been connected to anyone besides Clarence, the 12 men who had swiped right on her, and the two other men she had matched with. She couldn't even find Anthony when she tried to do a search. It was as though he had disappeared into thin air.

Goddammit! What the fuck was I thinking? I am a fucking detective for fuck's sake. Why did I encourage her to join a dating site? Why didn't I do a little sneak background check on this guy? Sure, it's illegal. Technically. But who would know? If that bastard did anything to her, I swear on my life, I will kill him.

Mendy slammed the lid of the laptop down and pulled out her phone again. She called her partner in the Missing Persons Unit. "Hey Robert, it's me. I know it's late. I'm sorry. Annalise is missing."

"What? How long? I saw her at work yesterday."

"Since about 10 a.m."

"Come on, Mendy. You know better. You know a report can't be filed for 24 hours. How do you even know she's missing?"

"I am standing in her dark, empty house. I talked to her earlier, just before she went out on a date with a guy she met on Tinder. It was just supposed to be a jog and a lunch date. You know her, she wouldn't be out this late... period... let alone on a first date. She was supposed to call me as soon as she got done. She never did."

There was a brief pause on the other end of the line, then: "This is a conflict of interest. Because of your relationship with her, you can't be involved with the investigation—even if one is warranted. You should get out of her house now, so nobody can say you tampered with any potential evidence—that's if there is any evidence to be found."

Mendy opened her mouth to say something, but Robert must have known what she was about to say, because his voice softened as he tried to reassure her. "If you don't hear from her by 10 a.m. tomorrow, we can file a report, and I promise I will go investigate. You know I care about her, too, just like everyone does here at the station. I'm sure there is nothing to worry about. Go home and try to relax."

"Okay. You're right. I don't want to interfere. I'll see you tomorrow."

Mendy turned off the kitchen light and locked the front door again, leaving the house as she had found it. She drove home with her stomach in knots. Mendy turned her volume up to the maximum before turning in for the night, so that she didn't miss any calls. At 4 a.m., she woke with a start to her phone buzzing in her palm and "Feel Good, Inc." blasting from the speaker.

"Annalise! Are you okay?"

"Oh God! Are you worried about her, too?"

"Belinda?"

"Yes, it's me. I was getting the kids ready for school, grocery shopping—you know, all the usual errands—and totally forgot I was waiting to hear from Annalise about her date. I should have heard from her over 12 hours ago. She isn't answering the phone. I'm worried. Why did you think it was her calling?"

"Because she never called me either. I went to her house, and it doesn't look like she has been home all day. I was hoping it was her."

"Did you file a missing person's report?"

"Not yet... I can't. It has to be 24 hours, so I will at 10 a.m. My partner is ready to investigate as soon as a report is filed. We all love her here. We will find her. I promise!"

"You have to find her. You know how much she means to me. Please, call me as soon as you know something, no matter the time."

"I will, Belinda. Try to get some rest."

Mendy settled back in bed, waiting for the next

interminable two hours to pass when it would be time to get up. There would be no more sleeping tonight.

Annalise would have called one of us, at least. Something is wrong.

Mendy rose an hour later and took her shower, before settling down on the couch with her laptop. She logged into the station's server and started a search on Anthony Carreras. Except there was no Anthony Carreras in the Southern California area. In fact, the only person by that name she found in the state of California lived just outside of San Francisco. He had moved to the U.S. from Italy five years ago and recently obtained his citizenship. But he looked nothing like the man who had contacted Annalise. He was 15 years older, just beginning to grey, and a couple of inches shorter than the height Annalise's date had used on his Tinder profile.

She called the corporate offices of Tinder to have them look up the Anthony Carreras profile. She was referred to their corporate lawyer to discuss the issue. Mendy called him immediately, but she had to leave a message with her cell and office numbers. There wasn't much else she could pursue at the moment without an official case file started, and she remembered her partner's warning about getting involved.

One way or the other, this was going to be a long day. Mendy forced herself to eat some oatmeal and a banana to go with the four cups of coffee she had already powered down. After she cleaned up, she grabbed her bag and headed out the door to get an early start.

Engrossed in her phone as she tried to send another text message to Annalise, Mendy didn't notice Detective Mills walking by as she entered the station, until she ran into him. Mendy looked up, surprised to see him standing there.

"Sorry, Mills. I'm a bit distracted right now."

"No problem, Detective Hoffman. I... I heard about Annalise. Have you heard from her? Is she still missing?"

"Yes, she is. I'm getting really worried. You know her... she's the most responsible person around here. She is quiet and keeps to herself. I'm her best friend, and we don't even spend that many hours together at one time."

"I understand. We're all worried here. We will find her."

"Hey, how did you hear about her?"

"Your partner. He came in about an hour ago. He told the rest of the Missing Persons Unit, and it spread around the station like wildfire. Mendy, let me know if I can help. I'm available anytime."

"No offense, but I hope I never have to ask for your help. It will kill me if this gets to the point where your kind of help is needed."

Mills smiled sympathetically and nodded before heading down the hall back to the Homicide Unit. Mendy turned the other direction and entered the door to the right, where the Missing Persons Unit was located. Everyone looked up, the concern in their eyes deepening when they saw Mendy's stoic face and wrinkled brow.

Captain Peters rose from the corner of his desk in the back office, where he had been sitting and talking with Mendy's partner, Detective Robert Stevens.

"Hello, Detective Hoffman. We've been discussing Annalise. Has there been any news?"

"No, Captain. The only update I have is late last night I talked to her sister, Belinda, who lives in Australia. She called me because she was worried, too. She had been expecting a call as well, but it never came. I am assuming Robert told you I went to

Annalise's house last night?"

"Yes, he did. We need to discuss your findings."

"Unfortunately, there isn't much to report. When I arrived, her house was dark and locked up tight. There was no sign that anyone had been there since she left yesterday morning. I used her laptop to log into her Tinder account so I could find out how to contact her date, Anthony, but I couldn't find any communication between them. In fact, it was like he had never existed. No sign that they had ever matched... no sign of his profile at all."

"Are you sure about who she was going to meet? Could she have given you a fake name?"

"No, sir," Mendy sniffled, before rubbing the back of her hand across her nose and sighing loudly as she stomped her foot. "I was the one who convinced her to try finding a date on Tinder. I helped her set up her profile. We went through all the matches together and swiped right on the ones that interested her. We even sent a message to Anthony together, inviting him to talk. I'm quite positive of who she was going out on a date with yesterday—or at least who he said he was. I can even sit down with the sketch artist, so we can get his sketch out to the press. Maybe we can develop a lead that way... someone has to know him."

"That all sounds great. We'll work on contacting Tinder to see if their technical support can find him. Let's get all the details together, so we're ready to go when we can file the official missing person's report at 10 a.m. We are going to find her. You know we all love her here, just as much as you do."

Mendy sat down at her desk and began to compile all the information she had for the report. Her day was just beginning, and a migraine was already setting in. She wouldn't stop until they had a lead and brought Annalise back home.

Sharon Marie Provost

Ten

The Eagle Has Landed

July 2022

What a difference a month makes! You send them a short, slightly threatening letter and a photo of your next work of art, and suddenly they're listening to you. Best of all, you take one of their compatriots, and the world stops while they search for her. Yet. they still aren't taking me seriously enough. I am sure there are others who will listen to me. Wonder what will happen when they get my next present?

Seated in front of the television, eating breakfast, Stellan couldn't believe how much coverage Annalise's disappearance was still getting a month out, as the third broadcast of the day asked for calls to the tipline. As soon as her story ended, the story on the continuing search for "the killer or killers" of Arizona Hutchins and Millie Simpson started.

Their "tragic" deaths were finally being reported, but the police were still withholding key details. They weren't admitting the cases were connected, nor had they mentioned the letters sent by the killer. Stellan couldn't understand why they were so reluctant to tell the truth. He was losing patience with their stall tactics, and it was time to make them understand that he meant business.

Stellan stared into space, lost in thought. *So many questions to ponder... Was Annalise's case getting so much coverage because she worked for the Police Department? Or did the delivery of Two-Faced and his threat to publicize it make them worry? Or was it a combination of the two?*

Further, had they even considered the possibility that Annalise was connected to those other two cases?

The police were strangely tight-lipped about Annalise's case as well, or maybe they just didn't have any leads. They had reported her last "planned" destination as Sanford Meadows State Park, but it was clear they couldn't corroborate that yet.

There had been no mention of Anthony Carreras' name, as he had expected since he had erased all traces of him. They were depending on the pleas from her colleagues at the station and the tearful video by her sister to persuade people to call in with tips. Little did they know, Stellan had been so careful that there was no evidence for anybody to call in about. They had even tried offering a reward through Secret Witness.

Stellan enjoyed all the coverage of the three cases, but it wasn't enough. People weren't scared, because the police hadn't given them sufficient cause to be worried. Most importantly, the police hadn't acknowledged his prowess and didn't seem afraid of his lethal potential. He didn't expect to see the photos of his art released to television, given their graphic nature, but they weren't even mentioned. The works of *Le Créateur* were worthy of respect and admiration; In fact, they were just as groundbreaking and innovative as his sold-out exhibition had been in New York. It was time to bring his *Dark Arts* collection to the world.

Stellan beamed as the perfect idea came to him—he knew just how to get their attention. He congratulated himself for keeping one little trophy from Annalise. He'd never been one to keep trophies before, other than the videos and photos of his works of art, but this one time he was inspired. Just before he'd thrown her in the incinerator, he had lopped off one of her taloned toes and placed it in the freezer. It was time to pick up that gift.

Dark Arts

Stellan gathered a few supplies before making the trip down to the warehouse. Upon arrival, he put on rubber gloves and went into his darkroom to print three more copies of *The Eagle Soars*. While they were hanging on the line to dry, he addressed two manila envelopes, one to KTLA News Channel 5 and one to the *Los Angeles Times*. He also set aside a small box with three simple words written on the front.

"I warned you."

Then he drafted two identical letters for the press.

"First, let me introduce myself... I am Le Créateur. You have not heard of me before because the Los Angeles Police Department has not acknowledged my existence... yet. However, that is about to change. I am responsible for the murders of Arizona Hutchins and Millie Simpson. They were the subjects of the first two prized works of art in my Dark Arts collection. The inept Police Department did not listen to me when I warned them that they needed to let the public know the truth. I bet they haven't even figured out that the disappearance of Annalise Fischer is connected as well. So, here I am, delivering the scoop of the decade to the press in hopes that you will uphold your duty to inform the world. I have included a photo from my grandest work of art to date, The Eagle Soars.

Kindly, Le Créateur"

He placed the letters in the envelopes along with the pictures and sealed them with a damp sponge. Then he went to the kitchen and removed the toe talon from the freezer. Along with an ice pack, he placed it in a leakproof container that he had brought from home after removing all trace evidence or fingerprints from it. He wrapped the container in a clean cloth to prevent any condensation from ruining the photo and letter and placed it in the bottom of the box. After laying the photo on top, he printed out one final letter for this box.

"I warned you that I would contact the press if you did not live up to your responsibilities. You reported the death of Arizona Hutchins as I demanded, and that of Millie Simpson, when your hand was forced with my previous delivery. However, you are not letting the people know that they are connected, and the vital role they are playing in the development of modern art. It is too late now to fix your mistake... as you will soon see. In the meantime, I have enclosed a couple of gifts for you.

Thinking of you, Le Créateur"

He sealed the box using a fresh roll of tape and set it aside. Now, it was time to arrange for the delivery of his parcels. Stellan logged into the dark web and navigated to the anonymous delivery service he had started using for all his special packages. He scheduled the two envelopes to be picked up at midnight from an unused parcel box out on Route 518 near Santiago Canyon and then be hand-delivered to the press offices. The box he would set up for pickup himself.

He used a voice-modulating app that heavily encrypted the file so it could not be broken down to record a voice message for the police.

"Le Créateur has a special delivery for the detectives at the L.A. homicide unit. It can be picked up tucked under the bench on the western side of the park across from the station. Sweet screams, detectives."

Once the recording was complete, Stellan scheduled a call to be sent out to the station at 2 a.m. that night. The message would repeat three times to make sure the incompetent assholes received the information. The call would be encrypted and go out over Voice over Internet Protocol and routed continuously through proxy servers around the world, making it untraceable.

The last step was the most important. Stellan hacked into the city's traffic and surveillance camera system to set the system to crash at midnight. He installed a Trojan virus that would take hours, if not days, to track down and remove. He had scoped out the private surveillance camera situation on businesses, so he had plotted a route avoiding those and any bright streetlights as much as possible.

Stellan dressed in black and wore a hoodie to hide his features should he come across any unexpected cameras or potential eyewitnesses. He used public transportation to get near the area and then walked five miles to the park. Even in L.A., the city was pretty quiet at that time of night, so he dropped off the package without incident. He left the area heading the opposite direction he had entered and took an Uber back to his car after stopping in at a busy nightclub to discard his dark clothing. Nobody would pay attention to another young man leaving the club late dressed to impress the ladies on a night out on the town.

Stellan drove home, exhausted but satisfied with the day's activities.

The shit is going to hit the fan tomorrow. Now, it is time to get some sleep so I can watch it all fall down.

The alarm went off on his watch, signaling that it was 2 a.m. Stellan snickered to himself. *The eagle has landed.*

Sharon Marie Provost

Eleven

The Creator Task Force

Late July 2022

Every available officer and detective had been assigned different pieces of the investigation into Annalise's disappearance, but it didn't matter. What had been gained from the thousands of man hours expended over the past five weeks? Bupkis!

The first two weeks of the investigation had been the most frustrating weeks of Mendy's career. She couldn't be involved in the case directly, given her close ties with Annalise. No going out into the field to do interviews with potential witnesses. She couldn't even oversee the forensic examination of the home.

Instead, she had been assigned the small bits and pieces like handling the tipline and contacting Tinder... another case of nada, zero, zip, zilch. After obtaining the warrant that Tinder's legal team had required before releasing any information about Annalise's account, she'd spent countless hours with their administration and technical support teams. She'd repeated all the information she could remember about Anthony Carreras until she was blue in the face, but they couldn't find any trace of him ever having been in the system, yet alone talking to Annalise.

She knew she was reaching her limit when the sixth snarky technical support supervisor questioned her memory. She could still hear his voice dripping with sarcasm, "Well Detective, I don't know what to tell you. Far be it from *me* to tell you how to do your job, but I think the source who gave you the information about this Anthony person is mistaken or lying. It is patently impossible that a person with that name and profile ever talked to that woman you're looking for. That profile simply does not exist now or in the past."

She had felt the eyes of the entire unit on her when she'd raised her voice in response. "Well, shit for brains, I am going to make it my personal mission to discredit your whole fucking operation to the entire world. I am that FUCKING source. I know for a fucking FACT that his name is Anthony Carreras, and he talked to Annalise. I was there with her, helping her decide how to respond. By the way, her name is Annalise, not 'that woman.' Is your system so fucking poor that you can't see her name right there in front of you when you're supposed to be looking at her profile? Your system is shit. Your company is shit. You are shit! Fuck off, asshole!"

Captain Peters was just leaving his office as Mendy's tirade began. "Hey, Detective Hoffman, can I speak to you for a moment?"

Mendy looked down and sighed heavily, mumbling under her breath, "Fuck! This is the last thing I need," before grabbing her coffee and calling out, "Be right there, Cap." She rose from her desk wearily and trudged over to the captain's office.

"Will you close the door, Detective?"

"Yes, sir. Is something wrong?"

"Have a seat, Detective... uh Mendy."

Mendy closed the door and deflated into the seat in front of the captain's desk. Her mind was whirling as she pasted a smile to her face and looked up at the captain.

Get your shit together, Mendy! What the hell are you doing? This is not the way to convince them you are ready for a promotion to Homicide.

"Mendy, how are you doing? I know she is your best friend, and I understand you are struggling. We all are. She was... I mean is, important to all of us."

"I am doing well, Captain."

"It didn't look like that a moment ago."

"I apologize, Captain. I didn't mean to lose control there for a moment."

"Don't misunderstand me. I agree with you. They need to get their thumbs out of their asses and figure out their system. They have the private information of how many tens of thousands of people in their system? And they can't even find one missing profile. It scares a person to think about their security. I am just concerned about your stress level."

"To be honest, I *am* struggling. Of course, I am. I'm terrified about what might have happened to her. My frustration level is through the roof because I can't really get involved in the meat of this investigation. I feel useless."

The captain nodded. "Do you need to talk to the precinct's counselor?"

"No, sir. I am truly fine. I just needed to blow off a little steam in that moment. I did, and I am ready to get back to work," Mendy said as she rose, her voice growing stronger with each word.

"Great. I am not done yet though, Detective."

Mendy turned around and sat back down with a sigh. "Oh, Captain?"

"There is one more matter we need to discuss. You applied for a promotion to be a detective in the Homicide Unit."

"Yes, sir. Please don't think I can't handle that because I lost my temper for a brief moment."

"That is the last thing I would think. In fact, I think you are by far the most qualified candidate for the job. That is why, as much as we all will miss you, I recommended you for the job. I just heard back this morning, and your promotion has been processed.

"Oh my God! Are you serious? Thank you, Captain."

"They expect you to report Monday for your first day on the job. I would like you to finish filing any reports and tie up any other loose ends today. Then take off the next four days to rest and recharge. I want my best detective to walk in and kick ass on the first day. Show those Homicide detectives how it's done. Is that clear?"

"Thank you, sir! Thank you so much. I will make you proud."

The next few hours were a whirlwind of activity as Mendy completed her report on her final call with Tinder and the calls she had received on the tipline the past two days. Then she packed up her desk and made the rounds, saying goodbye to the other members of the unit. As 4 o'clock rolled around, she heard her partner begin to sing. She looked up to see the other members of the unit surrounding her desk with a cake in hand and singing "For She's a Jolly Good Fellow." With tears in her eyes, she cut the cake and passed around slices to the only family she'd had, besides Annalise, for the past five years.

Mendy returned home that night with her box of belongings in hand and dropped them on the living room coffee table. She'd sort through them over the next few days. She walked into the kitchen and poured a glass of wine to celebrate, and then turned to grab the phone to share the good news... Except the only person she had to call was the very person that wouldn't answer her now. Or possibly ever.

Instead, she grabbed the bottle of wine and a quart of ice

cream from the freezer to bury her feelings. She turned on the television and cried when *Help! I'm in a Secret Relationship* came on the screen. She turned the television off and hurled her wine glass at the fireplace. She began drinking straight from the bottle and finished off the ice cream just before falling asleep on the couch.

Mendy's eyelids fluttered open slowly, and she grabbed her pounding head as she sat up. *What is that fucking incessant ringing sound?* The sound stopped for a moment, and then began again with earnest. *The phone!* She looked at the clock and saw it was only 6 a.m. *Who the fuck is calling me at this hour? They better have a good reason.*

"Who is this?"

"Mendy... uh Detective Hoffman, is that you?"

"Yes. And who am I speaking to?"

"It is Detective Mills, from Homicide. By the way, congratulations on your promotion."

"Oh. Thanks. How can I help you?"

"I am really sorry to do this. I know you were given a few days off and supposed to start on Monday. But I could really use you down here. There has been a new development in the case. I need to talk to you."

"That sounds like more than just 'talk' about the case."

"Well, yes. It concerns Annalise."

"No! Fucking no! I don't want to talk to *you* about anything to do with Annalise. You're wrong. You must be wrong. Tell me you are wrong, for fuck's sake!"

"I am very sorry, but I can't do that. I think this would be better if we discussed it in person. And I truly do need your help. Maybe we can get a break in this case finally."

"Give me five minutes to jump in the shower. I will be there in twenty. Damn you!" Mendy spat as she hung up the phone. She jumped off the couch, grabbing her head as she did. She made a quick detour into the kitchen for three Ibuprofen before running into the bathroom and turning on the shower. While it warmed up, she pulled a new suit out of the closet and ran back to the kitchen to put a pod in the Keurig.

Mendy returned to the steaming shower and let the water stream over her face; the scalding water let her ignore the tears streaming down. When her skin was bright red, she climbed out and began to dress quickly, buttoning her shirt as she walked back into the kitchen. She poured the mug of coffee into her Thermos and started another pod. She had a feeling this day was going to require pots of coffee before it was done and a bottle of Jack when she got home.

Mendy grabbed her phone and placed an order on Instacart for a bottle of Jack Daniels, a two-liter bottle of Coke and a can of Chef Boyardee ravioli, her go-to meal of choice when she was busy on a case. The driver had the code to her garage, so the groceries would be delivered and left in there by the time she got home. (He knew her personally and gave her a pass on the require ID check for the liquor.) She strapped on her piece and poured the last of the coffee in the container before heading out the door.

Mendy slammed the door of the car as she turned the key in the ignition. She navigated to her least favorite playlist—the one she only listened to when times were dark—the one she used to let out all her pent-up frustration and aggression before she had to walk in and be professional. Her palms slammed on the steering wheel to the rhythm of the thumping bass and screeching vocals of *Immigrant Song* by Led Zeppelin.

She pulled into her parking spot and knocked back a couple

of more deep swallows of her coffee, checking to make sure her eyes didn't show the tears that had been pouring from her eyes since the call 20 minutes earlier. She exited the car and slammed the door shut as she stalked up to the station. She couldn't stand the pitying looks of the other officers or the muffled sniffles of Anita at the reception desk as she made her way down the hall to Homicide.

She breezed through the door and, before Mills could say a word, she said, "Just tell it to me straight now. What happened?" Her eyes drifted to the corkboard, and her knees buckled as she saw the photo of Annalise's body, disfigured into some sort of grotesque... was it a bird?... posted at the top. "Dear fucking God! Not him! I killed my best fucking friend in the world. She was like the sister I never had. My only family left in this world."

"It is not your fault. You didn't kill her. That sick bastard did."

"But she never would have met him if I hadn't pushed her into going on Tinder. No wonder they can't find him. It's not an accident that he's invisible to them. He's a much more sophisticated criminal than anyone gave him credit for. This investigation has been botched from the start, if you ask me."

Mills put an arm around her shoulders and led her into his office, shutting the door behind them. His sympathetic gaze met her eyes. "I don't disagree with you. This only became my case a few weeks ago. They initially put Detective Anderson, the man you are replacing, in charge because of his seniority and 'supposed' experience. But none of us in this office has ever dealt with this kind of situation. If you ask me, we should have brought in the FBI's Behavioral Analysis Unit from the start.

"Don't ask me why, but Anderson was well-respected around here. He is old guard... did everything by the book the old-fashioned way. But the world is changing, and the criminals are adjusting faster than we are. Not to mention, it just seems like this world is filled with more fanatics and twisted psychopaths than ever before—at every level of society and the government. Don't get me wrong. He's as nice as they come, but what we needed was competence to handle an investigation of this caliber."

"I'm sorry that I lost my composure out there. It was a momentary lapse, and I promise it won't happen again."

"I would be worried if you didn't have that reaction. I didn't intend for you to see that picture until I talked to you. That is my fault for not noticing that someone had posted it, even though I had told them to hold off. You wouldn't be the right person for this job if it didn't bother you."

"What did he do to her? There were meat hooks through her bod..." Mendy gulped before gagging as she tried to force the bile back down her throat.

"We don't need to go through the details right now. There is time for that later, once you've had some time to process your loss. There is one important step that we need to do next before the story hits the press."

"The press? What the fuck are you talking about?"

"Apparently, he sent that picture you saw to a news station and a newspaper. They contacted us in the middle of the night, shortly after we received his package. They have agreed to hold off until the noon news cycle on air and the online edition of the paper. We need to contact her sister as soon as possible. I know she's in Australia, but I'm sure she's watching the local news outlets for any updates. I know I would be if I were her."

"Oh my God. You're right. I know my involvement in this case, at least when it comes to Annalise, will be limited, but can I be the one to break the news?"

"Yes, of course. That is one of the reasons I brought you in here this morning. I wanted both of you to hear it from someone you knew and trusted."

"Thank you. I'm sorry I was a bitch on the phone this morning."

"Apologies aren't necessary. It was perfectly understandable. Now is there anything I can do for you before you make that call?"

"No. You've done enough already. I appreciate your understanding. But can I use your office to make the call?"

"Absolutely. I was going to offer it anyhow. I will be out with the others when you're ready to get started. It is high time that we get you up to date on all the specifics of the case and what little we've found through our investigation. Besides, it wouldn't hurt for the rest of us to get a refresher on the case before the next intense phase starts. Today is Day One for the Creator Task Force. Fuck his pretentious use of French! This fucker is going down if it's the last thing I do."

"That fuckface better hope he doesn't come across me in a dark alley alone because only one of us will leave that meeting alive, and I'm not leaving this world anytime soon."

Mendy pulled out her cell phone and found Belinda's number in her contacts list. The phone rang five times before it was answered in a breathless rush. "Sorry, I was just wrangling the kids into the car. They didn't want to leave the playground after school. What's up? Do you have news about Annalise?"

"Hey, Belinda. Can you give me a call back when you get home and the kids are settled?"

"What's going on? You sound upset. Talk to me."

"It's not the time. The kids shouldn't be around for this."

Mendy heard Belinda's sharp intake of breath as she stifled a sob. "Give me a minute. Don't go anywhere." Mendy could hear the phone shuffling, and the car door shut, followed by muffled voices.

"I'm back. I caught up with my friend. She is going to take the kids for the night and send her husband by to pick up a bag for them. Now tell me what's wrong? Is Annalise hurt?"

"Belinda... oh God, Belinda. I am so sorry."

"No! Don't you dare! I don't want to hear it. It can't be true."

Mendy sobbed into the phone before clearing her throat harshly. "I had the same reaction earlier this morning. I am so sorry to tell you Annalise has been murdered."

"What in the hell happened to her? Who? Why?"

"I don't have all the details yet about what happened to her. Well, nobody has all the details at this point. We don't know the perpetrator yet, other than it is a serial killer that we've been looking for the past nine months."

"Why don't you know what happened to her?"

"We haven't found her yet. No autopsy has been performed."

"Then you could be wrong! Maybe she isn't dead. Why would you say she is dead when you don't know for sure?"

"No, Belinda. We are sure."

"How? How the fuck can you be sure? Tell me."

"Don't make me tell you. Just trust me. I would never say it unless it was true."

"Motherfucker! Tell me... I can handle it."

"Oh God! He sent us a picture of her. There is no doubt. I can't give you any more details than that. I really can't. This is an active investigation. You must keep this to yourself for now. More details will come out soon, but until then, please don't tell anyone anything."

Belinda's gut-wrenching sobs broke Mendy's heart. As she gasped for breath, Mendy desperately wished she could reach out and hold her. She knew how Belinda felt, but she needed to hold it together. She could mourn when the case was solved and that bastard was in the ground.

"So you haven't found her body? We can't lay her to rest? When will that happen? When can we let her rest in peace?"

"To be honest, I don't know. We have no leads. She's not the first victim. The first one disappeared almost a year and a half ago, and we still haven't found her. I want to be honest with you. I don't know if we will ever find them. I want you to be prepared."

"No! We were raised Catholic. She needs to be buried in consecrated ground."

"I am not giving up... none of us are, but I won't promise you something that I'm not sure we can deliver. I will promise you this, though: As long as I am alive, I will never stop looking for him. He is not going to get away with this. I will find him, and I will make him pay."

"Thank you for calling me personally, Mendy. I know this isn't easy for you either. I need to go. I need to call my husband. Please call me anytime if you find out anything."

Mendy pressed 'end' and held the phone to her heart. She took a few deep breaths before heading out to her new family, the members of the Homicide Unit.

"Okay. Notification is complete. Now, let's get me caught up on this bastard. Start from the beginning. What do we know about Arizona Hutchins' disappearance?"

Sharon Marie Provost

Twelve

Aella

Mid-August 2022

Aella, the "whirling dervish" to her mother, danced through the club in a manic series of twirls and shuffling steps. At times, these were punctuated by esoteric rhythmic arm movements. At others, her arms were crossed over her chest, as if she were stuck in a coffin, as she twisted her body from side to side. The thumping industrial music interspersed with punk, ambient, and darkwave spoke to her soul. Lost in thought about her upcoming date, she wondered if she might have finally found the one person who could understand her.

Most of the time, she wore the typical goth wardrobe: antiquated dresses and corsets with flowy sleeves, fashioned out of black leather, PVC, lace and velvet. She accessorized with old-fashioned cameos of ivory and coral with black-accented raised-relief carvings of Victorian ladies, skulls, and roses. She was rarely seen without her black sunglasses, their frames adorned with skulls and pentagrams. Her rosy red cheeks and blood-red lips were offset by the heavy black mascara and eyeliner, the starkest contrast of all being her long wavy locks of platinum blond hair that looked Malibu Barbie-ready.

Aella, the definition of an introvert, spent vast amounts of time at work—not that she was a workaholic, instead preferring the company of her favorite life forms: animals. She'd always avoided spending time with other people besides her family. During her childhood, her mother had been called into the counselor's office more than once to discuss Aella's lack of socialization, and she'd been referred to a child psychologist.

Aella's mother adored her child and found nothing wrong with her behavior. She was perfectly able to interact in an appropriate manner with other children—and, especially, adults—if the situation dictated it. Instead, she chose to play by herself or with the family pets. Her adoration of and gentle nature with animals only grew as she did.

Her arrival in high school had brought with it a fascination with the dark counterculture of the goth lifestyle, but the kind, loving person she had always been inside didn't change. She even acquired a few goth friends; while not close, she at least had someone to spend time with occasionally. She'd never been one to go out on many dates, but as of late she'd become interested in a life companion to enjoy *all* her pursuits.

Still, no one knew the true Aella, the enigmatic, self-professed goth Barbie. They saw her style and assumed they knew her personality, as well as her likes and dislikes. No one knew about her darker side—inside—the side that gravitated toward dark horror, both in the movies and reality. She didn't know if it was possible to find someone that could actually accept all the facets of her, especially the dark interests she hid from everyone.

Aella was not at all fond of most humans, so she knew the typical dating scene would never work for her. After doing extensive research, Tinder seemed like the best way to swim through the dating cesspool with the least amount of contact. She knew she was unlikely to find the profile of the goth man of her dreams just sitting there waiting for her. She would have to be more discriminating and look beyond the bland, normal pictures and personality profiles posted to find the hidden person inside. For that matter, she also knew she would have to post a toned-down version of herself to prevent men from running away at the first sight of her. She decided to upgrade to the Gold membership, so she could see the profiles of any men that showed interest in her.

She was prepared to set her profile to incognito if she started receiving too many unwanted propositions, so she would be visible only to those profiles she'd swiped right on. But for now, her profile picture showed her wearing a black velvet babydoll dress with candy apple red lips and delicately applied black eyeliner. She was honest in her profile but careful not to appear too extreme. In the end, her profile identified Aella Mattias as an introvert who listened to Bauhaus, Depeche Mode, and The Cure (to appear more mainstream), loved animals, dancing at clubs, and traveling.

Aella's profile went live just before her twelve-hour shift at the emergency veterinary hospital where she had been employed for the past five years. That was for the best because she was nervous to see who might swipe right on her, and if the day was anything like normal, she would be much too busy to check her phone. She headed to work exhausted after staying up most of the night working on her profile. To her relief, the day passed by in a blur of activity when the hospital received two hit-by-cars, one emergency C-section, and multiple pets sick with a variety of ailments, most of which could have waited until their usual veterinary office opened the next day.

Aella walked in through the door of her small apartment at 7 p.m. and flopped on the couch. She pulled out her phone to order Thai food on DoorDash, and she noticed she had a notification from the Tinder app. While she waited for her food to arrive, she logged in, expecting to see a notification telling her she needed to make her profile more interesting. Instead, she found that three men had swiped right on her. But she was disappointed to find that the first two were clearly not a match for her. They both looked like the Ken to her Barbie. They were handsome businessmen in suits and ties with the kind of smarmy, egotistical smile that screams out, "I'm God's gift to women."

Well not this woman. Keep stepping.

The third one had the most promising profile, and it belonged to Anthony Carreras. Only five years her senior, he had these penetrating icy blue eyes that hid way more than he was trying to let on. She could see the depth and a darkness behind that knowing smile. She couldn't help but think, "I've been a bad girl, Mr. Grey." Maybe it was just a sadomasochistic vibe she was picking up on, but there was definitely more to that Anthony than candlelit dinners and nights at home watching reality TV. She swiped right and created a match.

Now to see how he responds.

Aella set her phone down on the coffee table when the doorbell rang. She tipped the delivery man and headed back to the couch after grabbing a Mountain Dew Voltage from the fridge. She reached over to grab her laptop off the side table and then set it up on her lap table next to the cartons of Pad Thai and Chicken Panang Curry. She pulled the chopsticks out of the bag and began to eat as she scrolled through the listing of men on Tinder.

It came as no surprise that during a quick overview she found only two men that outwardly looked as if they might be interested in an alternate lifestyle. One appeared barely out of his teens and had the immature profile to match. The other appeared mildly interesting, so she swiped right on him. Now it was time to do a more thorough, discriminating look at the pictures and profiles.

Dark Arts

Aella had a bad habit of staying up all hours of the night and then stumbling through work like a zombie the next day. Three hours later, her alarm went off, reminding her that it was 11 and time to start cleaning up. During that time, she had found two men who looked like they might be hiding a darker, more twisted lifestyle than their profile pictures suggested. She set down the laptop and threw away the trash from dinner, then spent the next 45 minutes doing housekeeping and feeding her dog, cat, snake, and rats.

When she was done, she looked back at the two profiles she had chosen to like. One belonged to a man named John Peters who had similar musical taste and was wearing black jeans and a T-shirt. The second man named Tommy—annoyingly just Tommy like he was Prince or Madonna—was 15 years older than Aella and looked like he had lived the hard rocker life. She was not overly impressed with his profile; he was a last-minute selection in an effort to avoid being overly critical. Neither of them was an Earth-shattering, definitive lead, but she hoped one might be more like her than he was trying to portray. In the meantime, she couldn't help but feel a tingle of excitement when she thought back on Anthony's profile.

She logged off her laptop and plugged it in for the night before heading to bed, determined not to think any more about the dating site until tomorrow night. She had a restless night's sleep wondering if anybody would even respond to her likes. Despite her reservations, she rose early to check the site and found that all three men had responded to her. As she had assumed, John Peters was a poser trying to appear cooler than he really was, and Tommy was a well past-his-prime old rocker and roadie. Neither interested her, so she didn't respond to their messages.

Anthony though... now, he had only sparked her interest

more with his message. He asked her if she listened to The Damned, Clan of Xymox, or Victorian Witch. He had picked up on her gothic vibe and demonstrated his own interest. He had even sent her a picture of him outside The Cauldron.

Aella typed out a quick message inviting him to come hang out at The Veil on Friday night where they could have dinner, drinks and enjoy one of L.A.'s hottest goth clubs. She hit "send" before she could reconsider. She also left her phone number, inviting him to call her that night after 8 p.m. when she returned from work. She closed the computer and raced to get ready for work, pushing all worries out of her mind.

When she managed to take a quick lunch break late that afternoon, she looked at her phone to see if Anthony had responded. He had texted her directly, accepting her invitation on Friday and promising to call later that night. As she packed her lunch bag, her boss stopped by to ask her if she could start her shift an hour early the next day. She couldn't suppress her smile as she agreed to his request—or for the rest of the afternoon, garnering multiple odd looks from her co-workers, who were used to her usual stoic disposition.

Several emergencies requiring all hands on deck came in just before the end of her shift, so her day ended 90 minutes later than expected. She hurried to her cubby to check her phone to see if she'd missed Anthony's call. She had received a call from an unknown number, and a voicemail was waiting.

"Hey there, dark beauty. This is Anthony. I hope this doesn't mean you changed your mind. I am a creature of the darkness myself, so give me a call later if you are free. Take care."

Aella breathed a sigh of relief as she hung up the phone and finished changing out of her scrubs. She stopped at Taco Bell to pick up some dinner on the way home. As she drove the 45 minutes across the city to her apartment, she called Anthony. He picked up on the second ring.

"Aella?"

"Hi, Anthony! Yes, it's me. I am really sorry about earlier. We had some emergencies come in late, so I was roped into overtime."

"You work at a hospital?"

"No, I guess I never told you what I do. I work at Spring Creek Veterinary Emergency and Specialty Center. I am a veterinary technician there."

"Ahh... now that makes more sense. I hope everything was OK?"

"Two of them are not out of the woods yet, but their prognosis is good. Unfortunately, we did lose one to congestive heart failure."

"I'm sorry to hear that. I do remember your profile saying you are passionate about animals. That must be hard for you, I am assuming."

"No... well, yes. Now I probably sound weird. Ignore that."

"No, tell me more. I am interested."

"I just mean that I'm not like most people. I don't fear or dread death. Death will come for me when it's my time. I see beauty in both life and death. It's the natural order. I only care that animals don't suffer. Tonight, we tried to save a pet that couldn't be fixed, and then we did the humane thing and put an end to his suffering. Does that make sense at all?"

"Yes, it does. I would have never said that on my own because most women would flee from a man who said there is beauty in death. However, I feel the same way. Still want to go out with me on Friday?"

"Absolutely! Now more than ever. I have never met someone that understands me. They're repulsed by my dark side when I express it. I am used to looks of revulsion when I show the real me. Most men are just drawn to what I look like on the outside; they're seduced by my unique, exotic look. They don't want to hear what I have to say. You asked to know more... even when I probably sounded bizarre."

"Not bizarre. Fascinating! I had to know more. I am drawn to you, Aella. To me, you are an alluring tempest in this humdrum world."

Aella was shocked to hear her own hearty laugh. It was not that she didn't find joy in the world, but she was just never one to laugh. She found that people's laughter was far too often false, and they laughed out of a sense of expectation or in an attempt to be coquettish.

"That's the first time I have heard the word tempest used as an attempt at flattery."

"Only an attempt?"

"Fine. You got me. I must admit that is probably the most honest, appealing compliment I've ever received. You're not simply using words to impress me; you're not afraid to call it as you see it. You know, Aella does mean whirlwind. My mother gave me that name for a reason. She always said that from the moment of my birth, pandemonium ensued."

"Well, call me mayhem, because I am ready to join the fray."

Aella was shocked to find herself laughing again. The two of them fell into an easy rhythm of conversation, passing from one bizarre topic to another. They discussed their favorite horror movies and books, their outlook on life and death, their own experiences with the loss of a loved one, and the dark sense of humor they found they shared.

"Okay. Don't judge me here, Anthony," Aella began with a snort that devolved into a belly laugh. "I once had a co-worker that I befriended, and she had colon cancer. People who overheard us thought I was a monster when I teased her about having ass cancer. We even named her tumor after the misunderstood name of a pet that came into the clinic. It became Jorje, but was pronounced George. While she waited for surgery, I joked that she was going to hug it and love it and squeeze it, just like in that Bugs Bunny cartoon with Hugo the Abominable Snowman."

"That is classic. You have to laugh at the dark side that you can't escape. Being depressed and sad sure doesn't help. Besides, they say laughter is the best medicine."

"The funny thing is that she was just as bad as me. When her cancer metastasized to her lungs, she gave her mother, a smoker of over 50 years, crap for her not having lung cancer when my friend who had never even looked twice at a cigarette now had multiple mets in both lungs. Now that is dark but hysterical."

"I can't believe how long we have been talking. Did you realize that it is past midnight?"

"No, I didn't. I didn't even notice my 11 p.m. phone alarm beep in on our call. I'm sorry I kept you up so late. I am a creature of the dark, so the late hour didn't faze me."

"Well, I am the Dracula to your Vampira then. I rarely go to bed before 2, even though I have to work early. I should let you go, though, because I know you have to work early, and it sounds like you have crazy days at the clinic."

"Unfortunately, that is true. I still need to take care of the animals and do a few things around the house before I lie down for the night, so it is time for me to say goodnight. I really enjoyed our conversation. I am looking forward to Friday night."

"Me too. I will check in with you to finalize our plans on Thursday. Goodnight, my queen of chaos."

"Goodnight, my prince of darkness."

Aella's day had a turbulent start when she walked into the middle of a dispute with an angry client. They were unhappy with the high bill they had received, even though they had signed a treatment authorization and agreed to a high-end estimate $500 higher than their final bill. Aella, who generally detested interactions with people she didn't know, had learned how to deal with difficult people to minimize the time she had to spend with them. A few minutes of in-depth explanation later, and the day ground nearly to a halt.

Her boss sent her to a full one-hour lunch, on him, at the deli across the street. Engrossed in her phone as she walked in the door, she failed to notice the man at the table in front of her rise and turn to leave. She bumped into him and, when she looked up to apologize, she was surprised to see Anthony in front of her.

The man grumbled and began to sidestep her.

"Uhh... hi, Anthony. What are you doing here?"

"Are you talking to me?"

"Yes, Anthony. Don't you recognize me? It's me, Aella. We talked on the phone last night."

"You have the wrong person, Miss. I don't know no Anthony. Excuse me."

"I... I'm... uh sorry. They say everyone has a doppelganger."

"Yeah, whatever," the man said in a brusque tone as he pushed past her and out the door.

Aella turned around and watched him go. *What the actual fuck? I have seen people look alike, but that man looked just like Anthony. I am sure of it. He didn't mention having a twin. Besides, that man denied knowing him.* Aella's brow furrowed as she watched Anthony's spitting image sprint across the street toward the bus stop. She ordered a pineapple splash smoothie and sat down. She found that her appetite had disappeared. After a few minutes, she decided to return from lunch early to get her mind off the puzzling mystery.

When her workday ended, she checked her phone as she changed and found no messages. She returned home and turned on one of her favorite TV shows, *Evil*, to watch as she prepared macaroni and cheese. She couldn't convince herself that she had not encountered Anthony that afternoon, but she also couldn't explain why he would treat her that way. The evening seemed interminable, so she cared for the animals and turned in early for the night.

When Aella rose the next morning, she found a message on her phone from Anthony, as if nothing had happened. *Did it? Am I losing it?* She reread the message multiple times as she walked out to turn on the Keurig.

"Hello, mistress of the night. Just checking in with you to see what time you want me to pick you up tomorrow for dinner. I hope your week is going well. Text me when you get a chance. I have a business meeting tonight, so I won't be able to call."

Aella felt flummoxed as to how to handle the situation. Had she seen him that day? Why had he pretended not to know her? Was it even safe to go out with him?

She finished getting ready for work, determined to answer him later in the day when she had more time to think. She had expected that he would pick her up for the date, but now she didn't know if she wanted to be at his mercy. To make matters worse, she had agreed to let her mom borrow her car for the weekend because she was moving. She could always take the bus across the city. She had done that many times in the past.

When lunchtime arrived, she sat down and sent a response

to Anthony. "I am dropping my car off for someone to borrow after work tomorrow. I'll just catch a bus and meet you at The Veil at 7 p.m. If you get there before me, find us a table, and order me a Bloodlust and some pizza rings for us to start with as an appetizer. See ya tomorrow!" She put her phone back in her cubby and returned to work after she finished her lunch.

She didn't look at her phone until she returned home that night. She found he'd sent a reply back late that afternoon. "Sounds great. I will be happy to drop you off at home tonight after our date if you like. Hmm... Bloodlust sounds intriguing. I may have to order one myself. I can't wait to see you in person."

Maybe I'm just being paranoid. Maybe it was a stranger who was an uncanny look-alike. We'll see how tomorrow night goes before I agree to a ride home.

Aella had talked her boss into letting her off early on Friday. Her shift ended at 4 p.m., and she drove home. Her mom was getting a ride over at 5 to pick up her car. That would still leave her with about an hour and a half to care for the animals, take a shower and get dressed for her date. After another night's sleep, she had decided to enter the date with no preconceptions and see how it flowed. She would be herself and see if Anthony could handle her.

After her mom left, she jumped into the shower as she pondered how to arrange her long pale locks. She pulled her hair back into a ponytail and then twisted it to create a large bun on the back of her head that she pinned in place. She left the last 5 inches of hair hanging loose and curled it. She wanted to draw attention to her long, swan-like neck. If her heart kept beating so hard and fast, he would be sure to see the blood vessels in her throat throb with every beat of her pulse. Overall, she was quite pleased when she had finished.

Aella used flaming red lipstick to draw Anthony's eyes to her full, pouty lips. Then, she applied the usual heavy black mascara, thick black eyeliner, and a smoky eye shadow.

She looked through her closet for just the right outfit to attract the attention of everyone in the room. She settled on a low-cut, black, lace-covered corset with small blood-red ribbon rose accents. The ribbon used to tighten the corset had skulls printed on it. She paired this top with a black velvet knee-length burlesque bustle skirt with a slit up the right side that cut all the way up to her hip. The last piece needed for her ensemble was a pair of black combat boots with the embroidered skull and roses design. Every eye in the club would be on her.

She might be an introvert, but she liked the attention... as long as it was from a distance. Besides, it would make her look all the more desirable to Anthony.

She boarded the bus a few blocks from her home to the catcalls of a couple construction workers on the street and a few men on the bus. She flashed them her biggest smile before raising her middle finger prominently. She chose an empty seat near the front, glancing at her watch as she sat down. Aella sent a quick text to Anthony, "Just got on the bus. Should be there close to on time... maybe five minutes late," which she followed with a skull and crossbones and red lips emojis.

He replied simply with a flaming heart and the star eyes happy face emoji. Traffic bogged down more than expected when they entered the 110 freeway, but they made up time hitting green lights down 6th Street. She got off the bus, adjusting her corset as she sidled down the steps.

The host greeted her when she entered the club: "Well hello, gorgeous! We're getting pretty busy, but I think there are still a few tables left in the back."

Aella scanned the room and found Anthony's eyes locked on her body before slowly sliding up to meet hers. "I see my date right over there," she purred seductively as she sauntered over, her hips swiveling with every step. Anthony pursed his lips and whistled as she approached.

"You are smoking hot! I take it back. You are not a tempest in a humdrum world... you are a temptress. Dare I say a succubus, but I'm not dreaming, am I?"

Aella's smooth, breathy laugh drew him closer as she slithered into the booth next to him. "How did I ever find you?" he whispered into her ear, his bottom lip brushing her earlobe as he spoke.

"You looked on the dark side," she growled as her tongue darted into his ear. Anthony moaned and wrapped his arm around her shoulders, drawing her closer. The waitress winked at the two of them as she stopped by to deliver the drinks and appetizer he had already ordered.

"I just know this is going to be one hell of a night. I can feel it. You have inspired me."

"Inspired you how?"

"I want to share my passion with you. I have a feeling you will love it! Were you set on having dinner here or can I take you somewhere special? We can order in if you are hungry."

"To be honest, I'm not all that hungry. I had a late lunch today because the clinic was busy. The pizza rings should be perfect. Let's eat and finish our drink; then I am all yours."

"Yes, you are. I can't wait to show you."

Anthony and Aella spent more time staring and caressing each other than talking. Aella's few inhibitions drifted away on the breeze from the window as she imbibed. Anthony fed her a pizza ring and leaned forward to lick the tomato sauce off her lip as she giggled. He smoothly poured most of his Bloodlust into her glass when her attention was focused on kissing his jawline. Half an hour later, she was tipsy and more than ready to leave the club with him.

Anthony slid out of the booth and came around to grab her hand to help her up. He placed his arm around her waist and led her out to his Jaguar in the lot behind the club. At that time of night, the traffic had died down, so it was a quick ride over to the warehouse.

"You have my curiosity piqued. Come on! Tell me. What are you taking me to see? The suspense is killing me," Aella whined as her hand caressed his thigh

"You will just have to wait and see. It won't be long now."

A short time later, he made the turn into the warehouse parking lot, pulling into the slot directly in front of the door. Anthony jumped out of the car and walked around to her door, opening it to help her out. He unlocked the door and led her inside, stopping about six feet in. "Wait right here while I get the lights."

"Oooh... so mysterious," Aella cooed. She heard some metallic clanging and the sound of a lock clicking into place. "What're you doing over there? Locking me in?" she giggled.

"Oh yes, this is not the best neighborhood. Don't want just anyone walking in here. One moment while I find the switch."

Anthony flipped the switch, and Aella strained to see ahead of her as she squinted in the blinding light that surrounded her. "Where are we?"

"Welcome to my very special studio, dear," he replied as he ushered her forward to his creative space.

Aella's eyes widened, her pulse quickening, and her breathing became more ragged, as she took in the scene before her. Her eyes flashed from the hoist to the surgical table and instrument tray, then over to the computer station. "Wait! I know this place. Oh my God! You are *Le Créateur*." Her mouth widened, preparing to scream, as Anthony's hand wrapped around it, strangling the cry before it could escape.

"Very interesting, my dear. We need to have a discussion."

Thirteen

Chipping Away

Mid-August 2022

Aella's body stiffened as she felt his grip around her tighten. A tear slid down her cheek and came to rest on his hand pressed against her mouth. "There's no need for tears. Right, Aella? Let's just sit down and talk. Can you do that?"

Hell no, I don't want to talk. Calm down, you idiot. You have to try to reason with him. Make him see you as a person.

She took a shaky breath before slowly nodding her head. He pushed his body up against her back and led her over to a chair against the far wall. "Now, can you sit here like a good girl? I don't want to have to restrain you. I don't think you want me to do that either. Am I right? I think you know what I am capable of."

Aella tried to suppress a small whimper as she nodded once again. When they reached the chair and he turned her around, she sat down and placed her hands in her lap. "Let's have a nice discussion now, shall we? No need to scream, because no one will hear you anyway," he reminded her as he slowly released his hand from her mouth.

Aella knew she was beginning to panic again so she took a couple of gasping breaths, trying to clear her head before she looked up at Anthony. "What do you want to talk about?" she asked in a steady voice.

"You know who I am?"

"Anthony."

"Let's not play games. You won't like the games I like to play."

123

"You're *Le Créateur*," she spit at him.

What a prick! We both know I recognized him and this awful torture chamber.

"Correct. How do you know that?"

"Now who's playing games? How do you think? I subscribe to your channel on the dark web. I told you I was dark and twisted, and people don't know the real me."

Stellan chuckled. "I guess this is not a good way to build my subscription list."

Aella couldn't help but laugh in her own head, her dark sense of humor almost getting the best of her. "No shit, dickhead. Are you going to let me go then? I won't tell anyone. Clearly, we have similar interests. How about I just leave, you give me a free year of membership, and we go our separate ways?"

"I can't let that happen. You already put me at risk when you called attention to me the other day and used the Anthony name. That Tinder profile is hidden to everyone, except for my beautiful subjects. I nearly killed you that night without the benefit of turning you into a sublime work of art. That would have been a tragedy."

"So that *was* you? I knew it. I almost didn't come to meet you tonight because of that. Now, I wish I'd listened to my intuition instead of giving you the benefit of the doubt."

How could I be so dumb?

"Anyhow, getting back to your offer, it sounds good, but we both know that is not a viable option. This lifestyle does not afford me the opportunity to trust people. One false move, and I spend the rest of my limited days on death row. And the point of this whole show is not *my* death."

It could be... if I get a chance, this show is going to be all about your death. Splash your blood all over the fucking place!

"Well, I sure as hell didn't volunteer to be the subject. What about what I want?"

"Get real, Aella. Do you honestly believe any of those other women volunteered to be my subjects? You know damn good and well they did not. You told me you were a subscriber. Why were you watching? What gave you enjoyment? The begging... the pleading... the crying... the pain... the blood?"

Aella dropped her head in shame and refused to meet his eyes as she mumbled, "All of it." She had never meant for someone else to enjoy all those things at her own expense.

"Exactly, my dear. Tell me something."

"What?"

"We had a long talk on the phone earlier this week. You told me you didn't fear death. That death would find you when it was your time. And your outfit tonight shows that, while you may not like to deal with most people, you do revel in their rapt attention on your body. Did you mean what you said?"

"Yes, of course I did."

"Then what better way to have eyes glued on you than if you are the subject of my next work of art? Your beauty will be immortalized forever. Do you know how many people pay to download the videos? Death has come for you. Your time is up. If you don't fear death, then walk toward it with your head held high, ready to greet me, your grim reaper. The audience will eat it up. You know better than anyone they will."

Maybe it is my time. I always said I wouldn't fight death. I could give them quite a show—be the best one yet—ever for that matter.

Stellan's body trembled with excitement as he spoke. Aella saw him literally salivating at the idea. From the look of longing on her face, he could see she was being drawn into his excitement. She had never looked more sultry and intoxicating;

the reactions of the other patrons, men and women alike, in the restaurant earlier showed she was irresistible. Stellan stroked her cheek as he stared deep into her eyes.

"Let's do this together, dark beauty. We can make this unforgettable. You can help me finalize the plans of how to carry out your death. I have an exceptional, unique idea for my one-of-a-kind girl. I am going to hold an auction for three small canvases that will be part of the work we create today. Would you like to be part of the creative process?"

A dark smile crept onto Aella's face. "Really?"

"Of course. Would I lie to you? Have I, *Le Créateur*, not been completely up front with you about all of this?"

"Yes, you have. So what is the plan? How can I help? Where is the camera anyhow?"

"It is set up in a different spot than usual. I told you this was a very special episode. Follow me."

Anthony grabbed her hand and helped her up, leading her over to the far back corner, where the camera was set up facing a large white metal wall. Three canvases hung on the wall right next to each other. Approximately ten feet in front of the camera sat a massive, construction-orange piece of heavy equipment with a large chute on the back and the word "Timberwolf" emblazoned on the side. There appeared to be a spindle with large, sharp circular blades inside the chute.

"What is that, Anthony... er I mean *Le Créateur*?"

"Have you ever heard of the famous abstract expressionist artist Jackson Pollock?"

"I've heard the name."

"He is known for doing drip or splash paintings: He would drip, pour, or fling paint onto the canvas using his brush."

"Okay. What does that have to do with me or that *thing* over there?" She was afraid to hear the answer... already suspecting what it was, but she had to know.

"That is a woodchipper. It breaks down organic material, typically tree branches and leaves, into small chips and mulch and then shoots it out of that smaller, curved metal chute in front there."

A shiver ran up Aella's spine, and then she shook it off. "Wow... uh... I don't know what to say."

Fuck no! That is what I want to say. What the actual fuck? Is he serious?

"It will be epic. The blood, the gore... a memorable spectacle."

"Th... the pain." Aella's head spun as she contemplated the exquisite pain that would accompany such an ending. She felt lightheaded but fought to maintain her composure. In for a penny, in for a pound... of flesh.

"Well, yes. We need to talk about that part. That is where you come into the planning. You are my macabre muse. I can drug you or kill you before I put you into the woodchipper. Still gory but not as dramatic and sensational, but you wouldn't feel pain. Or you can choose to enter it alive... awake... in all your glory... stoic and brave... at least for a while. 'Do not go gentle into that good night' as Dylan Thomas said.'"

"I'm scared. What should I do?"

Run... fucking run is what I should do.

"I can understand your feelings. I will not make this decision for you. It is yours, and yours alone. Although, I will remind you that this is about making you immortal—searing your image onto the retinas and brains of those who watch *forever*. What would you want to see as a subscriber? How do you want to be remembered?"

"You're right. I want to enter this experience of my own free will. Where is my purse? Can you give me an hour?"

"You dropped it by the door earlier. What do you want? Why the delay?"

"I have some medicinals in my purse. I want to smoke a joint and, once I am relaxed, I am going to take some shrooms to enhance the experience. Is that okay?"

"Of course. Let me get it for you. Why don't you have a seat again? I need to prepare before we go live anyhow. Let me know if you need anything."

Stellan led her back to the chair before grabbing her purse and returning it to her. She pulled out a small bag of weed and papers and began to roll a joint. Stellan walked over to the control center and powered up the monitors and his computer system. As the system booted, he walked over to the surgical table and released the brakes so he could roll it over to the woodchipper. Then he opened the door to his private quarters to retrieve a fresh pair of black coveralls and his mask. He placed them on the surgical table before turning on the large video camera.

Stellan returned to the monitor bank to verify the camera angle would capture all the splendor that was to come. He retrieved a small Wi-Fi camera from the wire shelving behind his control center and set it up on the instrument tray a few feet to the right of the surgical table, out of sight of the camera's view. He wanted to be sure to catch every scream, every tear, every agonized facial expression.

Once he had finished the setup of the studio, he proceeded to the computer to login into the admin page of the Dark Arts site. Stellan posted an announcement with a 30-minute countdown timer, letting his subscribers know he was about to go live with a new episode of *Dark Arts*. He grinned as he saw an immediate spike of activity on the site.

Stellan got up and went to check on Aella. She was sitting in the chair, calm and relaxed, with her pupils dilated. "Hey there, Creatooooor! How are you? Those lights over there are so pretty, spinning and twisting around each other." Aella pointed across the warehouse to the painted over windows that did not even let moonlight shine through.

He smiled and shook his head as he responded, "Yeah, they're great. How you feeling, darling?"

"Great, great, great." Aella had visions of her blood and bits of bone spraying out of the woodchipper in a psychedelic rainbow with little black, hairy demons dancing around.

"Seems like it. You just about ready to go live? I just need a few more minutes, and I will get you set up in the studio."

"Oh yes, I can't wait for my moment in the spotlight."

"Good. I will be back in just a moment. When I start the intro to the show, I need you to be very quiet. Okay? Then you can scream or do whatever you want once we start. But there is one super important rule that you can't forget. Don't let on that you know me, so don't call me Anthony or *Le Créateur*. Is that clear?"

Aella giggled. "Aye aye, captain! So, I can call you dickhead, asshole, or motherfucker?"

"Yes, whatever."

Stellan turned and walked back to the surgical table to don the coveralls and mask. He then retrieved the camera's remote before returning to Aella to bring her into the studio. Aella followed him and climbed onto the table. He walked over to the small Wi-Fi camera and turned it on to check its positioning in the monitor before the broadcast began. A quick adjustment brought her face into full view. He returned to Aella's side. "It's showtime, baby," Stellan murmured before clicking the record button on the camera's remote.

"Welcome once again, my loyal followers, to the fourth episode of *Dark Arts* hosted by the one and only, *Le Créateur*. First, I want to thank you for your continued patronage. Tonight is a one-of-a kind, very special installment. I am paying homage to one of my favorite artists, and there is an opportunity for three lucky viewers to own an actual piece of this artwork.

"Once again, we have something tailor-made for all my gore lovers and sadists. This episode is filled with blood, bodily fluids and tissues of every kind. And don't worry, I will also be offering ten prints of the completed piece as well as the opportunity to download the video in 24 hours.

"I know some of you out there love to see the total domination of the subject, but please welcome our sublime subject tonight. She has given herself to us to create this wondrous work of art. She is conscious, as you can see, so you will experience her terror and pain once we begin. As always, I seek to satisfy your basest, most deviant need for gratification with pulse-pounding entertainment.

"Let me go activate the split screen and the closeup cam, so you can see her every reaction in exquisite detail."

With a few taps on the keyboard, he activated the second camera and started the split-screen view. He proceeded over to the woodchipper and flicked the power switch with a flourish. The woodchipper roared to life, its ragged blades visible as they spun inside the chute. Aella jumped when the engine began to race. She cried out when *Le Créateur* threw a chunk of wood into the blades to demonstrate its power. Aella was determined to follow through, but her stomach was in her throat. Her pulse raced, and she felt dreamy and light-headed.

Le Créateur looked over to the monitor bank at the screen where his subscribers could send him messages. There was a flurry of activity as people responded to the dramatic scene unfolding. *Le Créateur* walked over to Aella's side and swept a strand of hair off her forehead. "Are you ready, my deviant diva?"

A few errant tears slid down the side of her face as she nodded. *Le Créateur* unlocked the brakes on the surgical table and moved it up right against the chute before clicking them back in place. He then put pressure on Aella's shoulders to prevent her from rising as he began to slide her feet down into the chute toward the whirling blades.

As her toes entered the blades, the rapid revolutions began to pull her body further down into them, as *Le Créateur* kept her from rising. Aella let loose an ear-piercing shriek as the teeth tore the flesh and muscles from her bones, pulverizing them into a crimson red mush. The pain tore through her body; all rational thought left her mind as she swam through a sea of blood, waves crashing around her.

The discharge chute began to shoot a thick coagulated mixture of blood, flesh, and smalls chips of bone onto the left side of the wall and first canvas. The clumpy mess slid down the wall in snail trails of gore.

Le Créateur fought to hold Aella down when she tried to launch her body from the table as the powerful blades dug in and gnawed her ankles. She wailed in pain and gasped for breath, begging for the torment to end. "Just kill me now please. I can't do it. I changed my mind."

"It is too late now, dear. We must finish. Everyone is loving you. See that screen over there? All those people are talking about you."

"Really? Me? Oh fuuuucccckkk! It really is kind of pretty."

As the machine continued its inexorable march up her legs, a river of blood flowed into its giant maw. As it met the cyclone at the bottom of the chute, it sprayed a torrential rainstorm of blood back onto *Le Créateur*, what was left of Aella's body and every object in its path.

Aella smiled as the pain began to dissipate. She couldn't feel anything at all anymore. Swirls of electric blue crackled across her vision as she watched the macabre, nightmarish ingestion of her body, before it all began to fade to black. All color faded from her face as her frantic movements slowed and then stopped when she lost consciousness. *Le Créateur* used this opportunity to turn the crank and adjust the path of the discharge chute farther to the right to begin covering the middle section of the work.

When her struggles ceased, the machine pulled her body in faster, only bogging down a little as it began to pulverize her thighs, rending her flesh into a bloody, soupy oatmeal-like glop. As her heart rate became more erratic, blood sprayed out of the femoral vein in fits and spurts before slowing to an ooze as her heart stopped.

He turned the crank a few more times to finish covering the last canvas. As her abdomen proceeded down into the teeth, they began to draw out loops of bowel that were torn to thin threads as if they were being drawn through a pasta maker. Her lungs collapsed down and shriveled like raisins as the teeth tore open her thoracic cavity. As the blades chipped away at her cervical spine, drawing ever closer to her thick skull, *Le Créateur* used a small rubber squeegee to put pressure on the top of her head and push it through the powerful blades.

As the last of the grinding finished and the spray from the

discharge chute ceased, *Le Créateur* turned to the camera and bowed deeply.

"Well, my gruesome groupies, I present to you *Tempest.* The auctions will be posted for the ten limited edition prints and the three resin-coated canvases tomorrow morning at 9 a.m. PDT at the main Dark Arts site on the dark web. The auctions for the canvases will close at 9 p.m. tomorrow and for the prints at 3 p.m. tomorrow afternoon. As per usual, only cryptocurrency will be accepted, and secure anonymous delivery will be arranged. This video will be up for streaming on the Dark Arts gallery for the next 24 hours. After that, a heavily encrypted digital download can be purchased for $2,500 USD. I hope you savored every moment of tonight's presentation. Goodnight and sweet screams to you all!"

Stellan pushed the button on the remote to end the recording session and then moved over to the small camera to turn it off as well. He was drawn to the monitor bank as he saw comment after comment flashing up onto the screen.

"You are the bomb!"

"*Le Créateur* is vicious and sadistic. My kind of man, although, I do hope to never run into him."

"Best episode yet!"

"Have to ply my body on the uptown side tonight to earn the money for that download."

"Encore! Encore! When will we see you with your next masterpiece?"

Stellan was beaming with pride as he pulled off his mask and stripped out of the coveralls.

I'm going to be the most famous artist in the history of the world. They love me! How can I top myself next time?

Stellan removed the canvases from the wall after a few minutes of letting the excess detritus fall off them and laid them out on a large metal table to dry for the next day or so. Then he would have to start the painstaking process of mixing up a vast amount of resin to completely cover the art, preventing putrefaction and masking any odor from the blood and fecal material that covered them.

He ran through the events of the evening as he used a large industrial squeegee to scoop all the flesh and bone bits into a large stinking pile. He wheeled the wheelbarrow over and used a large deep shovel to transfer the mess into it and over to the kiln.

That stupid bitch! She seriously had some mental health issues. I can't believe how easily I convinced her that it was time for her to die, and that she WANTED to be my victim. Who in the actual fuck says, "Yes, please run me through a woodchipper while I am alive," hell, at all for that matter?

Stellan was busy late into the night cleaning up the warehouse before choosing and then printing the images for the auction. He also photographed the canvases separately so he could post three separate auctions for people to choose the piece that drew their eye. Then he uploaded the video file to the streaming link and set it to be available for purchase at 10 p.m. the next day. Stellan also printed three additional copies of the finished artwork to send to the police and media again in the coming days.

As dawn arose, he went back to catch a cat nap in his quarters before beginning the long process of removing any traces of interaction between him and the victim on cell phone records and clearing her from the Dark Arts subscriber database. He was a ghost on Tinder, so he didn't have to worry about any records of him being found there. Aella Mattias would never be linked to the *Le Créateur* case. She would just be another tragic missing person's case. And *Tempest* would just be a Jane Doe to them.

As excited as he was to create his next work of art for the *Dark Arts* collection, Stellan needed to get back to finishing up pieces for his next gallery debut in New York during the Christmas season. Meredith had been hounding him lately to see what he had completed so far, and she was hoping he could create an additional four pieces over the next three months. The collection titled *They Came from the Dark* was set to be picked up the Tuesday of Thanksgiving week, so it would be delivered just after the holiday. Then, he would have a little over a week to get it installed so it could debut the first week of December.

The gallery had already begun advertising his arrival with a new collection. The public was clamoring for the few available tickets to see the limited run of his new collection. All the biggest names in the art world—critics, other gallery curators, fellow artists, and private art collectors—would be in attendance on opening night.

Maybe though, I can find time to create something special for the All Hallows' season. Can't have them forgetting me just as I am gaining a foothold toward living in infamy for all time. I must strike again while the iron is hot.

Sharon Marie Provost

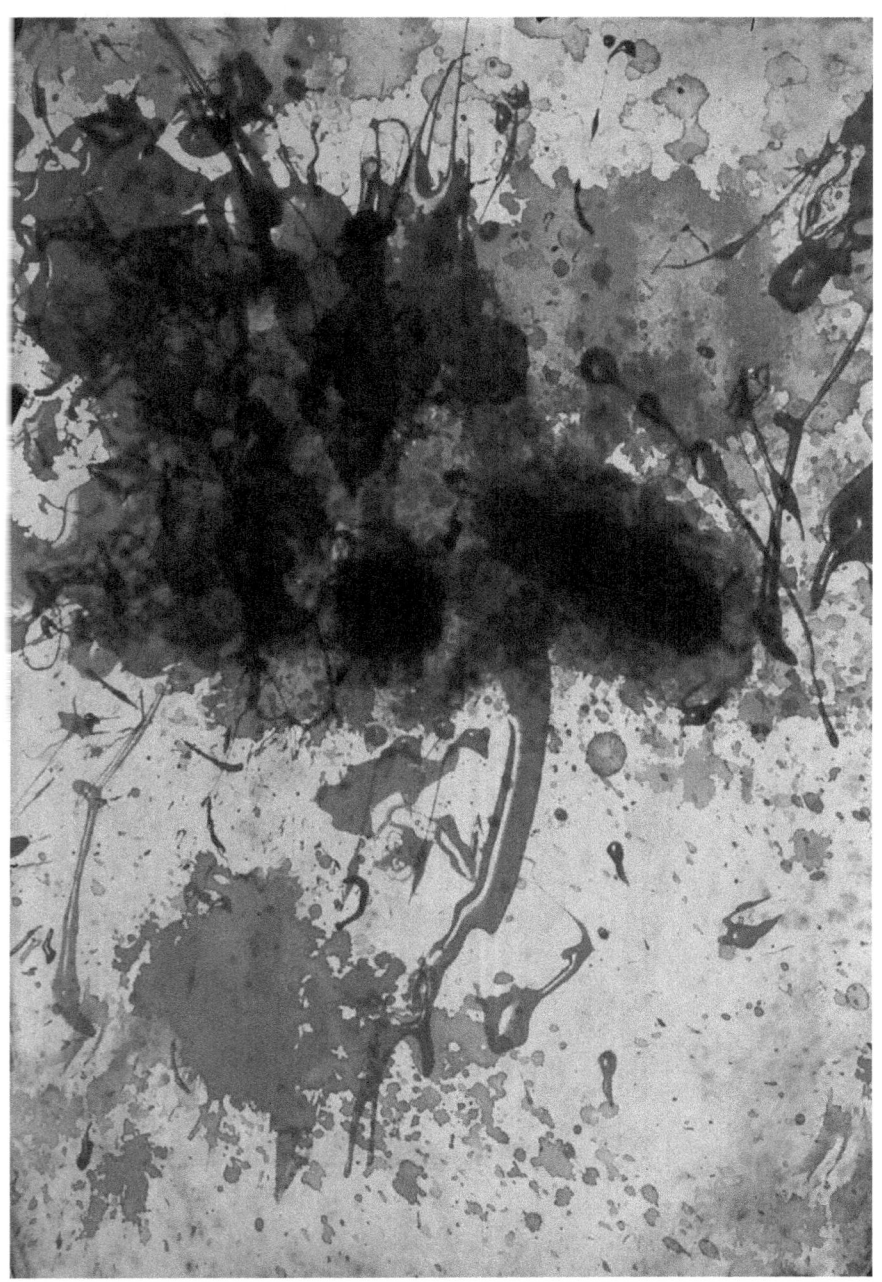

136

Fourteen

Ghost in the System

Late August 2022

The first two weeks in the Homicide Unit had been a blur for Mendy. After Mills called her in to inform her about Annalise, she'd spent the next 48 hours straight at the station reviewing the first two case files, only sleeping a few hours a night on the couch in the back of the office. Finally, Mills had insisted that she go home for 12 hours. She hadn't gleaned anything more from the case files than what she'd already learned during the team briefing.

The Creator case was a botched mess from start to finish. There were no leads at all in the Arizona Hutchins case. No one knew where she'd been or what she'd been doing just before she disappeared back in February of 2021. There were no viable suspects: no known boyfriends, no enemies, and no feuding co-workers since she worked from home alone developing apps. While she wasn't close to her extended family, they weren't at odds with one another. The only people Arizona interacted with regularly, if you could even call it that, were her fellow surfers down at the beach. None of them had a police record, and all of them had solid alibis.

The Millie Simpson case from July of 2021 wasn't in any better shape. Speculation centered on the boyfriend she had gone to see with her friend Alexandria, but there was no proof to support it. No witnesses had been found to corroborate that the girls had ever been on a bus that day, let alone indicate where they might have gotten off. They were never seen at the MAGA rally that day. Alexandria's roommate wasn't home until evening, so it couldn't even be proved that the girls ever met up.

Both girls had not been seen since that day, but Alexandria's flighty tendencies meant she couldn't even be classified as missing. Millie was reportedly dating someone, but there was no proof of it, and nothing to suggest who the man might be or how they might have met. The Tinder theory had been put on the back burner since there'd been no recent activity on her profile. One casual work acquaintance remembered hearing that Millie had a boyfriend, and he had seen the Tinder app on her phone, but he had no details.

No identifying details in the pictures of the two women could help them determine where the perpetrator might be— if he was even in Los Angeles at all. The setting looked like any one of thousands of old or abandoned warehouses in the 4,850-square-mile expanse that was the L.A. metropolitan area. All they knew for sure was that both pictures had been taken at the same location, and that it was the probable scene of the homicides themselves, as well as the staging of the bodies. They could break the case wide open if only they could find that location.

When it came to new leads since Mills had taken over the case, there weren't many. The packages with the pictures had been delivered to the media using an as-yet-unidentified bike courier service. Even more frustrating, there was no trace of who had delivered the package to the park. It was like a ghost had slipped into the area, or it had just materialized out of thin air. They had pored through hours of street cam footage and visited countless businesses in the area to look for private security footage that might help... all to no avail.

DNA testing had been performed on the taloned toe they had received in the package, and it came back as a match for Annalise.

Unfortunately, no other trace evidence was found, and prints had not been found on the toe, the letter, or any of the packaging. The bastard had used gloves. He was smart.

Hundreds of people had passed through the area on foot, on bikes, or in cars in the hours leading up to the delivery. Many of the pedestrians were dressed in dark clothing and hoodies despite the heat, so they were barely visible much of the time. None of them had acted suspiciously.

Then, to make matters worse, the entire city's traffic and surveillance camera system had crashed at midnight—hit by a Trojan virus that acted like ransomware. It had taken days to get the system up and running again and ultimately no ransom had been paid, which pointed to possible sabotage by the suspect. Few businesses in the area of the park had active security cameras, so no one was seen entering the park from the few vantage points that had been filmed. How could a vicious serial killer be so close to a busy police precinct and deliver a package unseen, like a phantom?

Mendy had once again been assigned to deal with Tinder regarding Millie's profile, and she received the same infuriating answer: There had been no activity of any kind on her profile in the past year, and certainly not with the non-existent Anthony Carreras. She had contacted the cell phone companies for all three victims, but no calls or texts were found with an unknown person.

The entire team did a deep dive into the personal lives of all three victims, and had found no connections between them. No business ties. No casual contacts. No friends. The only possible connection between two of the women was the Tinder dating. Nobody could verify if Arizona might have been dating someone at the time of her disappearance. A check on her cell phone showed she did have the Tinder app installed, but it didn't show she'd ever used it to connect with any men. A fairly bare-bones profile had been created two years ago but, given the nature of her job—creating apps—it could have been purely for research purposes.

The media had held off on reporting the pictures they had received until noon, as promised. After the team briefing, Mills had held a press conference at 11:30 a.m. to notify the public about the murders before the media did. He released the information that both previously reported murders were connected to the same killer.

Then he announced that the disappearance of Annalise Fischer had now been upgraded to a murder and linked to the same killer. Mills gave very few details about the killer other than the fact that he went by the moniker *Le Créateur*, and he was creating so-called works of art using the victims' bodies. Mills told them that the killer had made contact with the press the previous night in order to seek some sick fame.

The press room erupted in a flurry of activity as the reporters pushed forward, shouting questions.

How long had the police known about the murders?

How long had they known about the connection to the same killer?

How long they had known about what the killer was doing to the bodies?

What had the killer said to the press, and why had he contacted them now?

Mills declined to answer any further questions, citing the ongoing investigation. He asked the public to call the tipline if they had any information that might help the investigation.

The proverbial shit had hit the fan a mere 30 minutes later when the noon news went live with the lead story about *Le*

Créateur, followed by the afternoon update on the newspaper website. Thankfully, neither one showed the photo, but both described the picture in horrific detail. The focus of the stories was the fact that the Police Department had known for some time that both victims were murdered and by the same person, but they had neglected to inform the families or the public at large. The newspaper headline was especially damning: "What is the Los Angeles Police Department hiding about the murders of three local women?" The noon news led off proclaiming "Scandal at the LAPD!"

The department quickly became flooded with phone calls from the public condemning them for the handling of the case. The tipline became useless as a tool to gain valuable information, as all the calls coming in were critical rather than helpful.

The mayor held his own press conference, stating that Internal Affairs would be performing an investigation to determine who was culpable for mishandling the case. He was angry about their neglect in warning the public of the "real and present danger roaming the streets of our proud city."

Mendy's phone had rung about an hour after the noon news broadcast, and the caller ID showed it was from Belinda. She sighed deeply before answering it. The phone call was seared into her memory, and she replayed it often, especially when she felt like she was failing Annalise, which was daily.

"Mendy, my God. Why didn't you tell me? I asked how you knew for sure that she was murdered. You should have told me what he did to her! I asked you. It wasn't right to let me find out this way."

"I couldn't do that to you. I could barely process it at that moment. I had just seen it myself. I was hoping that the information wouldn't come out that fast, so I could find the right time and way to tell you. I'm so sorry. Please forgive me."

"I can't. I just can't. Who is the lead detective on this case? I will refer to him for my information in the future. I can't trust you."

"Detective Mills. I'm sure you know the precinct's phone number. His extension is 112. I hope you can forgive me someday. I promise you that I will find this bastard and take him down... for all of us but especially Annalise."

"B... bye," Belinda stammered through a sob.

That sob at the end woke Mendy up many nights, but it only strengthened her resolve.

Mendy became more determined than ever to solve this case. She was convinced that Tinder was the key to all of the women's disappearances. Annalise had definitely found her killer through Tinder, Millie had reportedly been dating someone from Tinder, and Arizona did have the app installed and had created a profile. The elusive "Anthony Carreras" had to be out there somewhere, even if he was a ghost in the system.

There had to be a way to find him or lure him out into the open. No matter how devious or intelligent, everyone made mistakes eventually, especially if they were given enough rope to hang themselves. The scope and breadth of this egomaniacal sadistic son-of-a-bitch's desire for infamy could lead to his undoing. Now they just had to figure out how to sink their hooks into him.

Mendy was still in the office at 10 p.m., long after the other detectives in the unit had gone home to get some much-needed sleep, when a call came into their office from the front desk. A package had just been delivered by a bicycle courier addressed to "The Inept Homicide Squad." The officer at the desk had held the courier for questioning. She grabbed her cell phone and dialed Mills as she headed over to the interview room.

"I need you here NOW. We just got another package. And this time we have the courier who delivered it."

"I'll be right there in five minutes. Wait for me!"

Dear God, what is it this time?

Sharon Marie Provost

Fifteen

Vanessa

First week of October 2022

anessa DuPre had never had difficulty finding a man—actually lots of men—to date. She had developed early, with the ideal measurements for bust, waist and hips. Her high cheekbones and the delicate curvature of her face made her a stunner from a young age.

Her parents had compared her beauty to that of Aphrodite, an assessment shared by the Randolph Modeling Agency that had signed her at the tender age of 14. She'd started out as a teen model before quickly progressing to high fashion at 16.

Her personality was certainly one befitting a goddess—love, passion, pleasure, lust, and procreation were cornerstones of her life. She never had to work hard to obtain what she wanted, whether it be men, power, money, or fame. She lived in the lap of luxury as a privileged child born to a family with old money.

Vanessa was soon able to maintain that lifestyle herself. She'd been legally emancipated at the age of 16—with a hefty trust fund—purely to make the logistics of her world travel easier on everyone. That way, she could go where she wanted whenever she needed without a chaperone. The jet-setting family rarely had schedules that overlapped, between her father's duties as a French diplomat and her mother's societal obligations and charity work.

In school, she passed her classes with easy A's as boys tussled over who would be the one to write her papers or get the exam key so she could have the answers. The ironic part of that was Vanessa was highly intelligent. She could have easily passed those classes without help, but why waste her time on school when it could be better spent having fun? When she moved on to home schooling when her modeling career started, the tutors were paid to submit her homework for her until she graduated early, a few months before her 17th birthday.

It wasn't long before Vanessa's hard partying and promiscuous lifestyle became more important to her than the fame she could gain from modeling. She couldn't pay someone else to work the long, grueling hours, often in less-than-favorable conditions, that were required of a model. She grew tired of feeling faint when she ate only a few carrot sticks after a 12-hour day in the heat or cold. Then there were the rules regarding alcohol consumption and early bedtimes. She had never been that tightly monitored as a child, and she certainly wasn't going to stand for it any longer as an adult.

At the height of her career, at the age of 22, she had retired from full-time high-fashion modeling. She'd occasionally accept a gig for the Victoria's Secret Fashion Show or walk the runway for a couture designer in Paris or Milan. Otherwise, she spent most of her time in Malibu at her mansion, meeting friends for lunch or shopping, attending red carpet events and pursuing her two passions in life... partying at night and adding to her body count.

Vanessa had become frustrated with the L.A. "dating" scene. Everyone saw her as a "catch" to add to their own social profiles and financial portfolios. She wasn't looking to become the trophy wife and checkbook on the arm of some L.A. businessman or second-rate television star. She just wanted to have fun with some hot player before moving on to the next. Desperate times called for desperate measures, so she had moved on the world of online dating with Tinder and FlingPals.

Lately, she had focused most of her attention on Tinder because it seemed to have a larger, more desirable selection of men. This had resulted in a handful of hookups that had lasted for a few hours and some she met up with a couple of times a week for a month or two, with no strings attached.

Vanessa had just returned from a month's vacation in the French countryside at her parents' villa prior to walking the runway at Paris Fashion Week. She was back in L.A. just in time for all the fun Halloween events and parties that started with the first day of the month. She had logged into Tinder on a long layover at the airport to find a partner for the Boos and Brews Crawl downtown on Saturday night.

She'd scrolled through what felt like a hundred profiles, swiping right on 20 of them. She was desperate for a hunk of man meat, but she did have standards. When she arose late Friday morning after sleeping in after her 3 a.m. arrival at LAX, she found that five of the men had matched with her. Three were handsome and exactly her type, but only one had the wild and sexy vibe she was craving.

She sent Anthony Carreras a message inviting him to meet her at the Rhythm Room, where the crawl was set to begin.

Vanessa met some friends for lunch and then went shopping for the perfect outfit for her adventure. If Anthony didn't respond, she would find someone to spend the night with. The crawls were always good for drunken hookups. As she walked out of the Nonna Boutique, she heard a small ping from her phone. She pulled it out of her Coach purse and found a response from Anthony.

"Hey there, sexy! I will see you at 8 outside of the Rhythm

Room. Maybe we can explore our own rhythm later at my place."

Vanessa smiled and typed a quick reply. "That was my intention."

She looked down at the dress she'd purchased and knew she had made the right decision. Every eye downtown would be locked on her rocking body.

I might be beating them off with a stick by the end of the night. But that might only get them more excited! Me too, for that matter.

Vanessa returned home and ordered Chinese food to be delivered. She relaxed the rest of the evening in preparation for her long night the following day.

She spent much of the next day lounging by the pool, followed by an hourlong workout with her personal trainer. Afterward, she made herself a healthy dinner with broiled salmon and garlic parmesan couscous, then ran into her sauna for a quick 10-minute steam to loosen her muscles before showering and getting ready for the night.

Vanessa got out of the shower and went to her walk-in closet to choose her outfit. She slid on a pair of black satin thong underwear, covering it with the new black low-cut, loose-knit crocheted sheath dress that ended just above her knees. The outline of her bosom was clearly visible through the holes of the loose-knit fabric, but a small crocheted flower covered her nipples. She paired the outfit with black 3-inch stiletto heels and secured them with the straps at the ankle.

She sat down at her vanity and began weaving her damp hair into a long, loose braid as she surveyed her makeup palette, choosing colors for her rendezvous. It was always a sexy move at the end of the evening to untie her hair and shake out the large loose curls that had formed as her hair dried. She used black eyeliner and mascara with a smoky eyeshadow and bright red lipstick.

Utterly stunning if I do say so myself!

She logged onto her Uber app to check on the status of her ride. The driver had just sent a message announcing his arrival. She dropped her lipstick into her black sequined clutch along with some cash and her debit card before heading out to the car. The typical one-hour drive took a little longer than usual because of all the Friday night traffic heading downtown. As the car pulled up in front of the bar, she noticed Anthony leaning against the wall near the door, looking at his phone.

Anthony looked up as she opened the car door and stepped out. His expression showed his appreciation as his eyes slid up and down her body, appraising her every curve, all of which were on clear display. Vanessa positively glowed under his lascivious gaze as he wolf-whistled at her, then came forward with his right hand extended.

"You are a knockout, baby!"

"Thank you. You're not too shabby yourself."

Anthony gestured toward the door. "Shall we go in?"

"Yes, please. I am dying for a cocktail."

Anthony opened the door and led Vanessa inside to a small intimate table at the back. Once he had helped her into her seat, he walked over to the bar to place their order. The song playing in the background suited the mood perfectly... "Bad Things" by Jace Everett. She'd noted his sharp intake of breath upon seeing her. They were going to do bad things to each other all night long if she had anything to say about it.

He returned with two lavender-colored cocktails in martini glasses emanating fog. "They are called Witch's Heart. I hope this is OK?"

Vanessa took a large swallow and smiled. "Perfect. I

absolutely adore blackberry."

Anthony pulled his chair closer to Vanessa and sat down with his arm around her. "I haven't been here before. I love the vibe of this place."

"They patterned it after an old jazz speakeasy that used to be here in downtown."

"Nice. So, what's the plan for the night? I haven't done one of these crawls before."

"You move from bar to bar over the next four hours. There are stops at Las Perlas, The Stowaway, The Slipper Clutch, and Kacey's Irish Pub. The path of the crawl takes you around Pershing Square, where you can stop in for the Fall Festival... if you can still walk by that point."

"I've heard a lot about Las Perlas. I am a tequila fan, and from what I hear, they have over 450 agave-based Mezcal spirits there."

"They are to die for. That's our next stop. I hope you don't mind walking tonight. We ultimately make a big circle, so we can come back to pick up your car."

"That's fine, baby. I hope you are up to it. Those shoes don't look made for walking."

"I was a high-fashion model for eight years, so this was pretty much all I wore for eight to 16 hours a day. I was born wearing stilettos with vodka in my sippy cup. To be honest, I don't know if I could walk in shoes with less than a 2-inch heel."

Anthony laughed as his hand caressed her knee. "I get it, baby. You are my kind of gal."

Vanessa knocked back the last of her drink and leaned forward, kissing Anthony passionately. "Shall we proceed to the next stop? I haven't even hit my buzz yet." Anthony laughed and downed the rest of his drink. He helped her to her feet and wrapped his arm around her waist, his hand resting on her pert little ass. He gave it a slap as they turned to head down 6th Street toward Las Perlas.

Anthony opened the door and led her inside. The bar was filled with people, so he held her hand as they navigated through the crowd to find two open barstools.

"I trust you. Ten out of 10 on that first drink," she replied as she made the OK sign with her fingers.

Anthony perused the drink specials created for the Halloween-themed event. After consulting with the bartender, he turned back to Vanessa and handed her a bright yellow drink with a small stalk of celery in it. "Hey, they have a horror movie theme going. I chose the Infinity Pool. Have you seen that movie? It is totally whack. It has that Skarsgård fellow in it that all the women find sexy."

"Well, he does have that hot Viking undertone and body going for him. And yes, I did see it. Tell me you don't find that Mia Goth chick hot. Men always go for the seductive, dark crazy bitch... that is until the crazy becomes too much." Vanessa's dark, throaty laugh rose above the din.

Anthony shrugged. "Well..."

"I knew it. You men are all the same. But I suppose I can't talk. Any one of those Skarsgård brothers could come pillage the city and drag me away in chains to be their woman."

"Oh, so you like a little bondage, eh?"

"Baby, you don't know the half of what I am into," she whispered into his ear.

"Maybe we should go explore that then." Anthony pulled her into him as he kissed down her neck.

"Slow down there. We have all night. I'm enjoying this refreshing cocktail right now, and I at least want to get to The Stowaway. There's a DJ there playing classic house, hip hop, and reggae music on vinyl."

"God, you know how to drive a man wild. You know just how to use your... assets to get a man to do exactly what you want."

"From the moment, I was born I had my daddy wrapped around my little finger... and everyone else for that matter. I was named after a goddess, you know?"

"Is that so?"

"Vanessa is a Latin variation for Venus, the goddess of love and beauty, also known as Aphrodite. From the first second my parents saw my beauty, they knew no other name would fit."

"I remember some Greek mythology from school. The goddess of passion, pleasure, and sexuality. That certainly fits you to a tee."

"I know," she said with a smile as she gave his inner thigh a squeeze.

"Let's finish this drink and move on to The Stowaway, you tease. I don't know how much longer I can keep my hands off of you."

"Who says you have to? This is L.A. Who is going to say anything if we have a little fun? As long as we keep our clothes on, that is."

Anthony's hand cupped her breast as he leaned forward, darting his tongue into her mouth. Vanessa playfully bit his lip as he pulled away and then picked up her drink to finish it up. "Are you ready, Freddie?"

Anthony took her hand and led her out of the bar. They turned right on Main Street and then headed up 4th to The Stowaway at Spring Street. They could hear the music pouring out of the front doors as they approached. They wove their way through the crowd of dancers and found a small booth off to the side near the bar. It was hard to hear each other over all the chatter and the thumping dance music in the background. Anthony leaned forward, and his lips softly brushed against her ear as he spoke, "Shall I do the honors again?"

"Go for it. Two for two so far," she replied as she made the OK sign with her fingers.

Anthony walked up to the bar and spoke to one of the bartenders, who pointed up to a blackboard behind him listing all the special event drinks. A few moments later, he returned with two drinks in red goblets. He presented hers with a flourish, "For your drinking pleasure, I give you the Mystic Brew. You enjoyed the last one, so I thought I would go with another sweet, fruity island-like drink."

"I can taste rum... lots of rum and tartness backed with a sweet molasses flavor. Is it brown sugar?"

"Good job. The tart comes from grapefruit."

"Mmm... you have outdone yourself. Saved the best for last. I love a nice stiff drink."

Anthony smiled and took another drink himself. She scooted closer to him and snuggled into his arms, rubbing his leg as she drank. After a few moments, she was disappointed to find her drink already gone. "One more for the road?"

Anthony nodded and started to slide out the other side of the booth.

Vanessa put her hand on his arm. "This round is on me."

She returned a short time later with the two drinks. The sexual tension between them was building, so they made quick work of the drinks. "You ready to go, beautiful?" he said as he came around and offered her his hand.

"Yes, I am," she giggled as she wobbled a bit on her heels. "Those were some powerful drinks."

"I parked in a long-term lot. I think maybe I should leave my car there for the night, and we can take an Uber back to my place. My head is spinning a bit. That OK with you?"

"Sounds fine to me. I know that Uber was supposed to keep a lot of drivers in the area for the event."

They walked out the door and sat on a bench in the cool breeze to wait. Anthony fiddled with his phone for a few moments before announcing, "Our chariot will be awaiting us down at the corner of Spring and 5th Steet. He wrapped his arm around her waist again as they made their way down the street.

They climbed into the red Mazda CX-3, and Anthony gave the driver an address. A short time later, they arrived at the Moxy Downtown. Vanessa looked at him questioningly. Anthony shrugged, "I thought we might as well stay near my car to make it easier for us to pick it up in the morning. Then as his hand grazed her breast and he looked into her eyes, he murmured, "Besides, I want you now. I didn't want to wait for the drive out to Beverly Hills." Vanessa smiled and led the way into the lobby.

Vanessa took a seat in the lobby as he went to the desk to get them checked in. He came back holding a key card. "Penthouse suite! Shall we?" The two of them fought to maintain some decorum as they made their way across the lobby quickly on their way to the elevator.

Outside the door to their room, Anthony grabbed her arm and spun her around. His body pinned her against the door as he kissed her passionately. She could hear him fumbling with the key card, trying to get the door to unlock. Finally, he wrapped his hand around the back of her head, his tongue twisting with hers, as he turned the handle and stumble-stepped with her toward the bed. In seconds, their clothes were strewn around the room in their race to the sheets.

Anthony wrapped his arm around her body, cradling her, as

he pressed against her, lowering her to the bed. The couple spent the rest of the night together, their bodies entangled in the sheets and each other as they passionately made love. Near dawn, they finally fell asleep with Vanessa's head on Anthony's chest.

Vanessa woke at 10 a.m. to the sounds of room service arriving. She squinted and blinked as her eyes adjusted to the sunlight streaming in through the windows. Anthony brought over a tray with an egg white omelet made with turkey bacon, mushrooms and Monterey jack, along with a fruit cup with a glass of freshly squeezed OJ.

"Well, thank you, kind sir."

"I knew I needed some food in my stomach to combat this hangover and nausea. Does it meet your satisfaction?"

"You picked well. I appreciate your thoughtfulness."

"I don't know what your schedule is like today. I just have a meeting at 2 p.m., but I can drive you home first."

"No, you don't have to do that. I live all the way in Malibu. I took an Uber here, and I can take one back. Besides, I need to stop in at the modeling office here downtown to discuss the show they want me to walk in anyhow."

"You can hit the shower first if you like."

"We still have some time. I thought we might take advantage of it. I saw the spacious spa shower in there with the double rainfall shower heads."

"I knew there was something I liked about you. Great minds think alike."

The two of them finished breakfast and took a leisurely, intimate shower before getting ready for their day. Anthony looked over as she rose from the vanity where she had been applying her makeup. "Do you want to get together again sometime?"

"Sure. What were you thinking?"

"Well, I didn't mention it before, but I am an artist. I have my first showing coming up next Friday. It might be nice to have a friendly face there amongst all those critics and all. Then we can go back to my place and enjoy each other."

"That sounds lovely. A chance to dress up and hobnob with all the bigwigs in the art world. It has been a while since I have done that."

"The show is at 7. I'll pick you up at your place then?"

"Actually, I will be here downtown all day. You mind picking me up at the modeling agency?"

"Perfect! Does 5 p.m. work for you? That gives us enough time to get to the gallery a little early to make sure everything is in place."

"I will see you then. Thanks for the fun evening," she said as she walked over and gave him a quick peck on the cheek. "Until next week, hottie."

After her dalliance with Anthony, Vanessa had signed on to do a runway show in Milan in three weeks. Somehow it seemed no matter how hard she tried to leave modeling behind, it kept dragging her back in... although there had always been a righteous party scene in Milan, so maybe it wasn't so bad after all. Their strict rules were much harder to enforce when she only signed up for shows piecemeal.

She had been busy all week tying up loose ends as she prepared to leave the country again. She would be gone for a month and a half because a couple of her friends had convinced her to do a five-week "eat, pray, love" whirlwind tour of western Europe, with stops in Spain and Italy. Now the date of Anthony's art exhibition had arrived, and she needed to concentrate on getting ready. She couldn't bear the thought of the art getting *all* the attention when a goddess was in attendance.

Vanessa took a quick steam bath to bring color to her cheeks from improved circulation, followed by an ice-cold shower. She moved to the large mirror at her vanity while she dried her hair and began to arrange it in a Victorian style with four large finger puffs pinned on the top of her head. In the back, she made one wide braid that she wrapped along the front at the bottom of the puffs and pinned in place. She used the iron on a few tendrils of hair at her temples to form delicate ringlet curls that framed her high cheekbones.

She then applied a thick black eyeliner with a smoky charcoal eyeshadow. She painted her lips a subtle rosewood shade that added some color to her face while playing off the raw umber color of her dress. Then she applied a light coat of blush in the delicate pink shade, Sweet Enough. She knew just how to accentuate her Grecian goddess features to make herself irresistible to men.

She moved on to her closet and pulled out her satin ankle-length deep V-neck tight bandage dress. It molded itself to every curve of her body, following the mounds of her breasts, along the curves of her buttocks, even the shallow depression of her belly button. The tightness of the dress prevented her from wearing any sort of undergarments, so her erect nipples could be seen protruding from the dress. The deep neckline formed two descending fan-shaped designs that ended in a V-neck a mere inch above her navel. She paired the dress with nude pumps and a layered gold choker to highlight her long neck.

Just as she packed the essentials into her black quilted Chanel clutch, she heard the horn signaling the Uber's arrival.

She slid the purse's chain over her shoulder and hurried out to meet the driver before he left, grabbing her keys and cell phone off the entryway table as she ran out the door. She sent a quick text to Anthony, reminding him to pick her up at the Randolph Modeling Agency downtown.

"Can't wait to see you at 5, my nubile enchantress," he replied with a winking emoji. Vanessa had to admit he was quite the charming gentleman. He knew how to compliment a woman without getting overly familiar since, in truth, they were merely bed buddies.

As they were nearing downtown, Vanessa's phone rang. It was her mother calling from France.

"Hey, Mom. How are you doing?"

"I'm doing well. How are you?"

"Other than your father driving me nuts with preparations for this party, I'm doing fine. You sound like you're in the car. Am I interrupting you?"

"I'm headed over to the modeling agency to go over some last-minute details for the Vogue photo shoot next week. Then I'm going out on a date."

"Date or hookup, Nessa? This is your mother. I know you better than anyone."

"Both... sort of. He was a hookup last week that invited me as a wingwoman to his first art show."

"And then?"

"Fine. You got me. Then we plan to hook up again. He is a very hot guy, educated and polite."

"I hope you are being safe, Nessa. So, how did you meet him anyhow?"

"Of course, Mom. We had the sex ed talk when I was 10, remember? I know I will never forget. I met him on Tinder."

Dark Arts

"Do you really think that is the best way to meet these men of yours?"

"How do you propose I do it, Mother dear?"

"There is the old-fashioned way. Go out to a bar or nightclub."

"How is that any safer, Mom? This way I can at least talk to them from the safety of my home. See if I pick up on the sleazy vibe without him following me out to my car."

"I suppose. You know me. I am not used to all this technology when it comes to dating and the end of in-person conversations."

"I know, Ma. I hate to do it, but I really have to get going. Call you tomorrow?"

"That's fine, sweetie. *Je t'aime! Au revoir, mon chéri.*"

"Bye, Mom. I love you, too."

Vanessa ran into the modeling agency and solidified plans for next Tuesday's Vogue photo shoot in New York's Central Park. She was happy to find out they'd booked her first class on United Airlines. The meeting finished just in time for her to run down and meet Anthony just as he pulled up in front of the building.

"Hey there, sexy! You look amazing. You must change immediately. You will take all the attention away from my art," Anthony teased.

"Babe, you invited the wrong girl then. How can you possibly compete with a daughter of Zeus descended from Mount Olympus?"

Anthony roared with laughter as he zoomed away from the curb. Their conversation continued easily until Anthony started driving into the mostly abandoned industrial area where his warehouse was located.

"Am I mistaken? I thought we were going to the opening of your first art show."

"Yes, that's right."

"But none of the city's art galleries are located out here."

"I never explained my art for you. It is a very gritty, dark subject. I think phantasmagoric was one of the words used to describe it. It is a true installation that one must literally experience, not just view. My agent and the gallery arranged to rent an old warehouse to house it in to add to the atmosphere of the exhibition."

"Strange. I've never heard of such a thing, but you have aroused my curiosity."

"Arousal is for later, hottie."

Vanessa laughed and slapped his arm as he made the turn into the parking lot in front of his warehouse. Her brow furrowed as she looked around. "There's no one here."

"The gallery people and my agent are parked in the back to save the parking for the guests that will be arriving in a little over an hour. Shall we go in?"

Vanessa nodded and turned to exit the car.

"One second," Anthony called out as he ran around to help her out of the car, pulling a rag out of a Ziploc bag stuffed in his pocket.

As he opened the car door and she turned to look up at him, she heard him say the most curious thing.

"Goodnight, Sleeping Beauty," Anthony murmured as he pressed the rag over her nose and mouth. Within seconds, she had slumped unconscious into the seat.

Sixteen

Scarlet Goddess

Friday, October 7, 2022

Stellan unlocked the warehouse door and pushed it open before leaning into the car to extract Vanessa, carrying her in and over to the chair. He placed her there and secured the leather restraint straps around her wrists and ankles and one across her chest. A short time later, as he was locking the door, she started to stir. Vanessa moaned, and her hands began flexing, as she tried in vain to free her arms.

"Hey there, sleepyhead! You rejoining the world?"

"Huh? Whaaat?" she mumbled.

Stellan snapped his fingers in front of her face. "Wake up, Vanessa! We have a lot to do tonight. We need to get started."

Vanessa's eyes fluttered open, and she struggled to focus on him. "Anthony?" She began to pull her arms toward herself, trying to slip her wrists through the restraints. She cried out as the leather straps bit into her flesh, creating deep red marks. As full awareness returned, she attempted to rise from the chair, but the chest strap barely let her wiggle. Vanessa tried to lift her pelvis up and push out with her legs to break the leg restraints loose, but to no avail. Grunting as she tried to slide down in her chair and slip free of the chest strap, she only managed to rub the skin around her ankles until it was raw and bleeding.

"I really need you to stop doing that. You are only hurting yourself and accomplishing nothing. I can't take a chance of you harming that stunning face of yours."

Vanesa's head was spinning, and she had a throbbing

headache. She was still confused and wondered if she was having a nightmare. *This can't be. It just can't be happening. Wake up, Nessa!* She imagined her mother's voice yelling at her to wake up as she used to do when trying to rouse her for school. But the burning pain in her limbs told her she was awake and her mind was screaming for help.

As Vanessa stewed in her feelings of helplessness and loss of control, she began to get angry. *People bow to my will, not the other way around. This is fucking ridiculous! It ends now.* She sat up straight in the chair, narrowed her eyes into slits, and furrowed her brow as she looked up at Anthony.

"What the fuck is your problem? You are going to remove these restraints now. I am not interested in this little game of yours. I want to leave NOW! Hurry up!"

Anthony's face twitched before he burst out in laughter. "Apologies, Your Highness! But you are confused. You think you are the one in control here, but you are wrong. I am!"

Vanessa was stunned. She had never been treated this way before. She was most scared by the fact that she could tell he meant it. The one thing she didn't know was the most important of all. *What is he planning to do to me?* She wracked her brain trying to determine the best way to handle the situation now. *Do I just play it by ear? Do I act subservient? Do I fight him when he removes the restraints? WILL he remove the restraints at some point?*

"I can see those gears grinding in your head, trying to figure out what to do next. Don't worry your pretty little head, Vanessa. You will find out soon enough. That I promise."

"Why are you doing this to me? I thought we were enjoying each other's company. Are you going to let me go at some point? Is this about money? I can pay you whatever you ask. My parents have even more money than I do."

"I wouldn't waste my last precious moments spewing all these questions. No question you ask—nothing you can offer me—will change the outcome."

"Last moments? Are you going to kill me?"

"Ding ding ding! Winner winner chicken dinner! My God, she finally figured it out."

Vanessa exhaled forcefully and sat there staring at him, stunned. She didn't realize she had forgotten to breathe again until her head began to spin faster, tiny pinpricks of light flashed before her eyes, and her chest ached with the desperate desire to breathe. She gasped for breath as tears flooded her eyes and began streaming down her cheeks.

"Now, now, now! Let's not do that. Your eyes will turn all red, which is not attractive on anyone. Does it make you feel better to know you will only experience pain for a brief moment?"

"No, you crazy asshole. I don't want to die! I don't want to experience any pain. Do you? What if the shoe were on the other foot? Fucking idiot!"

"You might want to shut that trap before you anger me. I can change everything. I can make you feel pain, the likes of which is unfathomable to you... make you beg for me to kill you and put you out of your misery. You don't understand who I am and what I can do to you."

"Who are you?"

"That doesn't really matter."

"Yes, it does!"

"Your worst fucking nightmare! That clear enough?"

Vanessa trembled as the truth of his words struck her. "Okay," she murmured.

"I need to prepare a few things before the show. I will be back."

"Show? I'm confused. I thought the show was all a ruse to get me here."

"That one was. I never lied about being an artist. My dear, you are going to be the star of a different, very special show called *Dark Arts*. They are going to love you. Aren't you excited?"

Vanessa just stared at him as he turned away. *This guy is a psychopath! What does he mean I will be the star? He said he was going to murder me. He wouldn't dare record that, would he? And who are 'they'?"*

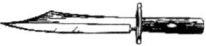

Stellan walked into the studio to post the 45-minute warning for the live show. He had a much more complicated set to prepare than usual. He was determined that this work of art for Halloween would be his greatest yet, the likes of which no one had ever seen. Next to the surgical table, he placed two large black plastic tubs. One was open and empty; the other was closed. Power cords snaked out of a small hole bored into the side of each container, and small holes had been poked into the lids.

Stellan dragged the instrument table over to the other side of the surgical table and laid out a variety of sharp surgical instruments, including a pair of bone-cutting forceps. Next to that, he placed a 3-inch push dagger with two wickedly sharp edges and a plastic grip that he could hold by placing it between two fingers and wrapping his fist around it.

Stellan reached into his pocket and pulled out a small box that he placed on the tray as well. A couple of large plastic buckets were placed next to the table, and he moved the wheelbarrow off to the side of the set, where he could conveniently dispose of the mess off-camera.

In the back of the set, sitting on the floor, he had a black metal base with a 3-foot pole attached—with several adjustable screw mounts on it. That wouldn't be needed until Sunday morning, so he left it out of the way for now. The rest of the supplies he needed for this one-of-a-kind piece would be delivered to his loft Saturday morning, and he would need to store them here in the industrial fridge along with one of the parts he planned to harvest.

He'd positioned the main camera in front of the surgical table and raised it to provide a view looking down on his work. That way, Vanessa's reactions would be on full display. He'd set up another small camera by the two plastic tubs. Now he brought a laptop over and set it up on a stainless-steel table in the back, so he could easily switch camera views when it was time.

Stellan returned to Vanessa's side. "Dear, you must stop your crying. It is making your cheeks all puffy. Besides, it's not going to make me change my mind. I want everyone to see how enchanting you are. We only have a few moments before the show begins. Let me grab you an ice pack to bring down the swelling."

Stellan walked into his private chambers and retrieved a small first aid ice pack. He took turns holding the pack to each side of her face. It brought even more color to her cheeks, and the swelling slowly receded. "There we go... much better. Nothing to say? You've gotten so quiet."

"I refuse to give you or whoever they are the satisfaction."

Stellan leaned down and looked her in the eyes. "You will. You won't be able to hold back for much longer."

"Go to hell, you sick bastard!" Vanessa spat in his face.

"That's more like it!" Stellan said between chuckles. "It is time we get you moved into place, but there is something I must do first. "You won't be needing these anymore." Stellan produced a pocket knife and began to cut off all her clothing. Then he removed the leather restraints from her wrists one at a time, so he could shackle her instead, and proceeded to do the same with her ankles.

Vanessa, usually so comfortable with her naked body, became self-conscious. She tried to pull into herself to hide her nakedness. She felt sick to her stomach, but she refused to vomit.

Once that was complete, he scooped her up from the chair and carried her over to the table, laying her prone on the surface. He secured a long nylon Velcro strap over her waist and another across the back of her neck to hold her face-down on the table. He spread her legs so he could secure them to the sides of the table with the leather restraints, and then he did the same to her wrists.

Unbidden, tears began to stream down Vanessa's face once more. Her mind was filled with dark thoughts of what was about to happen. She had seen the tools laid out on the table as he carried her over. She tried to rein in her emotions again as she heard him walk away.

Stellan walked over to the computer station to retrieve his mask and coveralls. It was time to get ready, only three minutes remained before the show would begin. He placed the camera remote in his pocket and walked back over to the head of the table. "Ready or not, it's SHOWTIME!" With that, he clicked the record button and started the show.

"Welcome once again, my faithful followers, to the fifth episode of *Dark Arts*, hosted by the one and only, *Le Créateur*. As always, thank you all so much for your continued patronage. I have something special planned tonight as a token of my gratitude. This will be a grand two-part episode that will conclude on Sunday at 10 a.m.

"I am going to keep the theme of this episode a mystery for now. I will tell you that the timeless beauty, as you will soon see, of this captivating creature is a key feature of this work of art. I will tell you that this piece is once again inspired by a famous work of art. If you can guess the piece, I will send a special reward to the first person to answer correctly. Post your answers on the chat board on the main Dark Arts site.

"This episode will feature something for everyone. As usual, I will cater to those who follow my own heart, my gore lovers and sadists. There will be blood, bodily fluids, and entrails aplenty. While physical pain will not be a main feature of this episode, our subject will experience enough *emotional* trauma that you won't even miss it.

"Our subject tonight will be unable to put up a fight and will be utterly at my mercy... not that any will be coming her way. Not only that, but our subject will once again be awake so you can experience her horror as we proceed. No need to trick-or-treat this year. This episode is all treat, as it is sure to satisfy your basest, most deviant needs with nail-biting entertainment.

"And the treats don't end there, I will also be offering 25 prints of the completed piece at a flat rate of $1,500—first come, first served—as well as the opportunity to download the video in 24 hours for the same price: a mere $1,500. Shall we begin?"

Le Créateur grabbed the push dagger off the tray and held it up for the audience to see. "My first step is to incapacitate my subject in preparation for what is to come. I don't want her to accidentally damage her flawless face by flailing about."

Vanessa's shrill scream filled the room as he slid the razor-sharp blade between her T6 and T7 vertebrae, severing her spinal cord. "That should do it," he said with a smile as he looked up.

Le Créateur leaned down and whispered into Vanessa's ear, "So much for holding back," as he began to remove all the restraints to turn her over. Once she was supine, he reattached the leather restraints at her wrists and one across her shoulders before elevating her head with a folded towel so she could see what he was about to do. "Front row seat, my dear." Then he turned to the camera "Behold, our goddess."

Vanessa was hyperventilating as she lay there unable to move from the waist down. She'd known that it was unlikely that she would be able to find a way out of this situation, but she'd still clung to hope. Now all seemed lost. Her pupils dilated as she watched him pick up a scalpel.

Le Créateur leaned over her so he could begin his incision on the far left side of her lower abdomen. A rivulet of blood bloomed as the blade entered her skin and began its trek up and across her abdomen and down the other side. Vanessa bit her lip deeply, drawing blood, as she tried not to scream again.

Spreading the skin of her abdomen apart, he plunged his hands in and laid hold of her bowels, pulling them to the surface.

Vanessa's hyperventilation worsened, her breaths becoming more rapid and shallow, depriving her of desperately needed oxygen. As *Le Créateur* pulled the bowel loops out further and draped them over the side of the table to fall into the waiting bucket, Vanessa grew pale and passed out. Her panicked breathing evened out once she lost consciousness.

Bright red blood oozed from the incision, squirting out in places where bleeders had been severed. As her pulse raced, blood began pouring from her disemboweled abdomen as *Le Créateur* began to sever her entrails. Her intestines and other organs landed in the bucket with a sickening slop, splashing blood and excrement onto the floor and his coveralls. *Le Créateur* scowled as the sickening odor of feces filled the room.

With a few last desperate pumps, her heart slowed and stopped. She took a few irregular, gasping agonal breaths as the last electrical activity coursed through her body and then stopped. *Le Créateur* removed the restraints, so he could adjust her body as he needed. He reached deep into the cavity to finish severing the last of her entrails, before flipping her over to continue the incision around her back until he met the starting point.

He pushed the fleshy flaps out of his way so he could use the large bone-cutting forceps to cut her vertebrae in the lumbar area between L4 and L5. Once he had finished cleaving her body into two parts, he brought the wheelbarrow over and pushed the lower half into it. Then he began the slow, tedious process of amputating her arms at the shoulder. He roughly hacked into the skin to get down to the muscles, ligaments and tendons to excise them. He threw both arms into the wheelbarrow as well.

Le Créateur then began a slow, precise incision across her throat just above where it connected to her torso, continuing all the way around. He folded back the flap of neck tissue so he could begin to cut out the carotid arteries, jugular veins and esophagus, which were thrown down into the buckets. Once the spine was exposed, he used the forceps to cut the cervical vertebrae between C5 and C6.

Now that the torso was free, he carried it over and set it inside the empty black plastic tub. He returned to the decapitated head and cleaned any blood off of it before grabbing a packet of suture off the tray and sewing the flaps of neck tissue tightly closed at the base of her chin. He left the cervical vertebrae protruding like a popsicle stick. From the small box on the tray, he removed a pair of blood-red contact lenses that made her entire eye, including the sclera, appear full of blood. He then picked up the head and carefully placed it in on a plastic tray on a table at the back of the set.

Le Créateur walked over to the laptop in the back and activated the smaller camera and switched to the split-screen mode. "Now for our final step of the night: I need the flesh removed from her torso, so we will be using these little guys here." *Le Créateur* removed the lid of the other plastic tub with a flourish. "Our friend, the dermestid beetle." He tilted the camera down so the audience could see inside the tubs.

Vanessa's torso was lying on a reptile heating pad with a layer of cotton batting on top. The other container had the same setup, but it was divided into two sections. One contained large chunks of Styrofoam with hundreds of tiny holes bored into it, and there were many maggot-like young larval specimens wriggling across the cotton. On the other side, crawling over every surface, were thousands of small beetles.

"This is my little dermestid colony, consisting of roughly 5,000 adult specimens, plus hundreds of larvae. The older larvae burrow into the Styrofoam while they pupate. Unless you feed them well, as we are about to do, the adult beetles must be kept away from the larvae to prevent cannibalism." At that, he set the pupating larvae colony aside on the lid while he poured the adult beetles and larvae over Vanessa's torso. "Her bones should be picked clean within a day and a half." He returned the Styrofoam to the empty container and placed the lids on both containers, after one parting shot of the beetles swarming over her body.

Dark Arts

"These creatures prefer darkness. So, after the episode ends tonight, I will be setting up a night vision camera inside the container. I will leave the live feed running, so you all can enjoy the feasting process.

"Well, that's it for tonight, my gory horde. I hope you are excited as I am to see how this work progresses. I am sure you are dying to know the theme of this project, but you will have to wait until 10 a.m. Sunday, when the show resumes for Part 2. Remember to post your guesses about tonight's theme for a chance to win a prize. I hope you relished every blood-soaked moment of tonight's presentation. Goodnight and sweet screams to you all!"

Stellan pressed the button to stop the recording. First step, he needed to get Vanessa's head into the refrigerator to arrest decomposition. After that was complete, he placed the night vision camera and restarted the broadcast with a countdown timer prominently displayed at the top of the screen. He set the containers aside while he began the deep-cleaning process, after taking the buckets and the wheelbarrow to the kiln for disposal of the remains.

After several hours, the set had been cleaned and set up for Sunday morning's show. The surgical table was lowered, and the mount placed on top. The two tubs were moved back into place. New tools were placed on the instrument tray, including a drill, a spool of 14-gauge galvanized steel wire, heavy pliers, a screwdriver, green floral wire, a 2-inch-wide soft paintbrush, and a small pair of pruning shears. Once he was finished, he changed out of his blood-soaked coveralls and closed up the warehouse for the night.

Stellan arrived at his flat and fell into bed, exhausted. He still couldn't believe how well it had gone. *That controlling bitch thought she was so tough, but she cried like a baby. She thought she was in control and could change the outcome all the way up until I severed her weak little spine. She thought she had me wrapped around her little finger because we slept together. Every man has needs that must be met every now and then. Her fate was sealed the day we met online. My only concern... that complicated dissection, but it really couldn't have gone any better.* He fell asleep, a smile on his face as he dreamed of the completed work.

The alarm went off at 9 a.m. so he could get ready before the flower delivery from My Secret Garden at 10. Stellan's friend Mary, the owner, was delivering two dozen large-bloom Kashmir red roses along with vines from a wild rose bush. He had looked long and hard through her floristry books to find the exact shade of scarlet red he desired. He packed the boxes into his Jag and drove over to the warehouse to place them in the industrial fridge along with Vanessa's pretty head. He had checked the video feed earlier and had seen that the de-fleshing process was proceeding nicely.

Stellan took the rest of the day off to relax and enjoy dinner at El Torito and then a late showing at the theater. He had been so busy lately creating art for one collection or the other that he hadn't let himself experience everyday recreational activities. He returned home and turned in early for the night in preparation for the next day's festivities.

Before heading over to the warehouse, Stellan checked the chat feed and found DarkBoy32 had correctly guessed the theme. When he arrived at the warehouse, he brought out the head and the boxes of roses from the fridge and set them on the surgical table, before starting the recording with a split-screen view of both cameras.

"Welcome, my adoring apostles, to Part 2 of the fifth episode of *Dark Arts*, hosted by the one and only, *Le Créateur*. I appreciate each and every one of you. Now to address this episode's special theme. I have always been fascinated by the intriguing mythology of the ancient Greeks and Romans. And to be honest, who wouldn't be drawn to the descriptions of the beauty of Aphrodite or, as she is known in Rome, Venus?

"This morning, I will be creating my interpretation of Alexandros of Antioch's pivotal work, the *Venus de Milo*. I hope you will come to adore her as much as I do. I am excited to announce that we did have a winner who correctly guessed the theme. Congratulations, DarkBoy32! I will be in contact with you to arrange delivery of your prize. Once I have finished photographing her, I will be sending you a piece of memorabilia: the actual contact lenses used. Plus you will receive a copy of the print."

Le Créateur grabbed the paintbrush off the tray before walking over to the tub and pulling off the lid, revealing the nearly spotless skeletonized torso of Vanessa. He used the brush to flick off any remaining larvae and beetles and then placed the torso on the table. The drill was used to make several small holes in the C6 vertebra on the torso and the C5 vertebra on the skull. Then, he used the galvanized wire to reattach the head to the torso.

He placed a towel on the table before rolling the body over so he could drill two holes an inch and a half apart in the back of the skull, repeating the process on the T4 vertebra and the L3 vertebra. *Le Créateur* carefully balanced the body up against the mount, using his body to hold it in place as he screwed the first adjustable screw mount into the skull. He then adjusted the height of the next screw mount so it matched the holes on the L3 vertebra and then screwed it in place. After he finished attaching the last screw mount, he stood back to let the audience see his work.

"Aphrodite had various symbols linked to her that each had a special meaning: roses, doves, apples, a mirror, seashells and various other objects. The rose symbolized love, passion, and beauty—or, more specifically red roses, which further represented the intense emotions associated with love and lust. One last step is required to finish this work of art."

Le Créateur opened the boxes containing the roses and the vines. He began to use the floral scissors to trim the stems of the roses so that he could weave the 12 most beautiful blooms through her hair, creating a crowning bouquet of roses atop her head. Then, he extracted the wild rose vines with leaves and began to weave them through her torso, creating a delicate cage over the ribs and spreading out from her sides with loops in the area where her arms had been attached. Some branches were tucked into the clefts between the clavicle, shoulder blades and collar bone, wending their way up to the rose crown on her head. Finally, one short vine filled with large leaves was tucked up in her hair amongst the roses over her right temple and draped down, mostly covering her right eye.

"Well, my twisted troop, I present to you *Venus in Bloom*. Isn't she majestic? The 25 prints will be available for purchase starting at 12 p.m. Monday at the main Dark Arts site on the dark web. Remember that it will be first come, first served, so don't be late if you want to have the chance to own a copy of this beautiful work of art. As usual, only cryptocurrency will be accepted, and secure, anonymous delivery will be arranged. This two-part video will be up for streaming on the Dark Arts gallery for the next 24 hours. After that, a heavily encrypted digital download can be purchased for $1,500 USD. I hope you reveled in every moment of today's presentation worshipping the scarlet goddess Aphrodite. I know I did. Good day and sweet screams to you all!"

Stellan spent the next couple of hours photographing *Venus*, uploading the files, cleaning the set and then disposing of the body. He prepared the package with the contacts and the picture and scheduled the delivery after he heard back from the winner.

He couldn't have been more pleased with how she had turned out. *She is utterly magnificent... everything I imagined and more. Now to get back to my work for my show in New York in just over a month.*

Seventeen

Clusterfuck

Halloween 2022

*A*ccording to Merriam-Webster, a clusterfuck is a complex and utterly disordered and mismanaged situation. That is the definition of how the start of the Le Créateur case was handled. I am the rookie on the homicide squad. Who is going to listen to me? How do we make up for all the lost time and forgotten or misremembered details that are common when dealing with witnesses long after an event occurred?

Mendy had been so excited the day the courier walked in with that package at the end of August. Finally, they had a witness they could question. Surely it would give them a lead to help them find The Creator. Little did she know how wrong she was and what awaited them over the next two months.

Mendy ran down to the desk, slipping on gloves as she ran, and grabbed the package from the desk sergeant on duty. It was the same handwriting: No doubt it was from him. She carried it back to the Homicide Unit office to wait for Mills, fighting the urge to rip into it. Two minutes later, he skidded around the corner into the office.

"What is it?"

"I don't know. You told me to wait for you."

Mills chuckled. "You have more patience than I do."

Mendy used a letter opener to open the package carefully. She slid out the photo and then looked into the envelope, expecting to find a letter, but it was empty. Mendy gagged as she looked down at the image.

"My God! What the fuck did he do to her? And who is she? Why no note this time?"

"I don't know. It makes no sense. He has always wanted to brag before. Unless... there's a reason he's hiding her identity from us. If we could just figure out who she is, maybe we could find him."

"How will we ever figure that out without more to go on? Sixty-five thousand women over 21 go missing every year in this country, and those are only the ones *reported* missing. We know he has a type: blond hair and green eyes. But that actually makes our job even more difficult. Do you know how rare that combination is? I looked it up. Globally, only 2 percent of the population, at best, has that combination... naturally. That's what makes it so hard. Everybody dyes their hair nowadays, and then with the advent of colored contact lenses, who knows how many women visually meet his criteria, even if it is only artificially? We could scan all the missing persons' files in the L.A. metro area and go right past a potential victim because we don't know she's changing her appearance."

Mendy studied the image, looking for any tiny detail they might be missing that could help them make some sense of it. Overcome, she spun in her chair, grabbing the wastebasket and vomiting up the Fritos she'd eaten an hour earlier. She flipped the photo over to hide the atrocity while she fought to regain control of her stomach. They both noticed that he had scrawled *Tempest* on the back.

"Egotistical bastard! Still had to give us the name of his masterpiece, even though he is afraid of us knowing anymore details," Mills growled, as he slammed his fist of the desk. "I'm going to take this all down to forensics real quick to see if they can lift any prints. I know... I know... it's useless, but we have to try something. Meet you in the interview room in a minute?"

Mendy nodded as she tied up the garbage bag to dispose of in the restroom. "I just need one moment." She went to the restroom and leaned under the faucet to gargle a bit, then splashed some water on her face. She popped a mint in her mouth and headed down to the interview room.

Mills had just opened the door himself and waited for her to enter first before following her in. "I am Detective Mills, and this is Detective Hoffman. Hello, Mister..." He paused as he looked down at the file.

"Phillips. But just call me Rod."

"Okay, Rod. Thanks for talking with us today. We need to talk to you about the package you delivered here 20 minutes ago. Who hired you?"

"I don't know."

"How can that be? How did you come to be in possession of the package?"

"I have an ad in Craigslist offering my bike courier services. A man, who never identified himself, asked me to pick up the package and deliver it to your office."

"Where did you pick it up?"

"He told me that I would find it taped to the underside of the slide in Griffith Park."

Mendy held up her hand to interrupt. "Didn't you find it odd that a man who wouldn't identify himself asked you to pick up a hidden package like that, and then deliver it to a police precinct?"

"Of course I did. But who am I to question it? I need the money to pay my child support. I'm not breaking any laws by delivering packages."

Mills broke in again with his calming demeanor. "You are absolutely correct, Mr. Phillips... Rod. How is he paying you?"

"He sent money to me through CashApp."

Both detectives jumped to attention and sat bolt upright in their chairs. "We need to know the name of the account that sent you the money!" Mendy demanded.

"Of course. It was Creator818."

"Did he say anything else to you?" Mills asked.

"No. It was a short conversation."

"'Conversation,' you said... so you spoke to him on the phone?"

"Yes."

"We need to pull your phone records to track that call. Do we have your permission? We will get a warrant if we have to," Mendy warned.

"No, that's fine. I have nothing to hide."

"Thank you, Rod. We may be in contact with you again."

It was just past midnight when Mendy and Mills returned to their office and called in the rest of the team to help them track the leads. Mendy called Verizon to obtain the cell records and kept refreshing her email, anxiously waiting for them to arrive. Mills followed up the on the CashApp profile. The rest of the team started working with Missing Persons to explore any recent reports to see if they could identify the victim. The Forensics Unit was sent out to the park to dust for prints or any other trace evidence that might have been left behind. Uniformed officers were sent to the area to see if any surveillance footage could be obtained that might show their perpetrator.

Sixteen hours later, Mendy yelped when she kicked her desk. "How the fuck can that be? Nothing. Nothing at all! He really is a fucking ghost." She had just gotten off the phone and found out that the call Rod had received couldn't be tracked. It had been received from a VoIP, Voice over Internet Provider. It bounced through 13 countries from one proxy server to another and then disappeared... completely untraceable.

Mills had the same luck earlier in the afternoon when dealing with CashApp. They could see the transfer of money, but it had appeared out of thin air. It was a legitimate transfer: They had received money that they then transferred into Rod's account. But there was no trace of its origin. They couldn't explain it.

Forensics had returned their findings by lunch: They'd found no fingerprint or trace evidence on the envelope, photo or in the park. Meanwhile, the uniformed officers reported that, in the five square miles surrounding the park, there were either no private security cameras or they had malfunctioned. Once again, the city's traffic cameras had also been down that day, mysteriously returning to normal once the package was delivered to the precinct.

The debacle with the way the investigation was being handled only worsened one day in early October. The whole office had been extremely tense ever since that call came into the captain's office shortly after 6 p.m. that day. His door had crashed into the wall when he came storming out.

"Mills! Hoffman! I need you in here now."

The entire office could hear him yelling, but they couldn't hear what he said. They soon found out the media had been busy in the six weeks since the story broke about a serial killer stalking the area.

At the 5 p.m. broadcast, KTLA had announced that the killer might be stalking his victims through the Tinder app according to the families of the victims. Belinda had told them that Annalise's killer had been her date from Tinder. Millie's family reported that she had been going to meet a boyfriend she'd reportedly met on Tinder when she disappeared. Supposedly, they even had a source reporting that Arizona might have been dating someone from Tinder as well.

The shit had hit the fan after the news report. The phones began ringing off the hook from callers questioning why the police hadn't warned the public to avoid the Tinder app. The mayor's office and the police commissioner had both called, criticizing the captain for the team's handling of the investigation. The captain was concerned that he was going to be forced into retirement.

The whole team had continued to pore through missing persons' reports, but no one stood out. Most didn't meet the physical profile of his preferred victim. Of those that did, there was no known connection to Tinder or any other dating app... or even a new boyfriend at all. They had all but given up hope of ever identifying her until they caught him and he confessed, or they found the murder site and could collect DNA evidence. Everywhere they turned, they seemed to run into a brick wall.

The situation had only worsened in the past two weeks. Late in the afternoon on the 10th of October, the DuPre family had walked into the precinct asking to speak to the police commissioner. The desk sergeant had explained that he was unavailable without an appointment, and then they had created a spectacle.

The family had just returned to the United States from France, and they were there to report their daughter, Vanessa DuPre, missing. They had been horrified when they saw the noon news and realized there was a serial killer in Los Angeles choosing victims via Tinder, information that had only come to light recently, thanks to the media. Vanessa's last known communication with anyone had been on the 7th when she spoke to her mother on the phone on the way to a date with a man she had met on Tinder.

The family was outraged that the police had not released the information about Tinder sooner. They questioned whether the last victim could have been saved. Then maybe their daughter wouldn't be missing now, if only she had known. Mills tried to explain that spreading potential misinformation could be dangerous as well, so they had been trying to investigate all leads before disclosing anything.

Jacques DuPre, Vanessa's father, was an ex-French ambassador to the United States. In recent years, since his retirement, he had obtained dual citizenship and spent his time going back and forth between the two countries. He threatened to sue the department and get the French government involved—pointing out that his daughter also had dual citizenship. He told them his next stop was the mayor's and governor's offices to insist that the entire power and financial backing of the city and state be put behind the investigation to find his daughter before she became the next victim.

If she wasn't already.

The entire Missing Persons Unit had been assigned Vanessa's case, but there had been no leads. Nor were there any new leads on The Creator case.

Now, here they were on Halloween, two months since the package with the unknown victim's picture was delivered, and no closer to solving the case. Mills had come to the office early so he could leave early to take his daughter trick-or-treating for the first time. Mendy had just entered the precinct at 8 a.m. after leaving late the previous night, when the desk sergeant called out to her.

She looked up to see the sheepish bike courier, Rod, standing there at the desk next to the sergeant with a package in hand.

"Please tell me you are not here with another package from him," she yelled across the lobby.

Rod looked down at his feet and couldn't meet her eyes.

Mendy pulled out her phone and texted Mills. "I hope you don't have plans. It is going to be a long night."

Eighteen

Only the Lonely

Halloween 2022

"Oh God! What now? I was going to take my daughter out trick-or-treating for the first time," Mills texted back.

"Meet me in interview Room 2. We have a visitor... again."

Mills sprinted out of the Homicide Unit and met Mendy, with Rod in tow, just as they were about to enter the room.

"Fuck! I was afraid that was who you meant."

"Rod, go ahead and sit down. We will be there in a few minutes. I need to speak to Detective Mills. Coffee?"

Rod nodded. Mendy asked a uniformed officer to take Rod some coffee before heading down the hall to Homicide with Mills. She held up the small box for him to see.

"That better not be what we think it is. Holy hell is going to rain down on all of us if that is Vanessa."

"I know," she replied as she carefully slit open the tape and lifted the flaps. A layer of dried rose petals covered what appeared to be a photograph at the bottom of the box. Mills held open a plastic evidence bag as she brushed the petals into it, revealing the horrifying image below. The stunning beauty of Vanessa had been transformed into some twisted, distorted combination of a bust and still-life art.

"We need to call the family immediately. There are too many prying eyes watching, waiting for us to screw up. And I hate to say it, but I am sure there are some loose lips around here. The press pays too much for a scoop like this for some of the uniforms with families to turn down. Then I need to hold a press conference. We have to confirm the Tinder connection. There is no longer any doubt... even if we can't prove it."

Mendy nodded and brought up Vanessa's case file on the computer to find her family's contact information. "I'll notify Missing Persons, too. And then I'll take all this down to Forensics, whatever good that will do," she said with a sigh. "I think I need to make this notification in person. I will be back as soon as I can." On her way out of the office, she gave Missing Persons a heads-up and told them to keep a lid on the news until after the press conference. Then she dropped off the evidence in Forensics along with the same admonition.

She made the relatively short drive into Westwood to the DuPre home. When she knocked, the housekeeper answered the door. She introduced herself and told her she needed to speak privately to the couple. The housekeeper led her to a wingback chair in the drawing room and turned to summon the DuPres.

Mr. DuPre hurried into the room, followed by his distraught wife. "Tell me you have some news about our daughter. Have you found her? Is she OK?" he spit at her rapid-fire.

"Yes, I do have news. I'm very sorry, but..."

Mendy was cut off by Mrs. DuPre's wail. "NOOOOOOO!"

Mr. DuPre looked over at his wife in shock, then turned to Mendy, disbelief on his face. "You're not saying?"

"I'm afraid I am, sir. I came here to notify you that we received evidence today that your daughter has been murdered."

"Have you found her body? Please tell me we can have a proper burial and lay her to rest."

Mrs. DuPre was so lost in her grief that she was no longer listening to the conversation. The housekeeper rushed in and led her away to her room.

"No, sir. We haven't found her yet... and, to be honest, I can't say if we ever will. We haven't located any of the others yet either."

"Others? So you are saying that she *was* a victim of that animal? The one the incompetent LAPD has been unable to find... hasn't even bothered to warn the public about?"

Mendy looked down and took a small breath, before raising her head again and responding, "Yes, sir. My partner is about to hold..."

"Get out! Leave my house now. I have nothing more to say to you. Your department will be hearing from my attorney."

"Yes, Mr. DuPre," Mendy mumbled as she turned to leave. The housekeeper had returned in time to lead her out of the house. Mendy climbed into her car and beat the steering wheel with her fists. She could understand their grief and anger. She had felt the same way when she'd found out that Annalise had been killed... and the police had been receiving photos from The Creator for the previous eight months.

How do we catch this sick fucker? He is always two steps ahead of us. Maybe we ARE incompetent. Fuuuuuuckkkk!

By the time she had returned to Homicide to check in with Mills—after stopping off to check on any progress at Forensics—the story had already blown up.

Thanks to the DuPre family.

He must have the press, the mayor and the governor all on speed dial.

The governor's office had called to say he would be arriving to speak to the police commissioner. He was flying down from Sacramento in the next couple of hours to address the situation personally. The mayor's office was trying to push the captain of the Homicide Unit into retirement and wanted everyone in the unit investigated.

The press had sunk their teeth into the story. Just as Mills had arranged a press conference, KTLA was already on the air, proclaiming "LAPD's incompetence responsible for murder of supermodel Vanessa DuPre!" The press room was standing room only, filled with reporters pushing and clamoring for a sound bite.

Mills called for quiet before he began to speak.

"We have an update on The Creator case," he began. "Unfortunately, we have to report that Vanessa DuPre has been identified as a victim of this perpetrator. Her family has been notified. We also need to urgently warn all the female citizens of the Los Angeles area to refrain from using the Tinder dating app. We have cause to believe that this is how the perp is meeting his victims.

"There is nothing more we can report at this time. If the public has any information that they think may be related to this case, please call us immediately on the tipline. A reward is being offered for any tips that lead to the identification and arrest of this suspect. Miss DuPre went out on a date with him approximately one week before her disappearance, so if anybody saw her out with somebody, please call us."

Mills turned to leave, but his path was blocked by the swarming reporters yelling out questions.

"Wasn't the Tinder connection first brought up with the second victim and then again with the third? Why didn't you warn people then?"

"Have you found her body?"

"Are you any closer to identifying the suspect?"

"Will Captain Armstrong be retiring after this because of his poor handling of this case?"

"What about Detective Mendy Hoffman? Should a rookie on the Homicide Unit be assigned to such a high-profile case? Has she had a role in mishandling this case?"

Mills returned to the lectern to address some of the issues. "First of all, Detective Hoffman is an extremely competent, well-respected member of the LAPD. She cannot be blamed for how the case has proceeded. She only recently joined the team, so she had nothing to do with what information was released initially. Secondly, Captain Armstrong has been a member of the LAPD for 30 years, serving the last 10 years as the captain of the Homicide Unit. He has handled many high-profile cases over the years.

"I cannot get into the details of an ongoing investigation, but I can confirm this case is much more difficult than the public is aware of. We have to consider what we release to make sure we don't spread potential misinformation. Many aspects of this case are very troublesome and can't be confirmed yet. We are handling the situation the best we can. Our first priority is always the safety and welfare of the citizens of Los Angeles. That is all for now."

Mendy slipped out of the back of the conference room before the press could notice her and met up with Mills in the hall. "Thanks for defending me."

"All I did was tell the truth. You are not to blame for any of this. You are an extremely capable detective and a valued member of the team."

The two detectives returned to Homicide to find a whole different hornet's nest. The governor, mayor and police commissioner were all in the captain's office, engrossed in a serious conversation. The captain gave them a subtle nod that they took to mean "scram," so they took advantage of the opportunity. They went back down to Forensics to check on the status of the evidence, and to their dismay found that nothing had been found once again... not a single fingerprint, fiber or hair.

As they headed back to the office, they ran into Mendy's old partner, Detective Stevens, in the hallway, who flagged them down.

"The shit storm around here is crazy. I can't believe they did that."

"Who? Did what?" Mendy asked.

"You guys didn't hear? The DuPres' lawyer filed a lawsuit against the LAPD. They raised a huge stink with the governor. Apparently, he even received a call from a senior staff member of the French president, demanding to know the status of our investigation into the murder of a French citizen. The governor talked to the upper brass, and they are 'asking' for your captain's immediate retirement. The police commissioner came down and talked to Captain Peters about you, and he personally vouched for you, as did your current captain. I think everything is OK for you. God knows what is coming next. Just keep your head down, Mendy."

"Thanks, Robert. We appreciate the heads up. I guess we should get back to Homicide and face the heat."

Mendy and Mills returned to the office to find the captain alone in his office, filling a box. "Hey Cap, what are you doing?" Mills asked.

"Take a seat, you two. We need to talk. I am being retired effective today. If I leave and keep my mouth shut, I get to keep my full benefits."

"That's not right, Captain. We should fight this. None of this is your fault. It is none of ours. We weren't the ones in charge for the first eight months of this investigation."

"No, it's OK, really. I have been talking about spending more time with my grandkids, so no time like the present. Besides, it is my fault. I am your captain, so everything any of you do... or don't do... is ultimately my responsibility. I trusted Detective Anderson, but obviously I should have been overseeing him more closely. You know that we all questioned his handling of it, but it was my job to intercede. And I didn't. Fuck! Why didn't I?"

"You can't blame yourself, Captain. Besides, even if it was handled better, I don't know it would have made a difference. We have all been investigating every possible angle, but this guy is too good. We hit one roadblock after another. He has to fuck up eventually, and then we will nail his ass to the wall."

"I know you will. That is why you are now in charge of the Homicide Unit. Your promotion has been accepted, and you are assigned here, effective... well, now."

"Are you serious?"

"Serious as a heart attack. Just don't give yourself one hunting down this bastard. You are the right man for the job, and you will finish this. I have no doubt. Congratulations, Mills."

"Congratulations, Mills," Mendy said as she slapped him on the back.

"Now for you, Detective Hoffman. The press and the DuPre family are trying to push some of the blame on you for being new to the unit. Your previous captain and I both gave our highest recommendation to continue on the team. You are not new to being a detective, and you haven't even been here for the majority of the investigation. They've agreed to let you stay on, but for optics they are requiring that Captain Mills oversee all of your work directly. Between you and me, that means continue as you have."

"Thank you so much, Captain. I don't know what to say."

"You said it all right there. Now get to work. Mills, I will be out of here in the next hour or so, and then you can move in. I know you were intending to leave early tonight for your daughter..."

Sadness flashed in Mills' eyes as he cleared his throat. "Yes, Captain. I already called my mother, and she will take her out trick-or-treating. She promised to take lots of pictures. She just turned a year old, so it's not like she is going to remember this anyhow."

"You're a good man... and father, Mills."

"Thanks, sir. Now we are off to see what is coming in on the tipline."

Mendy, Mills and the rest of the Homicide Unit worked until after 10 p.m., following up on any tip that seemed even remotely viable. Not even one of those tips panned out, and that—combined with a complete lack of physical evidence—finally became too much. Mills slammed his fist on the desk.

"Damn it! OK team, we are going to call it quits for the night. We won't accomplish anything if we're too exhausted to think. I want everyone here again bright and early at 7 a.m. Then we'll brainstorm any avenues we haven't explored. Goodnight."

The rest of the team gathered their belongings and filed out, bound for home. But Mills found Mendy still sitting at her desk when he came out of his new office. "Hey Detective Hoffman, let's go. Everyone out."

"Fuck it! I'm not leaving. This fucking mongrel killed my best friend in the world and all these other women. Now to top it off, my career in Homicide is at risk because of him. It's not fair what happened to Captain Armstrong. I can't let this asshole win. He can't be invincible. He has a weakness... somewhere... somehow, and I need to find it. Fuck him!" Mendy kicked her desk and yelped in pain, grabbing her toes and massaging them through her dress shoes.

"OK. I can see you need to decompress as bad as I do. Let's go to the bar for a drink. We can talk, not about the case, but you know, like real humans do. Deal? I get very little social adult time other than here at work, which just isn't the same. I love my daughter with all my heart, but I am tired of Peppa Pig. I'm about ready to turn her into peppered bacon."

Mendy broke out into uproarious laughter, punctuated by a snort. "I get it... I get it. I will take you out of here at least before I have to book you for hogicide."

"Ha ha... very funny! I don't know that I actually want a drink, but that bacon I mentioned does sound delicious. How about we go to Peggy's for a little late-night breakfast and some coffee? Let's face it... neither one of us is bound for much sleep tonight anyway. Am I right?"

"Well coffee, or caffeine in general, has never kept me from sleeping. But you're right, I doubt I'll sleep much tonight regardless. Most importantly, you had me at bacon."

The two detectives walked down the block to the old corner diner that had been around since the fifties and took a booth in the back.

"So, Mills..."

"Call me Brad. I don't think I ever introduced myself to you properly because everybody always just calls me Mills."

"Well, I saw your name on your plaque on the desk, but still, it's nice to meet you, Brad."

"I should've done it long ago. I've seen you struggle. You could've used a friend, and I should've reached out sooner. Your partner told me you lost the last of your family about five years ago, and I know how close you were with Annalise."

"I was never very close to my family anyhow, but it somehow

eats at you when you realize you suddenly have no one. No one to notice if you go missing. No one who cares if you eat at night. No one to talk to about your successes, like my promotion, or your fears, like losing said position in Homicide."

Mills reached forward and grabbed her small hand, enfolding them in his big bearlike-hands. "That's where you are wrong. All of us care about you. I... care about you. I would miss you if you didn't show up one day. I care if you eat. That's why we are here now. You haven't eaten anything since breakfast, that's if you even ate that. I know... I saw you work all day without a break. You pretended to eat some of the Chinese the team ordered in for dinner, but I saw you close it back up later, still full. As for your fears, you are going nowhere if I have anything to say about it, and guess what? I do."

Mendy's face grew red as she felt tears sliding down her cheeks. She turned away and brushed them off. The waitress approached, and they placed their orders for the Midnight Madness Breakfast, complete with two eggs any style, four slices of bacon, home fries, a fruit cup, and an English muffin.

"So Brad, tell me about your daughter. All I know is she just turned one and had croup a few months back."

Brad's face brightened into a huge smile. "She's the light of my life. My whole world to be honest. She, by the way, is Pandora. I got ahead of myself there. She is so intelligent. She was sitting, took her first step, and interacted with people weeks ahead of schedule. She's a happy baby who sleeps through the night most of the time... Listen to me going on and on with all this boring parent stuff."

"It's not boring. She means a lot to you, as she should. I do want to have kids myself one day. It's so stupid, but I would never admit to Annalise that I did want to get married and be a mother someday. I was much too absorbed and concerned about my 'tough girl' image to let her know it bothered me that I hadn't found someone yet. I think that's why I spent so much time trying to convince *her* to find someone, before it was too late. And look what I did, I sent her into the arms of a murderer. Talk about too late!" Mendy broke down in tears and hid her face behind her hands.

Mills leaned forward and wrapped his arms around her, pulling her into his chest. "You've needed to do this for months. That means letting go of that guilt. You know that none of this is your fault. I promise you that we will catch him, and he will get what he deserves."

"Yes, we will. He will pay dearly for what he has done, if it is the last thing I do." As Brad stared into her eyes, Mendy couldn't disguise the dark, seething anger just below the surface. She saw the apprehensive look on his face and fought to suppress the surge of adrenaline running through her body.

"I apologize for my outburst. She sounds absolutely delightful. May I ask what happened to her mother... your wife, I am assuming?"

Mills sighed as a pained expression crossed his face.

"Never mind," Mendy said. "Just ignore me. Tell me, 'Mendy, you are being a busybody.'"

"No, it's OK. We were two different people, to be honest. We loved each other deeply, but sometimes love isn't enough. She came from a wealthy family where her every need had been met, no questions asked. Cassiopeia was a world traveler—a born explorer—the kind that was never meant to settle in one place for too long. Or with one person for too long either.

"I met her on a sojourn here in Los Angeles, and we fell in love, almost overnight. We tried the long-distance thing, but that never works. I had too much pride to live off her trust fund and travel the world with her. Besides, I was meant to settle down. I was born to be a cop. I told her I could never live her jet-setting lifestyle. And she admitted that she couldn't settle down behind a white picket fence and spend her time raising 2.5 children with a dog in the backyard."

"That's hard. So, what happened?"

"We split up and tried to live without each other. Four months later, she showed up on my doorstep, pregnant and crying, and threw herself into my arms. She said she couldn't live without me... and neither could our child. She seemed happy enough throughout the pregnancy. We traveled on the weekends. She visited friends out-of-state until she was no longer allowed to fly. Then one blessed day, she went into labor and dear Pandora was born. Cassiopeia chose the name, in case that wasn't obvious to you."

Mendy giggled. "I did wonder about the name. You don't seem the Pandora type."

"She tried hard to be happy and dote on our beautiful daughter, but it wasn't meant to be. Cassiopeia withdrew into herself and sank into depression. One day, when Pandora was about three months old, I came home to find Cassiopeia and all her belongings gone. She left me a note explaining that being a stay-at-home mother was killing her. She'd left an enormous amount of money in our joint account for the care of our daughter and a signed document turning over sole custody to me. She only asked that when Pandora was old enough, I explain to her that her mother did love her with all her heart."

"I'm so sorry. I shouldn't have asked."

"It's fine. It helps to talk about it. To be honest, I've accepted it. I loved her so much that I wanted the best for her, even if that meant leaving Pandora and me. I have moved on, and I hope to find someone again one day. It didn't sour me on love." Mills looked away briefly to blink back the tears that threatened to come.

Mendy leaned in again to return the supportive hug he had given her, just as he turned back to face her. Their lips met, and Mendy started to pull back before leaning in to return the kiss his lips had sought when they felt hers. His massive hand cupped her face, drawing her in deeper. Mendy closed her eyes, and her mind drifted to all the times she had imagined just this moment.

The two of them jumped when the waitress set down their plates of food. "Sorry to disturb you, folks. Anything I can get you... a refill, ketchup, hot sauce?"

"No... uh no... we are fine. Thanks," Mendy stammered with a hot face that matched the red of the waitress' uniform.

Mills grabbed his fork and dug into his food, his eyes cast down on the plate. Mendy buttered her English muffin as she contemplated what to say. "Excuse me, Brad... uh I mean Mills. I don't know what came over me. Exhaustion probably. Maybe I should just go." She set down her knife and scooted around the curved booth to exit out the far side.

His hand darted out and grabbed hers gingerly. "No, don't. Everything is fine. Please eat. I will worry if you don't."

Mendy grabbed a slice of bacon and devoured it, followed by another and then another, until they were all gone.

"Now that's more like it." She looked up at the sound of his voice, and he met her gaze with a smile. The two of them sat in silence and made short work of their breakfasts. When the bill came, he reached over and grabbed it. "My treat."

"Thank you, Mills. I admit I feel much better now with some food in my stomach."

"Everything is better with bacon."

Mendy couldn't hold back her laughter as she agreed.

Mills grabbed her hand again. "Please don't misunderstand my reaction. I enjoyed kissing you. I started it, for God's sake. Our lips may have met by accident, but they stayed there because I wanted them to. I just think we both have a lot on our plates right now with this case, so it's not the right time to complicate things any further. Besides, I know there is a whole process we will have to go through with Human Resources if a superior officer dates someone on his staff. The press would have a field day with that. I like you. I want to pursue this with you... the sooner, the better. All the more motivation for us to catch this bastard and let him fry!"

Mendy smiled and nodded her head in approval. "It's time for us to get home and try to get some rest. And you need to kiss your baby girl goodnight. Thanks for dinner, um, Brad."

"You're welcome. Let me walk you to your car, Mendy."

Nineteen

A Dark Discovery

Monday, November 21, 2022

Meredith's head spun as she contemplated all the little last-minute details that needed to be finalized before Stellan's new collection, *They Came from the Dark*, was picked up tomorrow and his exhibition debuted the following week. It was a dicey enough proposition to send it across country during the busy holiday week, without any extra problems if something didn't go exactly to plan. She was one of the busiest, most sought-after art agents in the world for a reason: her attention to detail.

As she stepped off the curb to get in her car, the receptionist answered at the Weimar Gallery in New York City. "Hello, this is Meredith Price from the Price Artistic Agency. I was calling to speak to Charles about the Erikkson exhibition in December."

"One moment please, Ms. Price."

"Meri! How are you doing, darling?"

"Great, Charles. How about you?"

"Fine... fine. I'm very excited about this show coming up. His talent... his pieces... they are just beyond description."

"I know. I can't tell you how lucky I am that he just fell into my lap. These idiots out here in L.A. have proven once again that they have no taste. Can you even believe he's been denied a show at nearly a dozen galleries in the area?"

"How did you meet him anyhow? You never told me the secret to your success."

"We went out on a date. There was chemistry, but then he

happened to mention he was an artist. He had no idea I was an agent. You know me... I couldn't resist and asked to see his work. Mind blown! Date over at that moment. I am nothing if not professional."

"I bet he didn't know what hit him when Hurricane Meri swept over and picked him up."

Meredith chuckled. "Sometimes I forget how long we've known each other. You know me too well, Charles dear."

"So, getting back to the exhibition, how can I help you?"

"I just wanted to make sure everything was set on both our ends. The installation ships out on Tuesday afternoon. It's supposed to arrive at the gallery on Saturday evening after you close. Have they called to confirm that with you and find out who to contact to open the gallery?"

"Yes, Janice, the curator, talked to them," Charles said. "They're going to deliver Saturday night and come back Sunday morning to help her uncrate the pieces. Then Stellan will be here late Monday afternoon to set up 'the experience.' Is that correct?"

"Yes, I come in Saturday on the red eye to meet up with some friends, but if you need anything, give me a call. Then Stellan's flight arrives at 1:30 on Monday afternoon. He says he'll be able to have it completely set up by Tuesday evening, so you can go over the exhibition Wednesday, before its grand opening Thursday night."

"That all sounds great."

"Anything you need me to do for the reception that night?" Meredith asked. "The caterer told me he had talked to you the other day to make arrangements for delivery of the food and the open bar. I will be here all day though, so we should be fine regardless."

"Yes, it is all arranged. The guests have all RSVP'd, so we will have a crowd of the biggest collectors in the New York area plus some international guests, the best critics and a celebrity roster as well. It will simply be fabulous, my dear."

"So, anything you need from me then otherwise?"

"Not a thing. Just sit back and relax. Enjoy the fruits of your labor. This shooting star is going to make us all filthy rich."

"From your lips to the buyers' ears."

"I have already heard from one of my most proliferative collectors," Charles said. "He saw photos from Stellan's first show... 'Interested' doesn't begin to describe his reaction. He has expressed his desire to buy art from this exhibition if they have the same aesthetic appeal... multiple pieces."

"That's fantastic! I can't wait to see Stellan's face when I give him the news. You don't mind if I share, do you?

"Absolutely not! You have an excellent day, my dear. I must go. A VIP just entered the gallery."

"*Au revoir*, Charles."

"*Ciao, bella!*"

As she looked down at her list, Meredith realized all she had left to do was stop by Stellan's loft to measure the last two installations he'd created to make sure the shipping crates she had ordered were big enough, and confirm her travel plans. She stopped by The New York City Deli downtown to get some lunch while she confirmed her flight and hotel reservations online. While she waited for her DTLA Turkey Wrap to arrive, she called Stellan to see if he was home so she could stop by before she went to the gallery across town.

"Hello, you have reached Stellan Erikkson, *artist extraordinaire*. If you wish to purchase one of my pieces or schedule an exhibition, please contact my agent, Meredith Price, at Price Artistic Agency. If you know me personally, text me because that I will answer."

Damn! He isn't home. I don't want to have to come back into downtown later. Wait... my key!

Meredith disconnected the call and started a text instead. "Hey Stellan! I was hoping to reach you so I could come by to make sure those new installations will fit in the shipping crates. I just remembered you gave me a key to your loft, so I'm going to stop by in about 20 minutes to measure them. I will be in and out, so don't worry about hurrying home. Talk to you later in the week to finalize plans. Ta-ta for now Oh yeah, I have some big news for you."

Meredith's sandwich arrived as she set her phone down.

I wonder where he is. He's usually so good about being available when we make plans. Of course, he probably has a lot to take care of before going out of town for a month... or more. Well, no matter. I'm nothing if not resourceful.

Meredith finished her sandwich and drove the short distance to Stellan's loft. When she arrived, she noticed his Jag wasn't parked out front. She grabbed her purse, and then got into her trunk to retrieve the tape measure out of her tote bag. As she dashed up the stairs, she heard her phone's notification tone.

I'll get that when I finish here. I'm on too tight of a schedule today.

Meredith unlocked the door and entered the bottom floor of Stellan's loft, where his installation was kept. She didn't know how he could even move around in there... the place was packed.

This exhibition is going to be insane!

She maneuvered her way around the room and finally found the two new pieces. A few quick measurements, and Meredith was reassured to find they fit within the specs. As she skirted between two large pieces to leave, she noticed a partially unzipped photography portfolio on the desk.

Dark Arts

Don't tell me I found the Holy Grail. Has he been hiding it from me that he's a photographer as well? I'm sure he has an amazing eye. Surely, he wouldn't mind if I take one quick look.

Meredith finished unzipping the portfolio and flipped back the cover. She began to feel faint as her eyes skimmed over the top image. Her breath caught in her throat, and only sharp, quick inhalations followed. She slid the photos aside one-by-one, revealing one atrocity after another... five in all. She recognized four of the women. How could she not? Their photos had been all over the news the past year and a half.

"Oh God! No no no! It can't be."

Meredith heard a noise behind her. As she turned to look, a hand slid over her mouth. Another hand grabbed her shoulder and slowly turned her around to face Stellan. "I'm afraid so, Meredith. I wish you hadn't seen those. They were never meant for your eyes. I tried to stop you. I texted you to tell you I would be here in five minutes. Why didn't you wait?"

Tears welled in Meredith's eyes as the gravity of the situation descended on her. Hyperventilating, she found it difficult to breathe with his hand clamped tightly over her mouth. Her hands flailed at his, trying to get them to loosen.

"You want me to remove my hand?"

Meredith nodded.

"You've seen what I can do. Don't test me. Make one noise, and it will be your last. Got it?"

Meredith slowly nodded, pleading with her eyes.

Stellan removed his hand, slowly at first, but kept a firm grip on her shoulder. "I hate that it came to this. You've been pivotal in my career. But it happened, so now it's time we had a discussion, and you saw where I create my *real* art... my life's passion. Are you ready?"

Meredith didn't know how to answer a question like that.

Answer him dammit! I need to buy time to figure out a way to escape.

"I would love to, Stellan. This all just took me by surprise. This is by far your greatest work yet."

Stellan pulled the small push dagger out of his pocket and palmed it, pressing the tip lightly into her back. "There's usually no one around this time of day, but just in case, I need you to walk out calmly with me. We'll leave in your car. One false move, and I'll bury this in your kidney. You'll bleed out in a matter of minutes. Clear?"

"Crystal, Stellan. I wouldn't do that. I'm very excited to see your special collection."

Stellan and Meredith walked down the stairs and got in her car to begin the drive over to his warehouse.

How am I going to get out of this?

Twenty

Martyr to Art

Monday, November 21, 2022

Meredith began a steady stream of chatter, asking Stellan questions about his work. She could see his ego inflating as he described the pieces in detail. She took slow, deep breaths, trying not to catch his attention, in an attempt to suppress the waves of nausea threatening to overcome her. She'd always known he was a dark genius, but she never could've imagined just how twisted and horrific he could be.

She kept hoping that a cop would drive by as she navigated to Stellan's warehouse according to his exacting directions. She pretended to *accidentally* turn down the wrong street so she could head to a more populated area.

Stellan poked her in the side with the dagger, drawing a dot of blood.

"I hope you remember my warning. You turned too early. Turn left here and go up one more street before turning south again."

"Yes. Of course, I do. I was just thinking about the collection you were describing, and I misunderstood what street you wanted me to turn down. I am very excited about all of this. I would never betray you. Does your collection have a name?"

"It is called *Dark Arts*."

"So, what do you do with this collection? I mean... since you can't display it to the rest of the world."

"I have a show on the dark web where I broadcast myself

creating the works. It has been very lucrative. I do thank you for all you have done for my 'legitimate' career, but it is nothing compared to what I have created on the side."

"Wow. That's amazing. Maybe I can help you expand or advertise it more. I must admit, I don't know anything about the dark web, but you can teach me."

"Hmmm."

They had entered an old industrial area of L.A. Most of the buildings appeared long since abandoned and in need of repair. Help would not be found easily here.

Stellan directed Meredith to park in front of a large grey warehouse, demanding the keys when she shut off the engine. He came around the car and opened her door. Grabbing her elbow and directing her toward the entrance, he awkwardly unlocked the warehouse door with his one free hand and pushed her inside.

Meredith blinked as blinding light enveloped her when Stellan flipped on the light switches. She looked around as he locked the numerous deadbolts and slid the bars in place. He protected this place like Fort Knox... no one was getting in... or out.

"Welcome to my studio, Meredith."

"This place is amazing. You have so much room to work, and the technology appears top-notch. So, over here is where you film your show, I am assuming?"

"Yes. I have a variety of cameras to provide my viewers with different angles. The computer system over there encrypts everything and sends it through many different proxy servers, so my signal cannot be traced. I even have a little apartment in the back where I can stay the night. Most of these works keep me busy until the early morning."

"What do you do with them... you know, afterward?"

Dark Arts

"I have a kiln that cremates the remains and destroys all the evidence."

"Very smart. You have thought of everything."

"Come look at this!" With a broad smile, Stellan grabbed her hand and led her over to another room toward the back. He turned on the light and extended his hand as he swept it across the expanse. "This is my own private gallery. Those pictures you saw... I will be framing them and hanging them in here soon. What do you think?"

"It's great, Stellan! I can't wait to see it all finished." Her wide eyes betrayed her true feelings; she was horrified by the thought of the Dark Arts gallery. She turned and took hesitant steps toward the staging area. Her hands trembled as she reached out to run them over the surgical table and instrument tray, feigning interest. Her breath caught in her throat as she felt Stellan's hand grip her shoulder. "S... so... so how do you find your subjects anyhow?"

"I think we can let the pretense go, Meredith. You aren't fooling anyone, least of all me. I think we both know what needs to happen now."

"What do you mean? Do you have another victim... er... I mean subject that you are ready to create. Do you need my help?"

"Why yes, I do. And your help is absolutely essential."

Meredith screamed as she felt his arm begin to tighten around her throat, cutting off her air supply. Her hands clutched his arm in a desperate bid to pull it away, the fingernails digging into the skin at his wrist. She madly began to twist her body and kicked back with her high heels, hitting him in the shins and stomping on his feet. But nothing worked... he seemed impervious to all her attempts to hurt him. Her flailing died down as her world began to spin, and she felt lightheaded.

After another moment, she hung limp in his arms with her chest still rising and falling: unconscious but not dead... yet.

Stellan carried her over to the surgical table and applied the restraints to her wrists and ankles. He walked over to the metal utility shelves where he stored all his tools and art supplies. After a few moments, he found what he was looking for—a ball gag and a burlap sack.

He put the ball gag in her mouth and secured the strap over the top of her head, buckling it at the back of her skull. Then he placed the burlap sack over her head and cinched it shut around her throat, tying it tight to prevent her from sliding out. He moved the empty waste buckets over to the table and situated them under the drain hole at the top of the table. Stellan could hear her whimpers as she began to regain consciousness and realized the dire nature of her predicament.

"I am right here beside you, Meredith. You need to calm down, or you're going to choke with that gag in your mouth."

Stellan dragged over a large, rectangular box, the size of a coffin, and placed it near the table. Then he brought in the container that held the dermestid beetles and set it off to the side. He placed a scalpel on the instrument tray, adjusted the camera angle and then grabbed the remote.

Meredith's sniffling became louder as her crying intensified.

"I think we're all set here. I regret that it has come to this. I had hoped it would be different. But I could see it in your eyes—in your whole demeanor—that you could not accept my *Dark Arts* collection. I will not let you, or anyone else, deter me from my life's work. You won't be forgotten though. You will be the star of my next work of art. You will live forever in the minds of those who see your transformation. I promise your death will be quick and relatively painless. I owe you that much at least. I will make you proud at the next gallery exhibition... prove that I am your greatest discovery ever. Are you ready?"

Meredith tried to slide her hands and feet free from the restraints, but they wouldn't budge. She twisted her body on the table and tried to scream, but only a muffled whimper escaped from her lips. Stellan walked over to the shelving to retrieve his mask and a new pair of coveralls.

"Meredith, you need to stop that now. Nothing you can say or do will change the situation you find yourself in. I said I wouldn't cause you too much pain. But if you don't stop, I can't promise what will happen."

There was no time, given this sudden turn of events, for Stellan to start the countdown clock that was his custom prior to each episode. But he knew his fans would be monitoring the site. They were devoted, after all.

"I wish you could see my show. No matter though, you are going to be the star. It's showtime!" With a flourish, Stellan pressed the button and started the show.

"Welcome once again, my ghoulish groupies, to the sixth episode of *Dark Arts*, hosted by yours truly, *Le Créateur*. As always, thank you all so much for your continued patronage. Tonight, we are going to explore the concepts that beauty is only skin deep... and that, deep down, we are all the same. As they say, it's what inside that matters.

"This will once again be a two-part episode. We will meet again in three days, on Thursday, to celebrate Thanksgiving and finish the process. Today, we are going to take a bit of a different approach. We are not focused on the suffering of this subject. This episode is geared toward my artistic and philosophical aberrants.

"Our subject has voluntarily chosen to be a part of this work of art. You will not see her face or nakedness. Instead, you will witness her selfless, exquisite sacrifice as her literal lifeblood pours from her body. Her glorious form will be revealed to you Thursday when our thanks will be given to her for her selflessness.

"And I haven't even told you the best part yet. This work of art will be put up for auction; minimum bid is $1 million. Plus, I will be creating three one-of-a-kind small works of art during the process that will go up for sale after the show. The three smaller pieces can be purchased for $2,000, first come, first served, as usual. And of course, you can download the video in 24 hours for $2,000. Who's ready to begin?"

Le Créateur looked over at the monitor bank where a flurry of responses had begun appearing on the screen. He reached over and checked to make sure all of Meredith's restraints were securely fastened before releasing a lock that allowed him to tip the table downward, then turning a handle so her that her head hung just above the bucket.

Blood rushed to Meredith's head and pooled there due to gravity. She let out a strangled scream as the table thunked into place. Gathering her hair together, he twisted it into a tight knot at the back of her head and secured it with an elastic band.

Le Créateur picked up the scalpel and sliced open her throat with one swift motion, cutting the carotid arteries and jugular veins. Meredith's body jumped with the motion as she fought to grab her ravaged throat. Bright red blood squirted out onto *Le Créateur* and across the room. As her heartbeat raced when her body sensed its peril, blood fountained out and cascaded down her face and into the bucket.

Her respirations increased as she began to exsanguinate.

Each breath became a loud gurgle as she struggled to breathe through the blood that had poured into her trachea.

Little bubbles of blood appeared and burst as the ragged breaths pushed through the stream.

Meredith's body grew limp, the restraints biting into her skin, as she lost consciousness and then ceased to breathe. Her heart beat erratically and then ceased as well. *Le Créateur* left her hanging for a few more minutes, allowing all the blood to leave her body.

While he waited, he opened the large, rectangular box as he explained the next steps to his eager audience. "We will once again be making use of our friends the dermestid beetles. Since we will be placing her whole body inside, we will give them three days to completely clean the skeleton. I will arrive here early Thursday to do the last preparations before we finish the piece, and a time-lapse video will be provided to show you those steps."

He returned to the table and turned the handle underneath again, so he could return the table to its normal upright position before removing the restraints from Meredith's body. Then he picked her up and placed her inside the box, dumping the beetles and larvae across her body.

Le Créateur placed a camera inside the box before sealing it shut.

"Now I will be turning on an alternate camera while we proceed over to the canvases and the backdrop for this work of art. The bug camera will be activated at the conclusion of this afternoon's episode."

Le Créateur walked offscreen to the computer bank, where he activated the camera across the warehouse near the gallery he was installing. He had hung a large white cloth backdrop on the wall next to three canvases. He came into view a moment later, carrying in the bucket of blood, a few smaller paint buckets, and a caddy containing a variety of paintbrushes, tools and mica powders.

"Today, we will be exploring abstract art in conjunction with our installation. I will mix mica powders in with the blood to create different colors and a shimmer effect. Then I will use the different brushes and other tools to create interesting textures in the paintings."

Le Créateur turned away and spent the next hour painting the backdrop before creating three miniaturized versions on the canvases. The backdrop consisted of one large splotch of blood that looked like an ink blot from a Rorschach test. He accentuated the edges of that blot with a dark mica powder to create a dark reddish-brown outline.

That accomplished, he mixed in a black mica powder before creating another smaller splotch off to the lower right of the main one. At the top of the backdrop, he added to the original splotch with some blood that had been tinted with yellow mica powder, creating a shimmering burnt orange color. The angle of the light shining down on the backdrop created an eerie glow to the dark piece.

With a sigh, he set down his brushes and turned back to the camera. "That's it for now, my wicked worshippers. I bet you can't wait to see the finished piece like me. I know you are excited to see more, but you will have to wait until Thursday at 12 p.m., when the show returns for Part 2. Let me know what you thought of tonight's episode. Goodnight and sweet screams to you all!"

The next three days were busy for Stellan as he cleaned up from the unplanned, impromptu episode of *Dark Arts*, then packed and prepared for the next month or more in New York. His first order of business was disposing of Meredith's car, which he had left parked in the Projects, arranging for it to be picked up and taken to a chop shop later that evening.

He also couldn't afford to let the police discover that Meredith's phone had last pinged at his loft. Fortunately, he'd had her turn off her phone before they began the drive to his warehouse. After the cleanup, he drove to her house and used her keys to gain entry. Then he turned her phone back on, making it appear as if her phone battery had died and only been turned back on after charging later in the day.

The next morning, he walked over to her house from a few blocks away and sent a text to himself from her phone to establish proof of life for a day beyond her actual demise.

The delivery company had arrived early on Tuesday morning and begun the long process of packing up the installations in the crates. By early afternoon, they had been loaded on the truck and were bound for New York, set to arrive Saturday evening.

Stellan drove over to the warehouse to log into the dark web and make the arrangements for the pickup Saturday morning and eventual delivery of the *Dark Arts* pieces. He faced a tight timeline getting them ready, but he had no doubt he could make it work.

Stellan's alarm went off at 5 a.m. on Thursday morning. He needed to complete a number of tasks before he could start the second part of the episode at noon. He arrived at the warehouse by 7 and went to the computer bank. He turned off the camera in the bug box and put up a hold screen with a countdown until the episode resumed.

Stellan donned his disguise and began removing her body from the box, brushing off the beetles and larvae as he retrieved the pieces one by one. The beetles had done a thorough job, even removing all the connective tissue holding the skeleton together. He had placed a drill and an assortment of bolts and wires next to the box in order to reconstruct the skeleton as it was removed. The process was finished just in time for him to place the skeleton on the surgical table before the five-minute countdown began.

Stellan quickly transferred the beetles back into their container and removed the boxes from the set, then retrieved the last of the rose vines he had used in the creation of *Venus in Bloom*. Over the past month, the vines had dried up, appearing as long brown twigs from which the leaves had fallen. He made sure the camera angle was correct and then stood at the head of the table.

"Welcome back, my naughty minions. Thank you for joining me for Part 2 of Episode 6. As you can see, I have been busy preparing the subject for the last steps of this work. Those hungry little beasts simply devoured everything, including the connective tissue, so I had to reattach the bones. I recorded the process for you, and it will be spliced later today in between parts 1 and 2 on the streaming and download versions.

"Pardon me for a few moments while I switch cameras again and get the skeleton moved over for hanging."

Le Créateur turned off the main camera and carried the skeleton over, setting it on the floor. He placed the mounting hardware, drill, and dried rose vines on the floor next to it. Then he adjusted the secondary camera and started the broadcast once again.

"First, we need to install the main bracket that will support her skull." *Le Créateur* picked up the drill and screwed a double hook into the wall. The double hook consisted of two 4-inch hooks that projected from the wall about two inches apart, letting him slide the cervical spine between them, with the skull resting on the horizontal surface. He then drilled several holes down the length of the spine, in each side of the pelvic bone and the femur and tibia of the left leg. He inserted a screw into each of those and secured them to the wall.

For the right leg, he inserted a screw through the femoral head at an angle and bent the leg at the knee joint. He secured the lower end of the tibia with another angled screw, so the leg projected out, as if she were pushing off from the wall. He lifted both arms straight out at her side and affixed them to the wall in the position, as if she had been crucified. Once she was completely attached to the wall, he began weaving the dried rose vines into her upper ribcage behind her shoulder blades, forming "wings" to depict her ascension after her martyrdom.

Le Créateur stepped back to admire his work. She had turned out even better than he could have imagined.

"We have come to the end of this episode, my vulgar collective. I present to you, *Martyr for Art.* Isn't she splendid? The three small canvases will be available for purchase approximately one hour after the show once they have been posted on the main Dark Arts site on the dark web. Remember that it will be first come, first served, so don't wander away from the screen if you want to own a part of this work of art. Each canvas comes with a print of the completed artwork. The auction will begin promptly at 3 p.m. As usual, only cryptocurrency will be accepted, and secure, anonymous delivery will be arranged. This two-part video will be up for streaming on the Dark Arts gallery for the next 24 hours. After that, a heavily encrypted digital download can be purchased for $2,000 USD. Hopefully, you savored this episode as much as I did. Good afternoon, and sweet screams to you all!"

Stellan ended the recording and removed the mask.

There is no limit to the depths of my creativity. I didn't even have time to plan out this piece. Wait until the police see this one.

Stellan finished cleaning up his studio and set up the auction and the link for the purchase of the canvases. He would come back tomorrow afternoon to prepare them for shipping and get them transferred over to the pickup site for delivery arrangements.

I think I will treat myself to a delicious steak dinner out. I earned it. Then back home to finalize my alibi in regards to Meredith's disappearance. I only have a matter of days, at most, before someone notices her missing.

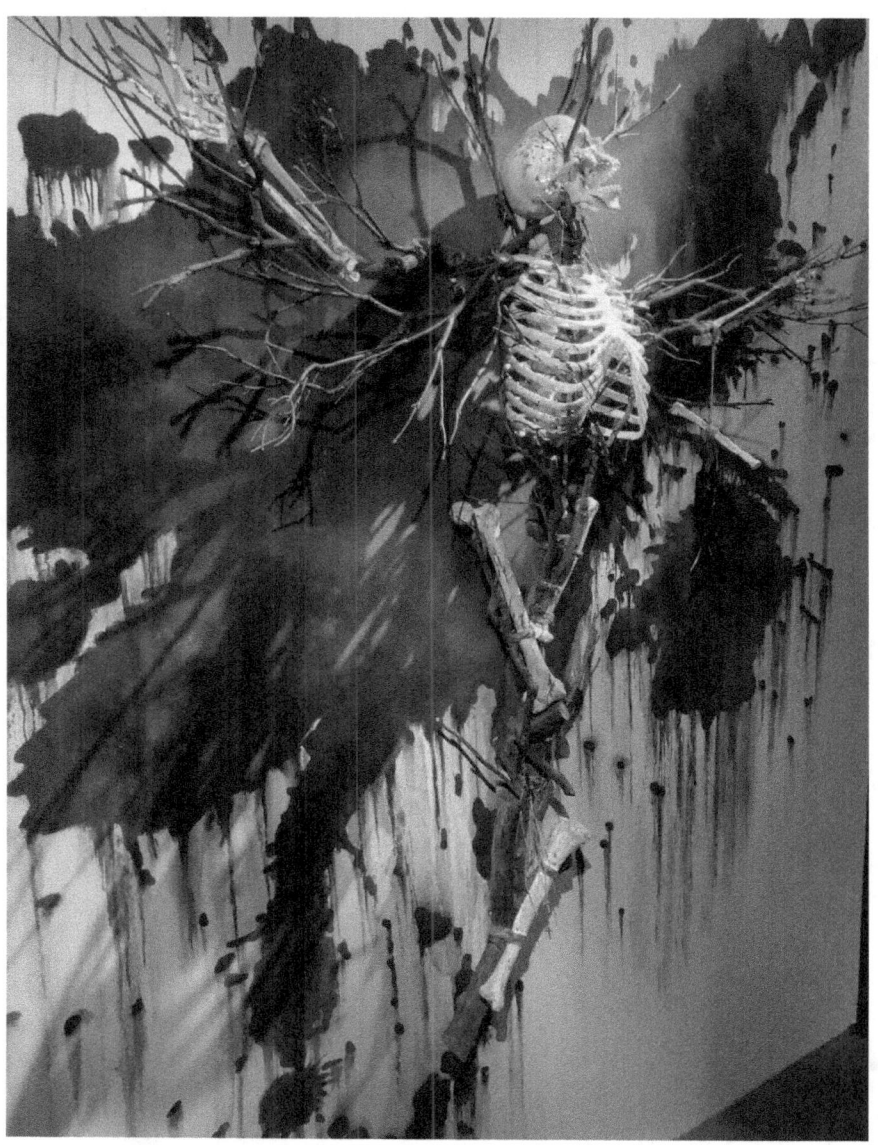

Sharon Marie Provost

Twenty-One

They Came from the Dark

Last days of November 2022

Sunday night arrived quicker than Stellan had expected. He went through his packing list one last time and felt assured that he had collected everything he would need over the next month or two. Meredith really had thought of everything, even arranging a private fitting for a new tux to wear at the debut of his exhibition. The tailor was coming to his hotel room at 9 on Monday night.

Stellan's flight was due in at 1:30, which meant he should make it to the gallery by 3 p.m. He planned to get the less complicated installations set up by 8 that night. Then he would have all day Tuesday to prepare the more involved pieces, setting up the lights and engineering the tight spaces designed to increase his viewers' unease.

Stellan was pleasantly surprised that no one had contacted him yet to ask about Meredith. He was sure he'd have to deal with that hassle the next day—which would be soon enough. He had to arrive at the airport early in the morning, so he scheduled Uber to pick him up at 4 a.m. and then retired early for the night.

He boarded his flight without incident the next morning and, with tail winds, arrived at JFK approximately 20 minutes early. He went downstairs to baggage claim and located the driver Meredith had arranged to pick him up, before collecting his many pieces of luggage. Since he was early, he had the driver take him to the hotel to check in and drop off his belongings. Then they continued on to the Weimar Gallery and arrived right on time.

Stellan walked into the gallery and was immediately greeted by the chipper receptionist. She blushed as she introduced herself.

"Mr. Erikkson, it's so nice to meet you. I am a big fan of your work."

"Hello, Miss..."

"Kelly. You can just call me Kelly."

An older brunette breezed into the reception area and interrupted their exchange.

"Kelly, let's not bother Mr. Erikkson," she said. "Charles is waiting to meet him, and we have much to do today." She leaned forward and gave Stellan a light peck on each cheek. "I am Janice, the gallery curator. Let me take you back to meet the owner, Charles."

Janice led him through the packed gallery filled with his installations. Stellan was relieved to see that they all appeared to be intact and undamaged. Her brow furrowed as she looked back at him.

"Is Ms. Price with you? I didn't see her in the reception area."

"No. I haven't met up with her since arriving in New York an hour and a half ago. Why do you ask?"

"It's just that we expected to hear from her by now. I know her flight was due in Saturday, and she was going to be seeing friends. But she is usually so conscientious that we expected she would check in with us at some point before your arrival."

"That is strange. I have been so busy getting ready the past few days I haven't talked to her myself. I can give her a call if you like."

"No matter. We have everything set up, and all the plans have been running like clockwork. I'm sure she will be here at some point today or tomorrow."

"Yes, I'm sure you are right. Thank you for coming in to receive my installations and oversee the unpacking."

"Don't mention it, Mr. Erikkson. I was happy to do so. Your work is very intriguing. I can't wait to see everyone's reaction on Thursday night."

"Hopefully it lives up to expectations."

"Without a doubt. Excuse me... Charles, I have Mr. Erikkson here."

"Stellan, please. It is very nice to meet you, Charles. Thank you for hosting my exhibition."

"The pleasure is all mine. I should be thanking you. You are going to make all of us famous, Stellan."

"You are much too kind. I suppose I should get to work."

"I have a crew in the back ready to help you move the pieces. If you need anything else, please let me know. Janice will be ordering in some food later. We can't have you passing out on us."

"That is very kind of you."

Stellan turned and headed out into the gallery to meet up with the crew coming out of the back. The ensuing five hours passed quickly as they set up the front of the gallery with the introductory pieces. The exhibition was designed to amp up the visitors' discomfort as they moved through the installation. Each piece grew darker and scarier, the lighting grew dimmer or more red and off-putting, the aisleways became smaller and were offset... even sometimes ending in a roadblock or a funhouse mirror. He had designed the pieces of *They Came from the Dark* so that each could be a standalone artwork, but they were best enjoyed as a whole... an "experience."

As 8 p.m. rolled around, Charles came by to see if Stellan needed anything before finishing the setup the following day. Stellan declined and thanked him for his hospitality.

"Stellan, are you staying at the same hotel as Meri, or should I say Meredith?"

"Yes, I am."

"Will you check in with her tomorrow and let her know I have a couple of questions for her? No emergency, but I would like to speak with her before the final show preparations Wednesday."

"Sure. No problem. She probably plans to meet up with me in the morning anyhow. Or maybe even tonight when I get my suit measurements done at the hotel. Speaking of that, I should get going, or I'll be late. I know traffic never totally dies down in New York. Thanks again, Charles."

Stellan returned to the hotel and checked in at the hotel desk to see if he'd received any messages before continuing to his suite. He had just settled on the couch when he heard a knock at the door. He opened it to find the tailor and an assistant wheeling in a wardrobe rack filled with a variety of tux styles and colors. Over the next hour, Stellan felt like a Barbie doll as he was dressed and redressed, arms lifted for measurements and otherwise manipulated. Finally, they settled on a classic black Ralph Lauren Polo Tailored Linen tux.

"Have you seen Ms. Price today? I thought she was supposed to meet us here. We were going to do some last-minute adjustments to her gown as well," the tailor asked as they packed up.

"You are the second person to ask me that today. No, I

haven't. I expected her here myself. Let me see if I can reach her." Stellan grabbed his cell phone off the coffee table and placed a call to Meredith—which, of course, went to voicemail. "Hey, Meredith. It's Stellan. Is everything OK? No one has heard from you. I am here with the tailor right now, and he says you were supposed to be here for a last-minute fitting. Give me a call."

Stellan turned to the tailor and shrugged. "That's weird. I've never gotten her voicemail before. She always answers, but I guess she must be busy. If I hear from her, I'll tell her to call you. Thanks again for stopping by so late."

"No problem, sir. Good luck with your exhibition. My assistant will drop off your suit on Thursday morning. If you have any issues, don't hesitate to call me. Here is my card with my personal number. Good evening, Mr. Erikkson."

Stellan let out the tailor and his assistant and followed them out and down to the front desk.

"Excuse me. My name is Stellan Erikkson. My rep booked my room for me as well as one for herself. She arrived Saturday, but no one has heard from her today. Can you tell me if you've seen her?"

"I'm not supposed to give out that kind of information."

"I'm not asking you to give me her room number or anything. I just want to make sure someone has seen her... that she is OK. She hasn't responded to my message, which just isn't like her."

"What's her name, sir?"

"Meredith Price. I am sure if you look up my room, you will see that she booked and paid for it."

"Sir, we don't have any guest here by that name. I show we had a reservation to start on Saturday, as you said, but no one ever checked in or canceled it. That's all I can tell you."

"Thank you very much."

Step one of establishing my innocence is complete. Now to place a call to her assistant, and then Charles.

Stellan returned to his room and placed a call to Meredith's assistant, Barbara. "Hey, Barb. It's Stellan. When is the last time you talked to Meredith?"

"She hasn't been in the office since last Monday morning. She texted me Tuesday to say she was busy with the plans for your exhibition so she wouldn't be in for the rest of the week. Why, may I ask?"

"She never showed up at the gallery today. Then she didn't come when the tailor was here tonight. I just checked with the front desk, and she never checked into the hotel on Saturday. Could she be staying with the friends she was going to visit this weekend? Do you have their number?"

"Yes, I do. I don't think I should give it out, but I will give them a call if you like."

"Yes, please. Then call me right back. I am concerned."

Stellan settled on the couch again and turned on the television, flipping through the channels for something interesting to watch. He sighed when the phone rang and answered with feigned concern in his voice. "Barb?"

"Yes. Her friends haven't seen her. She hasn't answered their calls either over the past two days."

"Do you have a key to her house? Can you go by and see if she's there?"

"Of course. I will head over right now. If there's no sign of her, I will call the police. I will let you know what happens. Oh dear, I am so worried. Thanks for calling me, Stellan."

Stellan prepared himself for another taxing conversation as he dialed Charles' private number. A weary-sounding Charles picked up after three rings.. "Um... Charles?"

"Yes. How can I help you?"

"This is Stellan Erikkson. I am sorry to disturb you at this late hour. I know you and Meredith are friends, so I thought I should let you know what's going on. She didn't show up to my fitting tonight, and apparently she had made plans with the tailor to be here. I checked with the front desk to see if they had seen her today. She never checked into the hotel at all.

"So I called her assistant, who hasn't heard from her in the past week. Barb then called her friends here in New York, and she never showed up there either. I am really quite worried. I didn't know if you had any ideas of anyone else to contact. Family? Other close friends? Barb is headed to her house right now, but I am not feeling very optimistic at this point."

There was a brief pause on the other end. "That is very disconcerting," Charles said, clearly fully awake now. "That is not like Meri at all. She is the most responsible person I have ever known. I knew I should have followed up when she didn't call me on Saturday. Let me see what I can figure out. I will talk to you tomorrow morning if one of us doesn't hear back from someone before that. Thank you for calling."

Stellan yawned and decided to call it an early night. He had a lot of work ahead of him the next day setting up the last half of the installation, not to mention dealing with all the missing Meredith drama that would follow. The shit was about to hit the fan, but they still had a show to put on.

Stellan groggily opened his eyes when his phone rang at 5 a.m.

What asshole is calling me at this hour? Don't I deserve a little peace when I am already fighting jet lag?

"Umm... hello?"

"Stellan, it's Charles. Barb filed a missing person's report last night. She went into Meredith's house, and all her belongings were there... purse, cell phone, car keys. Her suitcase was sitting out to be packed, but she hadn't even started. It looks like she's been missing for a whole week, and none of us even knew. Dear God! I hope she is OK. Where could she be? The police are checking with local hospitals. I am so worried."

"That's terrible. I feel awful. I should have checked in with her last week, but there was so much to prepare before I left. And you know Meredith, she had all the arrangements set up so perfectly that I didn't even have to check with her. It all went like clockwork. Is there anything I can do?"

"The police will be calling you at some point today to find out when you last spoke to her and if you noticed anything concerning in your conversation. It appears she never left the L.A. area. I really don't know what else we can do, especially being on the other side of the country. As callous as it sounds, Meredith would want us to forge ahead. As they say, 'The show must go on,' and we have a lot left to do before Thursday's debut."

"I know you're right, but it just doesn't *feel* right. I will get ready and head out soon. Meet you at the studio at 7?"

"That is fine. Thanks, Mr. Erikkson."

Stellan climbed out of bed and ordered room service before jumping into a hot shower.

I sure hope all this Meredith shit doesn't mess with the success of my exhibition. I have worked far too hard to be derailed now. Why the fuck did she have to ignore her phone that one time? Why didn't she see my message and wait for me? Now I have to find another agent for the future. What an inconvenience! I am a busy man.

Room service delivered his breakfast just as he finished dressing. He ate it quickly and called down to the doorman to have the driver come around to take him to the gallery. Traffic was heavy on a weekday morning, but he made it to the Weimar with five minutes to spare. As he got out of the car, he took a deep breath and put on the grave face of a worried friend.

Stellan walked into and was greeted by a much more sober Kelly. "Hello, Mr. Erikkson. Charles is waiting for you in his office."

He walked back to the office and found Charles finishing up a call with what sounded like the police. "Thank you, detective. Mr. Erikkson just arrived, so I will let him know to expect your call later today. Thanks for the update."

"Mr. Erikkson, thanks for coming down so early. That was the detective from Missing Persons assigned to the case. As we already knew, she never boarded her flight out of L.A. Her neighbor last saw her leave her house early last Monday morning. She said her car returned sometime late that afternoon, but she never physically saw her."

Stellan feigned a worried, puzzled look.

"She was OK until sometime Tuesday afternoon because she sent text messages to you and Barb, but nobody knows at what point she disappeared after that," Charles said. "They are pulling her cell records now. They say there was no sign of a struggle at her house, but where did she go and why?"

Stellan looked thoughtful.

"I've only known her for about a year and a half, but I know she wouldn't just disappear like this voluntarily without letting someone know. She was so excited about this exhibition, as all of us are. Should we cancel the exhibition?"

"No, no, definitely not," Charles said with a wave of his hand. "It is much too late at this point to change plans that are in the best interest of all of our careers. She would be mad at us if we did that. All we can do is help the police to the best of our ability, and make sure the show is a success. I hope that doesn't sound too callous. Can you do that?"

"Yes, I suppose I can. You are right. She worked too hard to set all of this up. I have to believe she is OK, and she deserves to celebrate in the fruits of her labor when they find her. That being said, I must get to work. Thank you, Charles."

"The crew will meet you in the lobby shortly. Let me know if you need anything. Janice will have lunch and dinner delivered."

Stellan and the crew worked steadily until after 3, setting up the installations, until he received a phone call.

"Hello. May I speak to Stellan Erikkson please?"

"This is he."

"This is Detective Robert Stevens from the LAPD Missing Persons Unit. I'm investigating the disappearance of your agent, Meredith Price. I need to ask you some questions about your last interactions with her. Do you have time to speak?"

"Yes, of course. I last spoke to Meredith via text last Tuesday morning. She was checking in with me to make sure that everything was going OK with the company that came to pack up and transport my art to New York for my exhibition that opens Thursday."

"When was the last time you actually saw her or spoke on the phone?"

Stellan had been expecting these questions and rehearsed the responses in his mind. But he knew he couldn't answer too quickly or make it *appear* he knew what was coming. "That would be last Monday afternoon," he said. "She dropped by my loft to measure my last two works to make sure the shipping crates were big enough. She let herself in, and I met her there a few minutes later."

"A neighbor said she saw you leave in Meredith's car with her at approximately 2 p.m. Where did you go?"

"My car was acting up, and I wanted to check out a new art supply store downtown. She offered to give me a ride on her way over to the gallery across the city."

"Can anybody confirm you were there?"

"Unfortunately, no. I forgot they are closed on Mondays. I stopped in the park to relax for a bit and then picked up some street food for dinner. I scheduled an Uber and arrived home about 7 p.m. I think. Uber should be able to confirm they picked me up in downtown and took me home if that is helpful."

"So what was wrong?"

"Pardon me?"

"With your car."

"Loose battery wire. Thank God! Last thing I needed was a car repair just before I had to go out of town. Do you have any leads, Detective Stevens? We are all very concerned about her. L.A. is a dangerous city. I would hate to think something bad happened to her."

"Nothing yet. She texted you and her assistant on Tuesday and then just disappeared into thin air. Nobody saw anything. Nobody talked to her after that. She left everything behind. I have to ask you. I'm sure you have heard about that serial killer in the area. Is there any chance she was seeing anyone?"

Stellan chuckled softly. "Excuse me. I'm not making a joke of this. It's just obvious that you've never met Meredith. That woman is a machine. I'm not sure when she sleeps... if she even does at all. She doesn't have the time or the inclination to date anyone. Her career is her lover."

"That's strange. I could have sworn that Charles Pitt, the owner of the Weimar Gallery, said that was how the two of you met."

"Exactly my point. That was the one and only date she has been out on in the past five years. We met at a market about a year and a half ago, and the attraction was banging. But during dinner, I mentioned in passing that I was an artist. She jumped on that little bit of news and asked to see my work. She was so impressed that she immediately ended the date and signed me to her agency. She can't pass up an opportunity to work, no matter how strong the sexual attraction. Ever since then, she's been so busy with my career and a couple of her other signed artists that she hasn't even thought about going out with anyone."

"Well thank you, Mr. Erikkson. I appreciate your help. I will be in touch if I have any further questions. You are going to be in New York for some time. Is that correct?"

"Yes, detective, for at least the next month."

"Good day, Mr. Erikkson."

Stellan hung up the phone, pleased with how the conversation had gone. The rest of the day progressed quickly as he and the gallery staff finished setting up the installation. As the clock struck nine, he stood on the circular stairway above the gallery floor and marveled at the completed exhibit. Charles came up the stairs and stood beside him.

"I have never seen anything like it. You are a genius, Stellan. It perfectly depicts the bleak, dark world we live in nowadays. The public has become obsessed with dark imagery. You are going to blow the art world away. I have no doubt! I just wish Meredith was here to see all this."

"I know. Me too. She was the first person who saw my genius. I wouldn't be here today without her, yet here I am without her. It doesn't feel right, but we have to honor all her hard work. Right?"

"Of course. It has been a long hard week already, and we have a very long day ahead of us on Thursday. Take tomorrow off. I can see that the exhibit is complete. All the preparations are in place for the party. Janice spent the day confirming all of it. Meet me here at 2 p.m. Thursday. The party starts at 5, but most people will be fashionably late, as is the New York way."

"Thank you, Charles. I will see you Thursday."

Stellan spent Wednesday doing all the sightseeing he had been too busy to do on his first trip to New York a year ago. In the afternoon, he called Detective Stevens to inquire about the investigation, but Stevens had nothing to report. Detective Stevens asked him what art shop Meredith had dropped him off at that day, and Stellan gave him the answer he had researched ahead of time, Jansen's World of Art. The detective said he would call if he had any news concerning the investigation.

He enjoyed a wonderful dinner at the Four Seasons, where Meredith had made reservations for them to have a celebratory dinner before the opening the next day. Then he returned to the hotel and watched television until he turned in late that night.

The day of Stellan's groundbreaking exhibition, *They Came from the Dark*, dawned early. His suit was delivered as promised and fit to a tee. He arrived at the gallery as the preparations were in full swing. Twinkling fairy lights had been strung through the lobby over tables brimming with delicious food. Several open bars were set up throughout the gallery, with bottles of Dom Perignon chilling on ice. His name was up in lights announcing his exhibition on the marquee over the front door. The public had already formed a long line down the street, hoping to score one of the few but cherished entries into the A-list party.

Charles took him through the exhibit, labeling and verifying the costs for each creation. Expectations were high that at least some of the pieces would sell on opening night to the high-end collectors in attendance. The critics were being granted early entry at 4 p.m. to talk to the artist and make their assessments before the place was barraged.

Stellan had just finished donning his suit and started descending the stairs when the first guests arrived. Within minutes, he was being sought out to discuss the artist's interpretation of his works—as measured against their own educated assumptions. He didn't even have a few minutes to rest before the rest of the guests arrived. The floor writhed with the movement of all the people surrounding his art. Gasps of delight or horror were barely heard over the oohs and ahhs of the adoring collectors. Stellan was passed from one A-list celeb to another, all of them clamoring for time with the "artist extraordinaire."

Stellan's head was spinning with all the attention he was receiving. Suddenly, he felt a hand on his elbow: Someone was trying to gain his attention. Turning, he realized it was Charles—who politely excused them as he led Stellan back to his office.

Once inside, Charles closed the door and directed Stellan to a chair. "I think you'd better sit down."

For an instant, Stellan panicked internally—though he managed to hide it. Had they gotten a lead on Meredith's disappearance? No, that was impossible. He had been too careful. He blinked. Charles was speaking again.

"We have much to discuss," he said. "This has exceeded all our expectations."

"I know. I must admit to being overwhelmed myself."

"First of all, two collectors have each bought a piece of the collection, lot 3 and lot 15."

"I'm already selling pieces? That's fantastic!"

"You didn't let me finish, Stellan. That's a mere drop in the bucket."

"Did Meredith get a chance to tell you that one of my most avid buyers had expressed serious interest in this collection? He missed your first show, and he was so enamored with it when he found the photos online."

"No, she didn't tell me. She was so busy that day I saw her. She must have forgotten and then..." Stellan turned away pretending to be overcome with emotion.

"I think you should sit down before I tell you. I must say I am a bit lightheaded myself. I've never seen this happen before. Mr. Klaus Reinhardt has bought the *entire* remainder of the collection... every last piece except for the two that had already sold. Not only that, but he wants to talk to you about commissioning two special pieces to replace those missing from the collection."

Stellan sat stunned in the chair that Charles had directed him to previously. He was at a complete loss for words.

"Yoohoo, Stellan. Are you in there?" Charles chuckled as he shook Stellan's shoulder.

"Yes, I think. Or am I dreaming? That's not possible, is it?"

"Very much so! He just wrote me an astronomically large check. Tomorrow, we will be very rich. And that check doesn't include the two commissioned pieces. He said he would be willing to pay whatever you want for them."

"That is astounding!"

"Are you feeling better then?"

"Yes."

"Well then, I need to go get Mr. Reinhardt. He insisted on a private meeting with you. Are you ready for that?"

"Yes... sure... anything he wants... a conversation... a pint of blood... my left kidney." Stellan laughed maniacally at his own joke.

"I will send him up then and keep the rest of the guests busy. Congratulations, Mr. Erikkson."

A few moments later, there was a knock at the office door. Stellan opened it and was greeted by the sight of an intimidating man of immense stature. His dark, penetrating eyes met Stellan's directly, not even blinking. He was dressed in a jet-black suit with a blood-red dress shirt. His hands were adorned with rings, one with a massive ruby and the other with a fearsome dragon's head. Stellan immediately reached out to shake the hand of a fellow dark soul, recognition instant in both their eyes.

"Thank you for meeting with me, Mr. Erikkson. I am a great fan of your work... for some time now I must say."

"It is very nice to meet you, Mr. Reinhardt. Thank you so much for your appreciation of my work. I am still stunned, in case you hadn't noticed. Charles mentioned that you wanted to commission two special pieces to replace the two that were already sold."

"Yes, that's correct. Well, sort of. We can discuss it all in more detail this weekend if you would do me the honor of coming out to my estate. I have very particular tastes, as I can see you do as well." Klaus' voice dropped to a deep menacing tone. "I've seen some of your *private* collection, and I would like to discuss what I am looking for. You have a unique eye for the dark, twisted side of the world. Your definition of beauty is exotic and fantastical. Your methods are one-of-a-kind and not for the faint of heart. A kindred spirit."

"You see me in a way no one ever has, Mr. Reinhardt. I would be honored to design your custom pieces to your refined tastes."

Klaus held out a business card. "Call me tomorrow. We will arrange a meeting on Saturday at my compound. Sweet dreams, Stellan." Klaus walked out as he winked one devilish eye at him, his open eye boring into Stellan's soul.

What does he know? If I didn't know better, I would think that he had seen my show. But how could he know it was me? Why do I feel as if I know him?

Stellan returned to the party and spent the rest of the night in a daze pondering what that meeting with Klaus Reinhardt might entail. He was a practiced social butterfly thanks to his mother's training, so he dazzled the critics and public alike. The exhibition's premiere didn't wrap up until late in the night, and Stellan returned to the hotel with his mind still spinning, unsure what was in store for him over the next few weeks in New York.

Sharon Marie Provost

Twenty-Two

Deep Delve

First week of December 2022

"**M**endy! How are you doing? You're always so busy with that Creator investigation that I never see you anymore." Robert, Mendy's old partner from Missing Persons, had bumped into her in the front lobby.

"I'm alive."

"You look exhausted, like one of those zombies you love to watch on that show."

"I can't afford to waste time sleeping. Annalise was murdered six months ago, and three poor women since then. I can't stop until we catch that bastard, even if it's the last thing I do. If the press, the politicians or Vanessa's family get their way, it just might be. It's fucking astounding! Every lead we think we develop goes nowhere. He is a fucking phantom!"

"I wanted to discuss something with you," Robert said. "It's probably nothing, so don't go getting all excited. Another woman was reported missing two weeks ago. She fits the profile physically. Unfortunately, there is zero evidence to suggest she was dating anyone. In fact, all reports seem to suggest it was impossible. But... she was an agent for artists. I am sure it's just coincidence and completely unrelated to your case, but what if..."

Mendy's eyes glowed with the news as she cut him off. "Thank you, Robert. I love you, I love you, I love you. I always said you were my best partner ever. This may be just the lead we need... finally." Mendy gave him a quick peck on the forehead before turning and running toward the Homicide Unit. "Tell your wife she is one lucky woman," she yelled back as she slid around the corner.

Mendy burst through the door to Homicide, bouncing it off the wall and startling the other detectives.

"Nice of you to join us, Mendy. You're five minutes late for the briefing, but no need to tear the place apart," Mills said grumpily.

Office interactions between the two of them had been awkward ever since their kiss. The lack of sleep from long work hours and a daughter with frequent ear infections didn't help his mood. Mendy would have taken the whole situation personally if not for the intimate conversations they shared via text or phone in their off hours.

"Sorry, Captain! I ran into my old partner, and he may have just given me the most promising lead we've had in a long time."

"Fine. We'll get to that here in a bit. Let's start with new evidence we received at the crack of dawn this morning. Then we'll discuss our progress in the case so far."

Mendy heard Detective Jackson's snicker in the background as he commented to the others, "You mean our lack of any progress... at all." She turned and glared at him, while Mills pretended he hadn't heard.

"What new evidence, Captain?" Mendy asked with a frown on her face.

Why didn't he call me in so we could look at this new evidence together? I've always waited for him in the past.

"We received a picture for a sixth victim. Her identity is a mystery to us like the fourth. Everything has been sent over to forensics for processing, but I'm not holding out much hope. When news of this latest victim gets out, the public is going to be rabid for our blood.

"We've been slogging through shit since the beginning of this investigation, and it's only getting worse. I know we've pursued every angle we have come across, but we have to go deeper. Think outside the box and look for something new. The pressure is on us from the top like never before.

"The DuPres have filed another lawsuit... now against that tabloid, *The Tattletale*. The Creator took his depravity one step further and sent the picture of Vanessa DuPre's desecrated body to them, and they printed it... in its entirety. The DuPres want all our badges. We're running out of time to save innocent women and ourselves."

"Shit, Cap! What do they want from us? We are doing everything we can," Detective Allen complained.

"I think we can all agree that he *must* be finding his victims through Tinder, but that has been a dead end so far. I talked to the captain over at Cyber Crimes, and he'll be assigning his best man to travel to the location of Tinder's server to see if he can make any headway on that angle."

"That's a great idea, sir," Mendy said as the others shook their heads.

"Next up... I know this won't be a popular idea, but we need to investigate the one and only Anthony Carreras that came up in the DMV database. I know he doesn't match the picture from the profile that Detective Hoffman had seen Annalise interact with, but we have to show the public and the politicians that we are doing our due diligence.

"Besides, we don't know what our perpetrator actually looks like. He may look like the picture Detective Hoffman has seen, like this Anthony does, or something else entirely. He might have been using a stock image he found somewhere or an old Polaroid he bought at a thrift shop. We just don't know. Likewise, he could have falsified his age and ethnicity. We have to see if this man has an alibi."

"I agree, sir. We should have done this long ago," Detective Jackson said, his tone decisive. "Who says he ever used that Anthony profile with any of the other women? He is a complete ghost to us at this point. Our best bet, honestly, is hoping that Cyber Crimes can find discrepancies in the lines of code showing that he hacked their system and find the communications these women had with him."

Mendy was shaking her head. "I think we are just going to be spinning our wheels again... wasting time and manpower," she interjected. "This guy is too smart. He knows how to cover his tracks. We have to cut him off at the pass. Attack him from an angle he isn't expecting and hasn't prepared for. Besides, there are other avenues of investigation that we haven't adequately pursued. We need to divide and conquer."

Mills sighed loudly and sat down heavily on the desk behind him. "Well, what do you suggest, Detective Hoffman?"

"I've always thought we didn't investigate the artist angle enough. From what I have seen, we've made minimal contact with the high-profile galleries in the area—and only regarding artists that might fit our half-assed, at the time, offender profile. We didn't contact the smaller galleries or any of the places artists can pay to have their art displayed. And we didn't follow up with any of the agents representing local artists. But this guy might not even be entirely local. We haven't even investigated outside the area. Just because he lives here doesn't mean that his work is shown here. The biggest art scene in the country besides L.A. is New York."

"That's like looking for a needle in a haystack," Mills said. "If you choose to pursue that avenue, feel free, Detective Hoffman. For now, the rest of the team will be assigned to help the detective from Cyber Crimes and to investigate the background of Anthony Carreras."

"But wait... I'm not done."

"What else, Mendy?"

"I told you my old partner had a very promising lead."

"And what is that?"

"He's the detective assigned to a new missing person's case. The woman has been missing since November 22. She's an art agent, and she meets the exact, rare physical type that our perpetrator has been targeting. What if one of her clients is the killer? What if she accidently found out something she shouldn't have? This can't be a coincidence.

"We have to work with Missing Persons to get more information about her disappearance. And most importantly, we have to continue to investigate artists. This guy has too much of an ego to only be producing this artwork. He's either a failed or recently successful artist who pursued fame in another way. He's sending the pictures to the media and us to become infamous. That tabloid proves it.

"We also need to uncover the identity of that unidentified fourth victim—and now this new one. From the start, he has gloated about each kill. He has identified them by name as he called us out on our lack of reporting. But now, recently, he has sent us two pictures of victims he doesn't identify. That can't be an accident. He's a conceited bastard, so he can't help but show us his handiwork, but he's scared to let us know who they are. There is a reason for that: He's concerned that their identity could lead back to him."

"Fine, Hoffman. That makes sense. I'll assign Jackson to work with you on discovering their identities. Get your old partner from Missing Persons to help you go through their files again and see if we can narrow it down. As for your desire to investigate artists and that agent's disappearance, I will leave that to you. The rest of the team will work on the points I laid out. Agreed?"

Mendy slammed the file in her hand down on the desk and turned away. "Got it, Captain Mills."

The din of the other detectives' voices rose as they began to discuss the case, but a loud voice from the doorway interrupted their chatter. Mendy looked up to see Nathan from Forensics calling out for Mills.

"Captain!"

Mendy shouted angrily, "Shut up, everyone! Nathan is here."

Nathan held up a file with a smile on his face. "We have our first break, Captain! We can't identify him yet, but he is starting to make mistakes. It's only a matter of time. There's a smeared fingerprint on the picture. We didn't find any matches in AFIS. That could be because the print was degraded, or maybe he isn't in the system, but it's a start."

"Hot damn! This motherfucker is going down," Mills said with a smile on his face. "He got a little too big for his breeches. We're coming for you, asshole. Just wait. We *will* find you, sooner rather than later."

Twenty-Three

You're on Your Own

Last week of January 2023

"Mendy, it's me, Belinda. Uh... how are you doing?"

Mendy hadn't heard from Annalise's sister since just after Annalise had disappeared.

"Not great, Belinda, but I am so glad you called me. I hated the way things ended that day. I just didn't know if I should call you back. I didn't want to make things harder for you."

"I understand. I know I was out of line. I can't imagine how hard this has been for you... as it is for me. Please tell me that you guys have been able to make some headway finding this monster."

Mendy felt herself gripping the phone tightly. She didn't want to tell Belinda they hadn't found her sister's killer. It felt like a personal failure to her.

"I wish I could. I don't even remember the last time I had a full night's sleep. This guy is like a phantom. The entire Homicide Department is working on this case, but no lead ever pans out. I have some ideas about how to pursue the case, but I've been told 'You're on your own' as they pursue other leads. I will never stop, Belinda. I will find this motherfucker and make him pay. I swear to you."

"I know you will, Mendy. There's a reason you were Annalise's best friend. I hope you know that she loved you like a sister. I have to admit I was a little jealous sometimes... all the time you spent together... the way you look more like my sister

243

than I do. Please keep in touch to let me know how the case is progressing and how you're doing. *I love you, too.*"

Mendy relaxed her grip on the phone slightly. "Of course, I will. How are the kids, Belinda? I know Annalise loved them so much. She was always telling me about their extracurricular activities."

"It has been hard on them, as you might imagine. I've been trying to keep them busy. That's why it took me so long to contact you. I have been working hard to keep myself together so I can be there for them."

"I understand. You are an excellent mom, Belinda. I will let you know *when* we catch this psychopath. I promise. Take care."

Mendy's level of frustration had reached dizzying heights. She'd worked with Detective Jackson for more than a month, trying to find out the names of the two unidentified victims. They'd pored through all the Missing Persons files with the help of her old partner, Robert. Only two women who disappeared during that timeframe matched the physical profile of the other victims: Aella Mattias and the agent, Meredith Price.

But people commonly changed their appearance, whether it be by dying their hair or wearing colored contacts. There were hundreds of missing women who might not naturally fit the profile but could have been altering their appearance. Still, they'd followed up on every woman who went missing during that time and, according to family, friends and co-workers, none of them had changed their appearance at the time to fit the profile. Likewise, none of them had been dating on Tinder.

In theory.

But people often hide their private lives from those closest to them, so it was impossible to be sure.

Aella and Meredith fit the physical profile exactly and had

disappeared at just the right time. However, once again, not all the pieces fit. Meredith was an extremely busy business owner who hadn't dated in over a year according to all her friends and confidants. In fact, one of her friends confirmed that she'd met the last guy she dated in person, rather than online. She had no Tinder profile at all.

Aella, on the other hand, did have an old Tinder profile... but it hadn't been used in years. No one had heard anything about her dating anybody, although her out-there goth lifestyle hadn't led to close connections with any friends or, especially, co-workers.

Meredith felt confident that both of these women were the victims in The Creator case, but there was simply no way to prove it without the bodies. And after doing an exhaustive dive into the personal lives of these two, they hadn't come up with any evidence that led back to the perpetrator.

To Mendy's dismay, Jackson had just been reassigned that day to work with the rest of the department, leaving her on her own to investigate artists and the clients of Meredith Price. The focus of their investigation, she couldn't fathom. It had hinged on tracking down the one Anthony Carreras they'd found and following up with Cyber Crimes. Just as she had predicted, their investigation had been fruitless.

Mills had contacted the man and set up a meeting with him at his home in San Francisco. The man hadn't even been in the country for two of the murders: He'd been visiting family in Italy. For the others, he had solid alibis in the San Francisco area. Mendy fought against her overwhelming urge to say, "I told you so."

The department had then focused all its energy on working with the Cyber Crimes unit, but nothing panned out there either. The detective assigned to spearhead that investigation had identified changes in the lines of code, but he couldn't track any of them back to see what had been changed. In essence, they now knew the real "Anthony"—or whatever his name was—was a ghost in the machine, but they couldn't prove what he was doing or trace anything back to who he was.

Mendy had pulled the names of all art galleries in the area, both large and small, to see what artists they were working with. The list of names was vast... more than was reasonable for one person to investigate, but she was determined to solve this case. If that proved useless, she was ready to move on to galleries in the New York area. She had put in a call to Meredith's assistant to get a list of all her clients, past and present.

Interactions with Mills had become more tense over the past month. Mendy understood that he was under a lot of pressure to protect his own job, as well as those of his team members. She just couldn't understand why he didn't trust her instincts anymore. He had recommended her for the position in Homicide, yet he wouldn't help her follow valid investigative paths.

Inter-office romances are always a bad idea. Plus, he has a daughter already. He doesn't have time for me. And to her, I would always just be an interloper—or, if things got serious, the resented stepmother. Besides, I just started in Homicide. Do I have time to pursue love anyhow? I think not!

Mendy struggled to remain on friendly terms with Mills but had to put all her focus on this case. She had fought too long and hard... worked too many years to receive this promotion. The DuPre family had started calling and threatening her job, as if the lowest man on the totem pole—or in this case woman—could be solely responsible for the entire department's failure. The police commissioner made several visits to the office each week to check on their progress.

But when it came down to it, Mendy was most concerned about finding the sick bastard who had murdered and mutilated her best friend, as well as six other innocent women. It had been almost two months since they had heard from The Creator. His absence had to have an explanation... one that could well lead to his capture.

Now to find out where he's been and what he's been doing.

Sharon Marie Provost

Twenty-Four

A Rose by Any Other Name

Second week of February 2023

Stellan still couldn't believe how fast two months had gone by. His exhibit's smash success on opening night was only the start of the crazy ride he had embarked on. On Saturday, after the show, he read one glowing review after another from the art critics in the papers. In the interim, while Meredith's disappearance was being investigated and he was busy schmoozing, Meredith's assistant took messages for Stellan from other galleries hoping to host his next collection. It took a few weeks, but he signed on with Angelique Masterson in New York to handle his art career on a "trial basis" while the search for Meredith continued.

The most important meeting during his time in New York had occurred on the Saturday after the exhibition. Stellan was invited up to The Hamptons to visit Klaus Reinhardt's palatial estate. Klaus even sent his private chauffeur to pick Stellan up from his hotel. The mansion looked like it belonged in the English countryside with its modern Gothic architecture, complete with gargoyles at the gated entrance and on the corners of the roof. Stellan was pleased to see his art would fit in with the ambience of the estate.

Klaus' house servant had met him at the steps when the car pulled up in front.

"Welcome, Mr. Erikkson. Mister Reinhardt is on a conference call, and he will be done in just a few moments. Let me take you to the sitting room. Would you like some coffee or tea while you wait?"

"Black coffee would be great. Thank you!"

The servant returned a few moments later, with Klaus close behind. He served Stellan and Reinhardt their coffee and then retreated, closing the sitting room doors.

"*Guten tag*, Mr. Erikkson. I appreciate you coming here to meet me and discuss the custom pieces I would like you to create. I am sure I told you that I am a great fan of your work. Your collection was delivered a few weeks ago and set up by the crew according to your detailed instructions. Thank you for including those. Would you like to see my private gallery? I have a few other pieces on display in there that fit in with your dark arts." Klaus' voice dipped into a low, sinister tone with that last sentence.

Stellan raised an eyebrow when Klaus said "dark arts" in such a suggestive tone. But that was the extent of his reaction. His mother had raised him to conceal his true feelings, even when baited. "Absolutely! I would love to see my collection one last time, plus I am always fascinated with the macabre."

Klaus led Stellan down the long hallway and out the rear door. They continued down a covered pathway to a large building with a bas-relief sculpture of the *Danse Macabre* carved into the stone archway above the entrance. Immense gargoyle sculptures perched on boulders positioned on either side of the black basalt stepping stones that led up to the door. Klaus removed a set of keys from his vest pocket and unlocked several durable locks. He smiled and stepped aside as he opened the door for Stellan to enter.

Dark Arts

Stellan walked in to find an immense room that had been darkened in the front half to perfectly suit the pieces of *They Came from the Dark*. Light pierced the gloom in the back of the building, where Stellan guessed the other works of art Klaus had mentioned were displayed. Klaus followed close behind Stellan as he made his way through the installation.

"Everything set up correctly according to your artistic vision?"

"It is astounding, Klaus. All the pieces are placed correctly with the proper lighting. Your gallery is set up in the most flattering way for my collection. I truly couldn't be more pleased."

As they rounded the corner from the last piece in the collection, the doorway that led into the next part of the gallery appeared. On the back wall, bathed in angelic lighting directly in front of the doorway, hung his most recent work, *Martyr to Art*. Stellan stopped abruptly, his breath caught in his throat, as he struggled to process the sight in front of him. He felt Klaus' hand grip his shoulder and squeeze.

"That is just the reaction I was hoping for. I mentioned I had seen your private art and had been a fan for some time, did I not?"

"Yes... uh. Yes, of course. But I never thought..."

"Never thought someone would recognize you."

"When I saw the pieces from your first collection in that magazine, they seemed so familiar to me. I had to attend your exhibition for this collection to see if I was right. As soon as I started walking through the installation, I knew. There was no doubt in my mind. Then, when I met you and looked into your eyes, I saw a fellow connoisseur: a master of the dark arts, as you so aptly named your show. I saw the recognition in your own eyes of my true nature and our kinship. Am I wrong?"

"No, of course not. I just didn't know it was so obvious."

"Only obvious to another dark soul."

"I had to buy your collection to go with the rest."

"The rest?" Stellan asked as his eyes roamed the room. He quickly realized that Klaus had bought a print from every single episode. His own gallery back at the warehouse paled in comparison to the beautiful display Klaus had created there.

Klaus smiled and nodded in response as Stellan's eyes returned to him. He pointed across the room. "That side of the room is where I intend to display those two custom pieces I commissioned from you. Have you recovered from your shock? Are you ready to discuss them?"

Stellan's mind was a whirlwind of thoughts and emotions, including fear for the first time that he could remember since he was a young child. *He knows everything about me... my true identity. What if he decides to turn me in?*

"I can see you are worried about me knowing about your... shall we say less-than-legal works of art? I would never betray you. Besides, how could I prove it other than to disclose my own collection? I don't intend to go to prison any more than you do."

"But what if someone sees it?"

"Do you think I invite all my friends and guests in here?"

"No. I don't know. What if someone breaks in?"

"Once again, does it seem logical that someone would disclose their own crime in order to expose mine? Seriously, you worry too much, Mr. Erikkson. There is only one entrance, and you saw the sophisticated, sturdy locks I have installed. The whole property is protected by an extremely advanced security system. The police would be here arresting someone long before they could find their way in here. I am the only one with a key, and it never leaves my person."

"Still... I would be an idiot if I didn't have my own safety net. I want to record our conversation regarding your custom pieces. Make sure it is known that you are asking for their creation and what that entails."

"You are asking for a lot there, Mr. Erikkson. But I trust you. I know that you have become quite wealthy through these pursuits, but your earnings don't compare to my personal wealth. I have enough money to buy my way out of any *complication*, even if it meant a change of location... which would not please me at all. I am sure that you have your own security in place to guard your studio, so I trust that you will keep this recording safe there as well."

"Absolutely!"

"Then let's get to it. I have one specific request, and the other I will leave up to your creative mind."

"OK. What's the first one then?"

"I fell in love with *Venus in Bloom*, as I am sure you meant for your audience to do. However, it was obvious that piece could never be sustained long-term. I would like you to redesign that piece with just the skull so that it can be kept here in my gallery. I will leave all the final details up to you."

Stellan nodded. "I know just how to do it. And for the other?"

"I want your most 'out there,' disturbing piece to date. I want to see the depths of your depravity and creativity, but once again, it must be able to be displayed here in perpetuity."

"You are a man after my own heart. Now for some specifics. Do you have a personal type? I am sure you have noticed that I choose only green-eyed blonds. Do you want me to broadcast the show as usual but indicate it is a commissioned piece that is not available for sale? If not, do you want a recording for you or just the finished work of art? Do you want her to suffer or die in a particular way? That is an important factor for some of my viewers."

"No, I don't have a type. I want your best work, so you need your inspiration. These works are for my eyes only. I will be paying you handsomely for them, so I insist that no recording be made, and that nothing be broadcast. I will be busy with some pressing negotiations and acquisitions over the next two months, so I will not have time to watch a video anyhow. I will leave all the specifics for how the work is actually completed up to you. Whatever inspires you is fine with me."

"That is perfect. My creative juices are flowing already. I think you will be very pleased. Now, what about the timeframe?"

"I don't want a shoddy, rush job by any means, but I would like to receive at least the first piece as soon as possible. I was thinking three months would be sufficient for the completion of both pieces. Now to get to business. I am going to pay you a $3 million deposit up front, with the final $7 million payment upon completion and delivery of the second piece. Is that agreeable, Mr. Erikkson?"

"Certainly. And you do realize I won't get back to my studio in L.A. until probably mid-January to early February?"

"Of course. If that is all settled, I do have some business to attend to, so my driver will take you back to your hotel."

"Thank you, Mr. Reinhardt. It has been a pleasure."

Stellan spent the next eight weeks in New York meeting with other galleries, private collectors, and fellow artists, and signing up with his new agent. Stellan returned home on the 3rd of February, with pressing work ahead of him following his consultation with Reinhardt.

Dark Arts

After spending a few days cleaning up his house and dealing with mail and messages that had arrived during his absence, Stellan began to search in earnest for the subject of the first piece. He had neither the inclination nor the time to waste establishing a pseudo-relationship with a new woman on Tinder. He didn't need to know her inner desires or fears to inspire the theme or for dramatic value when filming an episode. So he simply targeted the profiles of lusty women looking for a hookup or lonely, women desperate for any sort of companionship.

Within a week of arriving home, he found the perfect woman, Rosa Alvarado. Her Latino and Icelandic descent led to the most beautiful combination of the rare green-eyed blond combination in conjunction with gorgeous mocha-colored skin. He couldn't understand why this exotic beauty hadn't already been snapped up, yet there she was, shy and lonely. Then he spent some time talking to her and soon realized why. It was like accidentally walking into fly paper... he couldn't get free.

This girl is quite pathetic. I could tell her I was a psychopathic serial killer, and she would still go out with me. We've texted for a sum total of an hour the past two days, and she already told me she really likes me... which translates to "loves" me. What a loser! The poor girl even admitted she doesn't have any friends and doesn't get along with her family.

Stellan couldn't handle much more interaction with her, so he asked her out on a date via text. Rosa enthusiastically agreed to go out with "Anthony," and they made plans for him to pick her up the next day at the park across from her job at the grocery store, followed by dinner and a movie at his place.

The next afternoon, Stellan parked his Jag next to the bench and got out to greet Rosa. She sprang up and enveloped him in a hug.

What happened to her being shy?

He pasted a smile on his face and hugged her back. "Hello, Rosa. It is so nice to meet you. You are much more beautiful in person."

Rosa grinned like the Cheshire Cat before standing up on her tiptoes to kiss him on the lips.

"Thank you, sexy."

What the fuck? If I don't watch out, I will never get these tentacles off me. Talk about clingy.

Stellan led her to the car and held the door for her. She climbed in and started to chatter immediately. Stellan flicked the door shut with his wrist as he walked around to his side. When he sat down, Rosa placed her hand on his thigh and began squeezing it.

"It's so nice of you to cook me dinner. What are we having? And what movie did you pick for us?"

"I am making spaghetti with my homemade meat sauce. We are going to watch Texas Chainsaw Massacre."

"Oooh, a scary movie so I can hold on tight to my man!"

Stellan looked out the window as he rolled his eyes and said, "Exactly my plan."

A few minutes later, they pulled up in front of his warehouse. Stellan jumped out of the car and opened the truck to retrieve the rag. He balled the cloth up in his fist and made his way around to her door. As he opened the door, she looked up at him with her adoring, doe-eyes, never noticing the rag as he brought it up to her mouth. Within seconds, she was unconscious, and he left her sitting there while he unlocked the door.

Stellan propped the door open with the bar and carried her in, putting her on the surgical table before returning to lock up.

He strapped her down to the table in case she happened to wake up, while he changed clothes and retrieved the other supplies needed to complete this piece. He had found New York to be the perfect place to shop for the various, odd items he needed.

Stellan had found a place that stocked high-quality silk roses that could only be discerned from real flowers when one bent down to inhale the roses' intoxicating scent... and found it missing. He had chosen a dozen stems of the large-bloomed deep pink McCartney rose and had them shipped back home. In an occult store, he had found a candlestick that was composed of bundled-together animal femurs, which he also had shipped. It would make the perfect mount for the skull. The last item he needed proved to be a little more difficult to find until he noticed that The Oddities Flea Market was holding a holiday shopping event in New York City. He found the antique glass eyeballs he needed in the perfect shade of green.

Just as he returned to the table with those items, Rosa began to stir. "Anthony? What's going on?"

"I'm sorry, but this is just not your year. This will all be over quickly."

Rosa began to sob, gasping for breath, in between pleas for her life. "Please just let me go. I will do anything you want, Anthony." Her eyes grew wide as she saw him pick up a large syringe. Stellan reached over and injected her with an overdose of sodium pentothal, causing respiratory depression. She slipped into a coma and then ceased to breathe within a few moments.

Stellan walked over to the shelving and grabbed the chainsaw to make quick work of removing her head. As the chainsaw's teeth bit into her flesh, blood splashed onto his coveralls as bits of skin and bone were ripped away and thrown around the stage. It took less than a minute to saw through the neck. Stellan used the wheelbarrow to dispose of the body in the kiln before throwing the head in with the dermestid beetles.

Stellan wondered how far the police had gotten in their investigation. Last he had heard, the department was being threatened with a lawsuit after a lengthy investigation of an innocent man who just happened to bear the name of his alter ego, Anthony Carreras. The man claimed his reputation had been ruined. Fortunately, it didn't seem like they were any closer to identifying his two anonymous victims. The department was completely bogged down in lawsuits and bureaucratic nonsense, with detectives and politicians alike fighting to keep their jobs.

Their heads are so far up their asses, they will never find me. I bet those idiots think my victim profile stems from some Oedipal desire to fuck my own mother. Wrong! My mother was pale with blond hair and blue eyes. Or better yet, emotional trauma from a failed relationship when I was young. No again! I was the heartbreaker, and no one ever fit that combination of physical features.

I am a true artist. I want my work to be unique and use only the finest quality source material. What could be better than using subjects with one of the most rare hair-eye combinations—seen in only 2 percent of the world's population! And as luck would have it, the women I've found who met these criteria have also been strikingly beautiful. Luckily, California is a melting pot of cultures, so I've been able to find these elusive unicorns.

Stellan returned the next evening and found that the beetles had done their job. He removed Rosa's skull and threw away the few cervical vertebrae that had been attached. He placed the skull on the candlestick and adjusted it until it was at a cockeyed angle that lent a questioning pose, looking up at the viewer. He then drilled through the occipital bone and into the candlestick so he could place screws to hold it in place.

Dark Arts

Stellan slid the glass eyeballs into the orbital sockets and secured them with a little Gorilla glue. He also had them looking slightly to the right to accentuate the appearance of the skull looking up at someone. Then, he clipped off the stems from the roses and glued them in place across the skull, creating a crown of deep pink roses. On the right side, he glued a rose where her ear would have been to create the coquettish look of a single, island girl. He was proud to see what an astonishingly stunning bust he had created.

Stellan took a picture of the piece and posted it in a private message link on the Dark Arts website that could only be accessed by Klaus, using a security code. Then he sent a text message to Reinhardt, letting him know, and gave him the code. A short while later, he received an encrypted message back:

Mr. Erikkson, you have outdone yourself. I am very pleased with the piece. Please arrange delivery. I can't wait to see what you have planned for the pièce de resistance of my collection.

Regards, Klaus

The next few hours—spent finishing the cleanup process and performing the data wipe of all traces of communication with Rosa—went by in a flash. Stellan's thoughts were awash in the praise he had received from Klaus and plans for his upcoming artwork.

Now I just need to find the second subject and get this last work completed for Klaus. Angelique is very close to booking my next exhibition, and I will need to complete 10 to 20 works for that installation. I haven't even come up with the collection's theme yet. The work of a master artist is never done. And I can't forget my friends at the LAPD. They've been too quiet the past few weeks. I need to let them know I didn't forget them or move on.

Stellan printed a photo of his latest work. Klaus had never told him that he couldn't pass it on to the police. He placed it in an envelope with the name of the piece written on the back, *A Rose by Any Other Name.* He logged into the system and arranged anonymous pickup and delivery of Klaus' package to New York and the envelope for the LAPD.

I sure hope the detectives will enjoy my special flower delivery for Valentine's Day.

Twenty-Five

Anastasia

First week of March 2023

Reinhardt loved *A Rose by Any Other Name*! His effusive praise had raised Stellan's spirits more than he had expected. He missed producing *Dark Arts*, and the adoration of all his fans. Worst of all, the police seemed to have forgotten all about him—that is until he sent them the latest photo.

The angry furor from the media, the public and Vanessa's family certainly hadn't died down. The DuPres were determined to take down everyone involved with the case. It appeared they just might be successful in getting them all... everyone but him, that is. They hadn't the slightest inkling about the superior intelligence of their daughter's murderer.

I'm invincible! They will never catch me. None of them are smart enough to track me down.

The constant news reports had made it more difficult to find Stellan's next subject. The pool of available local women on Tinder seemed to be shallower. Before, it seemed, he could log on and find someone within minutes. Now, he was spending hours searching through the profiles to find someone who matched his type—but who wouldn't require him to spend days wooing her.

Reinhardt didn't care what the girl looked like, but it just wasn't as much fun if he used substandard material. Besides, Reinhardt wanted a true work of art that surpassed all others. After weeks of research, he had found the technique to create just such a piece—one he was sure would meet Reinhardt's discriminating tastes and his artistic designs. This piece demanded only the finest materials and a great deal of time.

Laid Bare would be the greatest work of his life. Except for one problem... the plastination process would take a year to complete between embalming, the desiccation process, the penetration of cells with the polymer, the positioning of the body, and then the final hardening process. Stellan felt unsure about whether Reinhardt would accept that kind of timeframe.

There was only one way to know for sure: Stellan called Reinhardt on an encrypted line. "Hello, Mr. Reinhardt. This is Stellan. I needed to discuss my proposal for the second piece of art you commissioned."

"Call me, Klaus. Is there a problem?"

"No, sir... er, I mean Klaus. You wanted something special... something to exceed anything I've yet produced. You said you wanted to explore the depths of my depravity with the creation of my most disturbing work. I have just the creative inspiration, but the question is, 'Do I have the time?'"

"What do you mean, Stellan?"

"You wanted both of them within three months. This particular work would take approximately a year to finish, but the result would be beyond even your wildest dreams. It will be difficult for me to part with because I will be instilling my entire dark heart and soul into this project. But I know it is exactly what you are looking for—the culmination of my creativity and dark desires over my lifetime."

"You have me very intrigued, Stellan. How can I possibly say no? How soon can you get started on this project?"

"I hope to get started in the next day or two. I think I found the perfect subject last night. Now I just need to obtain her."

"Please keep me apprised of your progress. Goodnight, Stellan. Hopefully, there will be sweet screams for both of us in the near future."

Stellan logged onto the internet and set about ordering the many supplies he would need over the ensuing months. They wouldn't arrive until the end of the week, so he had some time to arrange a meeting with this girl.

Her profile was listed under the name Anastasia, and that tight leather corseted dress couldn't be just a coincidence. She was used to taking a walk on the wild side... "50 shades of sexual positions" was her game. No need to spend days flirting with and getting to know her. Hooking up for the night was her end game.

Stellan updated his profile picture to one that showed him in a smart, dark-colored suit with a smug, sexy smile to match. He listed himself as a CEO of an investment firm. His commanding presence would be irresistible to her. He swiped right on her profile and sent her a message, "Hey, baby! Meet me for a drink at The Rooftop at The Standard on Saturday night at 8. You won't regret it."

Stellan turned away from the screen and began sketching out ideas for works for his next collection.

He hadn't been working long when he heard the notification on his phone.

He picked it up to find a short message from Anastasia. "Or you could just pick me up after work and take me to your place. Skip the pretense."

He smiled as he replied. "What's your address? And when do you get off?"

"Pick me up downtown outside the Eastern Columbia Building. I get off work at 7, but I expect to get off over and over."

"Oh, you will, baby!"

Stellan was quite pleased with himself. That had been even

easier than he had hoped. As long as everything continued according to plan, he would be a very busy man over the next year. His new agent was deep in negotiations for his next exhibition. There was even talk of it going international— although the thought of transporting his installations safely abroad caused him great anxiety.

Friday morning arrived quickly that week, and with it came the delivery of the supplies he needed for the plastination process. He sent off a quick message to Anastasia to confirm their plans, then proceeded to his agent's office to discuss the future of his career in the art world.

Stellan stepped into a pair of black Armani cashmere drawstring trousers and donned a light blue button-up sport shirt: the perfect look for the part... casual, yet well-to-do. At 6:30, he got in his Jag and headed downtown to pick up Anastasia. She was standing on the corner in a short miniskirt and crop top, looking every bit as hot as she had online. Her body would be exquisite for this work.

Stellan pulled up to the curb quickly and jumped out to usher her into the car. She greeted him with a smile and pressed her body up against his as her tongue slid into his mouth. "Hey there, sexy," she said as she climbed into the passenger seat. He closed the door and ran around to climb back into the driver's seat.

"You are smoking hot, baby!"

"Did you expect anything less?"

"No, I most certainly did not. You don't appear to be one to disappoint a man."

"Never, darling." Anastasia reached over to squeeze his leg and run her hand up and down it. "Shall we go?"

"Yes!" Stellan revved the engine before darting out into traffic. The 30-minute drive to the warehouse district passed quickly. Thankfully, Anastasia was not one for a stream of endless inane chatter; rather, she spent her time running her hands across his body and squeezing his shoulder. Stellan found her quite attractive—too bad there wasn't time to have a little fun first.

As they turned into the parking lot, Anastasia looked over at him, disappointed. "This is where you live, baby? I was expecting... more."

"Don't let appearances fool you. It is quite luxurious inside. My penthouse is being renovated, so I am staying here right now. Ready?"

Anastasia nodded, a look of disdain still upon her face.

Stellan stopped at the trunk to prepare the rag with the chloroform. He re-emerged with an expensive bottle of wine in one hand and the rag tucked inconspicuously in the other. As he reached the door, he placed the bottle of wine on top of the car and opened her door.

He reached around from behind, his hand drawing close to her face as he prepared to place the rag over her mouth. He was almost there when...

Anastasia grabbed his arm and jerked it down, slamming his face on the roof with a resounding thump. The bottle of wine fell over and rolled off the roof, crashing to the ground below. She twisted his arm up behind his back, turning him around and dislocating his shoulder in the process, then used all her strength to slam his head repeatedly on the car door.

Blood trickled down his forehead and across the spidery web of cracked glass in the passenger window. Stellan slumped to the ground unconscious as his head hit the window the third time. Anastasia climbed out of the car and stepped over him gingerly, before reaching down to search his pockets for the keys. She removed a pair of fuzzy handcuffs from her handbag and secured his arms behind his back.

Unlocking the door to the warehouse, she dragged his body inside, before returning to the Jag to wipe the blood off the window and close the car door. Anastasia went back into the warehouse and dragged his body over to the surgical table. She used her body for leverage to lift him onto the table, and had begun securing restraints on his limbs when she heard the door to the warehouse open.

She looked up as a booming male voice asked, "What the fuck is going on here?"

Twenty-Six

Laid Bare

First week of March 2023

"**M**endy, what the hell are you doing? Who is that man? Why are you dressed like that? You better speak up fast before I place you under arrest."

"What are you doing here, Mills?"

"I followed you. I've been concerned because you've been acting so strangely the past couple of days. Now I see why."

Mendy took a step toward him, defiant. "This doesn't concern you," she said. "Can't you just walk out and pretend you never saw any of this?"

"Are you serious? Of course, I can't do that. Explain yourself. NOW!"

"This is *him*. I caught him. It is The Creator. He doesn't deserve a trial... a chance to live or even possibly be set free. Just walk out of here. You don't have to be a part of this."

"I can't let you do this. We are detectives for the LAPD. We're not supposed to be acting as judge, jury and executioner."

Mendy finished applying the restraints and tightened them until Stellan's skin blanched.

"You know as well as I do that we'll never get a conviction. Hell! I don't think we can even convince the D.A. to press charges with what we've got... which is nothing. We take him in, and he walks free. This is the only way. This is what he deserves. To suffer at *my* hands the way they did at his. From the way they looked in those photos, the coroner said he probably mutilated them while they were still alive. No one who inflicts that kind of pain deserves to get away with it."

"How did you find him? How can you be so sure?"

"Because I was right. I told you we needed to follow up on artists outside of the area. I told you this was all somehow connected to that art agent who was murdered. This piece of shit was one of her clients, and she had a huge exhibition set up for him in New York. She disappeared a week before the show, and guess who the last person was to see her in person? Here... let me show you on one of these computers. You will see the connection. It is undeniable!"

"If you were able to track him down like you said, we can use that in court. Cyber Crimes can go through his computer system to find more evidence. He will be convicted."

"It's too late now. With what I just did to him, his lawyer will get them to suppress all this evidence... 'fruit of the poisonous tree.' It doesn't matter anyhow. He deserves to suffer the way he made those women suffer. Prison is not enough. Hanging out in prison for decades, filing appeals before they finally impose the death penalty—if they ever do—is not harsh enough."

Stellan moaned and began to move.

"Mendy, this is your last chance to get out of this before he wakes up. We could remove the restraints and leave him here, and then come pick him up later... legally."

"I don't care what happens to me. You can arrest me when I'm done. Claim that you tracked me down after I'd already done the deed. Just let me take care of this piece of shit first. If you don't trust me not to run, just wait outside for me. What if he had done this to someone in your family? To me? To your daughter?"

"I get it, but I'm sorry. I just can't be a party to this. It's not in my DNA. But I care about you, and I cared about Annalise...

everybody did. And you're right: This scumbag doesn't deserve a chance to work the justice system. I'll be outside waiting for you and keeping an eye out. Let me know when you're done, and we'll figure out what to do next."

Mendy walked over to Mills and fell into his arms, holding him to her in a vise-like bear hug. He leaned down and kissed the top of her head as he caressed her back.

"You can change your mind anytime. No judgements from me... one way or the other. I just need you to be OK when this is all over. Annalise would want you to be happy, and we need each other. I need you."

"I love you, Brad. Now go."

Mendy grabbed his hand and led him to the door. She stood up on her tiptoes to kiss him one more time before shutting the door. As she did, she called out to him. "Turn on the radio to drown out the noise."

Mills returned to his car and parked it in the dark alley between Stellan's warehouse and the abandoned one next door. He turned on the radio and started playing solitaire on his phone.

Mendy returned to Stellan's side as his eyelids began to flutter open. "Uhhhh... what happened, Anastasia? Why am I strapped to this table? What the fuck is going on here?"

"Welcome back, motherfucker! My name is not Anastasia. Just like your name isn't Anthony. I'm Mendy, and I'm here to pass judgement on you and carry out the sentence I deem fair."

"What are you talking about? Release these straps now. We can talk about this and figure it out. Did I do something to offend you?"

"Offend me? I wish. Why don't we establish your real identity first, *Stellan*? You're that pretentious bastard who calls himself *Le Créateur*. You're the sick fuck who tortured, mutilated, and killed eight innocent women."

Mendy turned away as a tear escaped from the corner of her eye and struggled to speak through the knot in her throat. "One of those women was my best friend, Annalise," she hissed. "You turned her into your own warped and demented version of an eagle. The coroner told me about the unimaginable pain she must have suffered during your sick '*creation.*' I intend to make sure you feel everything she—and every one of the other women—felt."

"How did you find me? I covered my tracks impeccably. Everything was encrypted, I used a VPN, and it passed through proxy servers around the world. The show was broadcast on the dark web. Everything was untraceable."

"Everything but your massive ego. Maybe you shouldn't have made such a big name for yourself in the legitimate art world as well—especially with art that contained such dark themes. Those pieces screamed out that they belonged with your underground art. But your biggest mistake? Killing your agent, Meredith."

Stellan closed his eyes and shook his head. "But how did you figure it out? There was nothing to connect me to her disappearance. There are other artists who produce art with horror-based themes. What tipped you off?"

She pulled in close to his ear. "As I said, your ego got in the way. You were so smug, thinking you had beaten the system by hiding your identity on Tinder. I still don't know how you did it. The best computer analysts in L.A. could detect that changes were made, but they couldn't track down your ghost. You had them flummoxed. Your mistake... thinking you were unbeatable.

"Do you know who convinced Annalise to try dating on Tinder? That was me. I even helped her create her profile and decide who to swipe right on. I saw your profile and many of the messages that passed between you. You were dumb enough to use your own picture, so I knew exactly what you looked like.

"Over time, as the pictures of your 'art' kept coming in to the Homicide Unit, I could see that you had a physical type. One I just happen to share with your victims. Diving into these women's backgrounds, I could also see that you gravitated toward those who were unlikely to share details of their personal lives with others. But you miscalculated with Annalise because she *did* show me.

"It was easy enough to create my own profile with my picture and highlight the kind of personality traits that would draw you in. Then I just had to wait for you to contact me. As soon as your ghost profile appeared, *voila*! There was the picture of the man I knew I had to hunt down."

"You mentioned my photos coming in to Homicide. Are you the detective she warned me about?"

"Yes, I am. You didn't realize when you picked Annalise that she worked for LAPD, and that her best friend was a detective in Missing Persons. Well, since then, I've been promoted to Homicide. You messed with the wrong person."

Stellan swallowed hard. "She told me that day when she begged for her life. She threatened me that the police would find me, but you don't act like police. This is illegal."

"You are correct. It is 100 percent illegal, but I don't care."

Mendy gulped as she tried to fight back tears once again, to no avail. She turned back toward Stellan and punched him in the face, regaining control when he winced in pain. She took a couple of deep breaths before she started using scissors to cut off his clothes.

"I have to make you pay. It's my fault that Annalise is dead.

If I hadn't pushed her to date... to use Tinder... you never would have found her. That was enough of a cross to bear, but then..." Mendy gasped and began to cry uncontrollably.

"What else? You have me fascinated here. What could be worse than that?"

"It's all my fault that Rosa Alvarado is dead. I could have stopped you, but my own selfish desire for revenge got in the way."

"Ooohh, tell me more."

"I figured out who you were at the end of January, just before you returned home. The rest of the Homicide Unit was focused on other leads. I alone had been assigned to follow up on artists and the missing agent to see if they were in any way related to this case. I saw your artwork and felt sure it must be you. Your name seemed familiar, and then I remembered you were connected to Meredith Price. When I investigated further and saw your picture in an article about your art exhibition, I knew I'd found you.

"I could have told my captain, and then we could have arrested you properly before you ever returned to L.A. But I was determined to make you pay. I was sure you would respond to my profile on Tinder right away, but you found Rosa first. I should have been tailing you, so I could have stopped you. I bear the responsibility for that innocent girl's death. I've been watching you since then to make sure that didn't happen again, and thankfully, you swiped right on me next."

"Ahhh, now I see. So what is your plan? Torture me and then turn me over to the police, even at your own expense?"

"No, that would be much too easy on you. I would never do that. I *am* going to torture you... and then, when you cry out and beg me to stop, I will torture you even more. When you are utterly and completely broken, only then when I kill you. Not out of mercy, though. You're not worthy of mercy. Merely to make sure you never hurt anyone ever again."

"I don't believe you. You said you're a detective. You wouldn't actually murder someone, would you?"

"With you... in a heartbeat. You shall see soon enough... well, maybe not that soon."

Mendy walked away, then turned back as she reached the end of the table. "You mentioned a show earlier... on the dark web. What were you referring to?"

"I had my own show called *Dark Arts*, where I broadcast the torture, murder, and then creation of my art work using my subjects. It was very successful, even more so than my legitimate art exhibits."

"You used that computer system over there to broadcast?"

"Yes."

Mendy turned away and began searching the shelving near the computer bank. She collected various instruments of torture he kept there and placed them on the instrument tray near the table. After that, she found a sledgehammer, which she placed on the computer desk before retreating to the back of the warehouse, into his private chambers. She made a racket searching through drawers and cabinets as she collected more of the tools she would employ in bringing her plans to fruition. Stellan tried to lift his head to see what she was setting out on the table, but the strap across his forehead kept him immobile.

Mendy walked back over to the computer bank and used the sledgehammer to begin smashing all his equipment. Stellan begged her to stop, but all she did was laugh maniacally until all the electrical components were barely discernible bits across the room.

"Well, that's taken care of. No one will ever see these recordings again, except on the dark web. That is, until I can find someone to destroy your site."

Mendy walked across the room and into the gallery he had been preparing for all his works of art. She pulled the framed prints off the wall and stacked them in the center of the warehouse, near the surgical table. She found some paint thinner in the back and placed the cans near the canvases.

"What are you doing?"

"It's really none of your concern. I do think it is time that we get started, though. My captain is out there waiting for me, and I don't want to keep him waiting too long."

Stellan's eyes widened. "That was your captain? He's not going to stop this?"

Mendy just smiled as she stepped up to the instrument tray and removed the pair of bone-cutting forceps. She could see the discomfort on his face; how exposed and vulnerable he must have felt lying there naked, strapped to the table. He flinched as she reached first toward his hands and then down toward his feet. He didn't have time to react when she suddenly reached down and grabbed his penis, lopping it off with one snip of the forceps.

"Ohhh no, that is a lot of blood. We can't have that now, or you will pass out and die before I am done."

Stellan's scream intensified as she flicked a lighter and began to cauterize the wound. "There we go. That's much better." Mendy grabbed a toe as she said in a sing-song voice, "This little piggy went to market," before snipping it off. Then, "This little piggy stayed home," and she lopped off the next one. Stellan ground his teeth as he fought the urge to scream. By the time she reached the second foot, he had lost control again.

"Fuuuuckkk! You said I was a monster. What about you?

You are supposed to be the law."

"You fucked with the wrong woman's best friend. Annalise was everything good about this world... all sweetness and light. She was the yin to my yang. We were a lot alike in many ways— but not all. She would have watched rom-coms with you. Me? I'm all about dark, twisted horror. I've seen plenty to inspire me... Little did I know I would use it one day."

The room filled with the bitter stench of burning flesh as she removed all ten toes before turning her attention to his fingers. Each bone-crunching snap of the forceps, followed by Stellan's whimpers and pleas for her to stop, filled her with glee. She rechecked the wounds to make sure he wasn't losing too much blood before picking up a cheese grater she'd found in the kitchen.

"I am quite looking forward to this part. I saw this in a movie, and it really freaked me out at the time. But now, the thought of doing it to you is just..." Mendy lifted her head and pressed her fingers together for a chef's kiss. "Mwah! It is sheer perfection."

She lowered the instrument to his kneecap and began the rhythmic motion of passing it over his exposed flesh as she pressed down hard, ensuring it did its job. Little by little, she shredded the flesh and muscle down to the bone, separating strips and strands of skin and raw sinew. She began with one knee and then moved to the other, ignoring Stellan's screams for help that reverberated through the warehouse. Blood flowed out of the torn flesh and ran down his legs, dripping onto the table below. Bits of skin flew from the blade and stuck to Mendy. Such was the force with which she tore through him.

"Whoops! Looks like we need a little more cautery."

Stellan begged her to stop, promising to do anything she asked. Mendy smiled down at him. "You are doing just great. Let's see. What shall we do next?"

Stellan closed his eyes and took deep breaths.

"Look at me."

Stellan refused to meet her eyes.

"I said look at me. Now!"

Mendy saw the muscles in his jaw and neck tense as he stubbornly refused to look up at her.

"Well, I can fix that."

Mendy reached over to grab another tool. She pulled up an eyelid, using the razor-sharp scalpel to slice it from his face. Then she moved to his other eye and repeated the process. "I bet that blood stings a little. Let me just wash it away for you." She reached down and grabbed an open can of paint thinner, pouring it liberally over his face to flush his eyes. Mendy plugged her ears as Stellan's screech tore through the room painfully.

"Please! Please stop! I give. I'm done. Just kill me now. I know you're going to kill me. Just please be done with it. You can call in my murder anonymously and make your career with your discovery of *Le Créateur* and his *Dark Arts* show. I will live on forever in infamy when my show is discovered... by you. Please, I beg of you."

"How quickly you forget. I told you I would only kill you when I had completely broken you. Your *spirit* may be broken, but your body? That is another matter. I don't think you have experienced enough pain yet... not nearly enough. Oh, and you can forget that 'living in infamy' part. I will not expose anymore of your atrocities to the world. No one will ever know your identity. They've seen enough of you already. I am going to destroy your body and everything here. No one will ever know the true depths of your depravity, except for me. I will make sure you are forgotten—not even a footnote in history."

"Noooo!" Stellan howled. "You can't do that! My work is my

life... my legacy."

"I can, and I will. They won't even be able to identify your body when I am done. Your sick work won't even be an epitaph on your pauper's grave."

"Now to work on that part about making you unidentifiable. First, your teeth." Mendy grabbed a bit of cotton he used to clean his brushes and stuffed it down into the back of his throat. "Can't have you swallowing those teeth."

She used a small hammer to bust every tooth, leaving only sharp, jagged peaks and bloody holes where they had been. She scooped the bits of teeth from his mouth and set them on the warehouse floor, where she pounded them into dust with the hammer.

Stellan lay there staring off into space, his eyes burning with a searing pain as he tried desperately to blink without eyelids, all will to live vanquished from his body. His body flinched, but he no longer cried out in pain. His eyes slowly rolled toward Mendy.

"Damn!" she muttered, shaking her head.

Mendy picked up some sandpaper to sand off his fingerprints, until the flesh was raw hamburger with no identifiable ridges. "I should have done that before I cut them off... although I don't know how much more pain you can handle before you pass out on me."

She threw the fingers down on the floor, next to the bits of teeth.

"I guess it's time to get down to the painful part of this process. Our coroner believes you dissected at least some of those women while they were alive. I think it is your turn now. I don't think this part will last very long. You have lost a lot of blood already. Any last words?"

Stellan shook his head no, almost imperceptibly.

"Now it is time to give you a taste of what you inflicted on some of those poor women." Mendy grabbed the scalpel again and began to carve marks into the skin of his chest and abdomen. Blood oozed from the wounds and snaked its way down his body, onto the table. "That is for Arizona."

Then she used the scalpel to flay a large swath of skin from his cheek before searing the wound with the lighter. "And for Millie." Stellan's body slumped as he lost consciousness from the pain. Mendy waited patiently for him to wake up. As he lay there, she looked around the room and noticed a large piece of equipment in the corner: Recognizing it as a woodchipper, she rolled it over to the end of the table and positioned it just above his head.

When Stellan awoke, he moaned when he beheld its twisted, terrifying blades mere inches from his face. "Hey there, Snoozy Suzy! About time you came around again. We aren't quite done with our fun yet."

Mendy approached from the side where she had been sitting at the now-defunct computer bank. She picked up the scalpel and began to make one long, deep incision from the top of his breast bone down to his groin. "Did I forget to warn you that this is going to hurt? Oopsy!" She spread apart the incised skin so she could see his internal organs and ribcage with his fluttering lungs as they hyperventilated.

She used her hands to begin scooping out his organs and spread them across his body and the table. She lifted a long loop of bowel high into the air so he could see it. Then she retrieved the bone-cutting forceps again to begin cutting his ribcage open, exposing his still-beating but slowing heart. "Oh no! You can't duck out on me yet." Blood was pouring from the massive incision in his body. Mendy rushed to the top of the table; she knew she had mere moments left.

She turned on the woodchipper and let the blades spin perilously close to his face for a few seconds. She moved down so she was staring down directly into his eyes. "Fuck you!" she screamed as she began to shove his body headfirst into the woodchipper. His head imploded as the chipper spat out shards of skull, grey mushy brain matter, and blood. She didn't stop until the last of his body had been pulverized to a bloody mush in the center of the staging area.

Mendy returned to the chair by the computer and collapsed, tears pouring from her eyes as she released all the emotions and stress that had built up over the past year and a half. When she finally regained her composure and caught her breath, she got up and went into Stellan's bedchamber. She used one of his towels to clean the blood off of her and dressed in one of his coveralls hanging in the closet.

She threw the towel and bloody clothes down in the pile of sludge that had once constituted *Le Créateur* before picking up the cans of paint thinner. She poured the contents of two of the cans over the mass of tissue, teeth, fingers and framed photos. Then she used the remaining can and a half to pour a trail into his bedchamber, over the computer equipment and through the rest of the warehouse. She would burn this unholy torture chamber to the ground. When she was done, nothing would be left of it but ashes.

Finally, she gathered herself together enough and walked out to Mills to see if the coast was clear. When he saw her, he jumped out of the car and wrapped her in his arms. He held her tight until she had cried herself out.

"So have you seen anybody out here?"

"Dead as a doornail. I think this area has been deserted for some time."

"I just need to go light the fire. We will call it in anony-mously with a burner phone when it's all done."

"Let me do that for you. I'll be right back."

"No, you can't do that. I don't want you to see what I've done. You'd never look at me the same again."

"I could never see you as anything but the woman I love. But I won't look if you don't want me to. I will just be in and out. Light a match and toss it... make sure it goes up."

"Thank you. I'm just going to go sit..."

Mendy collapsed into his arms, all the strength draining out of her. Mills helped her to the car.

"What are we going to do about his car?"

"I looked up his address when I found out his identity. I was going to drop it off outside his loft in the middle of the night."

"Good idea. Let me go move it a couple of blocks away, where it won't be noticed. Then we'll come back later and take care of it. When I return, I'll light the fire. You just rest here for now."

Mendy lay back in the seat and closed her eyes. But even with her eyes shut, she knew the visions of what she had done would be seared in her memory forever. The emotional toll of the night pulled her down into a restless slumber.

A short time later, Mills joined her in the car and drove down a few blocks to a dark, deserted lot. From there, they tracked the progress of the fire until it finally collapsed into a burning heap an hour later.

Mendy pulled out the burner phone and made the anonymous call to 911 to report the fire.

After they dumped the car, Mills drove her home and helped her into bed before returning home to his daughter. The Homicide Unit would be receiving a call before long, and he

Dark Arts

could use a little sleep.

Sharon Marie Provost

Epilogue

From a Spark to a Flame

Second week of March 2023

The previous week had passed by in a flash for Mendy. Three hours after they had retired for the night, Mills and Mendy had been called in to work a homicide in the old warehouse district. The Fire Department had responded to a report of a fire there. When they arrived, they found the building had collapsed, and it took a few hours to douse the remaining flames and cool off any hot spots.

An arson inspector was called in when signs of a pour pattern from an accelerant were found. A short time later, the call was passed to Homicide when bits of bone and tooth fragments were discovered. The coroner collected the remains, but it was no use trying to find a match in CODIS: The body had been almost completely consumed by the fire, leaving no fingerprints, usable DNA, or dental records to establish the victim's identity.

The intense heat had destroyed the building and all its contents, including any personal belongings that might have been used to identify the deceased. They had found melted electrical components, probably from a computer, but there was no way to retrieve any data. Property records were pulled for the building, but the owner had used a false identity to purchase it. The case appeared unsolvable—especially since all the resources of the Homicide Unit were being used in the hunt for The

Creator.

They had received a photo of an eighth victim back in late February, but she was as yet unidentified. The FBI had been called in to assist with the investigation at the mayor's insistence, but they weren't having any luck identifying the perpetrator either. Their presence had at least taken some of the heat off the LAPD Homicide Unit.

Mendy had started spending the night at Mills' house after they returned from that first night of the arson investigation. They started work late the next morning, exhausted after a long night spent discussing how Mendy had found The Creator.

In the morning over coffee, they agreed never to discuss it again.

A week later, Mendy walked to the park across the street to eat her lunch while she placed a call.

"Hello."

"Hi, Belinda. It's Mendy. How are you?"

"I'm doing OK. Dealing with all of this a little better each day as I focus on the kids. They are my lifeline. How are you?"

Mendy began to cry softly. "I'm... uh... I'm doing better."

"What's wrong? Are you really OK?"

"Yes, I am. It just has been a long year, you know? I just needed to call and tell you something."

"You can tell me anything. What is it?"

"It's done."

"What's done? What do you mean?"

"It has been taken care of. You don't have to think about him anymore."

"What are you saying, Mendy?"

"Nothing. Nothing at all. You get me?"

"Yes, I do. Thank you for calling. My family and I will be

coming to the States this summer to have a memorial for Annalise. Will you come?"

"You name the date and time, and I will be there. We need to celebrate... her life, I mean."

"Of course. Talk to you soon, Mendy. Take care of yourself."

Sharon Marie Provost

About the author

Sharon Marie Provost is the author of *Shadow's Gate* and co-author with Stephen H. Provost of *Christmas Nightmare's Eve*, *All Hallows' Nightmare's Eve*, and *Shades of Love*. Her stories have also appeared in the ACES Anthologies for 2023 and 2024, which highlight the works of Northern Nevada writers and for which she served as co-editor.

Chief operating officer of Dragon Crown Books, Sharon is a longtime resident of Carson City, where she lives with her husband and her pets. She worked for 20 years as a veterinary office manager and is the owner of champion of dog-trial poodles, and the creator of handmade dreamcatchers and chainmaille jewelry. You can find her at local craft fairs, author events, and at "Sharon Marie Provost, Author" on Facebook.

Books by
Sharon Marie Provost

Dark Arts
Evermore: Dark Soulmates (with Stephen H. Provost)
Shadow's Gate
All Hallows' Nightmare's Eve (with Stephen H. Provost)
Christmas Nightmare's Eve (with Stephen H. Provost)
Azrael's Assassin (with Stephen H. Provost)
Shades of Love Vol. 2

Did you enjoy this book?

Recommend it to a friend. And please consider **rating it and/or leaving a brief review** at Amazon, Barnes & Noble, and Goodreads.

www.ingramcontent.com/pod-product-compliance
Lightning Source LLC
Chambersburg PA
CBHW051245260626
47162CB00002B/612